Interior Format

LISA WELLS

Allyson,
Happy reading!
Lisa Wells

To MarVeena — You're one hell of a sister and medium. Thanks for bringing me messages from the other side. #Ibelieve

OTHER TITLES BY LISA WELLS

CONTEMPORARY ROMANTIC COMEDY

The Seduction of Kinley Foster
The Attraction of Adeline
Aggie the Horrible Vs Max the Pompous Ass
(*Releases Feb 24th, 2020*)

PARANORMAL ROMANTIC COMEDY

Hexes and O'S
Hand Picked – *COMING SOON*
Cup of Spirits – *COMING SOON*

PARANORMAL COZY MYSTERY

Be watching for more from the characters of
Hexes and O's as they break out into a Cozy
Mystery series.

ACKNOWLEDGMENTS

To David, thank you for never complaining about the hours I spend creating fictional worlds. I love you to Pluto and back.

To Margie Lawson, thank you for the highly-sought-after NYT in the margins as I worked on this book in your immersion class and for being one of my biggest champions. You've shaped and molded and occasionally – when needed - kicked me in the butt as a writer. ★The fact you use an excerpt from this book when teaching, gives me all the butterflies of happiness.

To Barb Bettis, thank you for writing with me every Tuesday. Your friendship rocks.

To Darynda Jones, your review has left me permanently floating on air.

A big thank you to the village who helped take this book from my computer to the world:

Killion Group, Inc. designed the magnificent cover and did the formatting.

Holly Atkinson and Amanda Grondski worked their editing magic on Hexes and O's. Their expertise gave me the courage to share this book with the world.

CHAPTER ONE

When life gives you a lemon…duck. It hurls them three at a time.
-Remington Smith, realist

REMINGTON SMITH, FORMER SEAM-STRESS FOR the stars of Branson, looked away from the legalese inheritance letter in her hand and stared at the wall like it held the secret to mind control. Who had died? Did she want to know? Would life really lob three more lemons at her today? All before noon?

Six lemons in three hours. A Guinness-book record.

Dear Ms. Smith: It is with regret I inform you of the death of Bethany Joann Henderson. After a brief battle with Stage IV breast cancer, Beth, at the age of twenty-four, passed away on September 12th of this year.

Remington stopped reading. Relief collided with grief in her heart. Relief because her never-known mom wasn't dead. Grief because her best friend growing up was. And Beth had died before Remington had a chance to mend the broken fence between them. The fence Remington had shattered.

Maybe she'd misread. She reread. No. Dead was dead. Tears welled under her eyelids, and a strangled noise escaped from somewhere deep in her soul.

This definitely counted as a three-lemon whammy. Beth was Remington's person. The one she could count on to bail her out of a predicament, no questions asked. Predicaments like today. Last night when Remington had gone to bed, she'd had a job, a boyfriend, and an apartment. This morning, not so much.

Why hadn't Beth gotten in contact with her? Damn it. Had she replaced Remington with a new best friend? Someone she'd met while away at college? Someone who didn't have so many flaws?

Why hadn't life given them time to make amends?

Remington blinked until her eyes were somewhat focused and continued reading.

As her attorney, I am carrying out her final wishes. Beth included you in her will. The attached letter will explain her bequeath.

Sincerely,

Caroline Leagle

Attorney-at-law, LLM

Remington dropped the letter, grabbed the tub of Ben and Jerry's Chocolate Therapy ice cream she'd nabbed from the freezer for moral support before opening the letter, spooned out an enormous mound, and quickly swallowed. She needed the cold treat to flash-freeze her heart. A frozen heart couldn't feel pain. Could it?

Oh, crap, brain freeze. Ouch. Ouch. Ouch.

She pulled her knees up against her chest and rocked back and forth. Beth Henderson couldn't be dead. She just couldn't be.

An ache seeped into her bones and burned a goliath hole in the middle of her soul. She forced herself to stop rocking, to pick up the letter, and to turn the page.

The letter was handwritten. *Beth's handwriting.* Orange ink. Cursive lettering.

Remington's mangled heart crawled up her throat. Was Beth going to yell at her for being a pathetic friend?

Dear Remington:

Pardon my French, but merde. I'm dead.

I thought I'd win the battle against breast cancer—even though they told me it wasn't likely.

I've missed you so much. I'm so sorry we stopped talking. And I'm sorry for whatever I did that made you not want to talk to me. You were the only one I could ever tell my secrets to.

Speaking of secrets, I have one last secret I need to share with you. I did something when we were little that has haunted me for years. Something that made me feel like I wasn't good enough to be your friend and no wonder you stopped talking to me.

Here it goes: I prayed really hard that no one would adopt you.

If someone had, you might have moved away. I couldn't handle the thought of you not being my best friend and not living down the road. It's my fault you never got adopted. God answered my prayers, not yours.

Remington, life isn't a given.

You can't just assume you have a tomorrow like Scarlett O'Hara did in Gone *with the Wind.*

My new prayer is for you to seize every breath life gifts you.

You are probably thinking I left you my half of our memory rocks. I didn't. I gifted them to Jonathan B. Jones. He's five and lives at the orphanage. He has humongous blue eyes and a dimple bigger than the hole we accidentally blew up in the town's golf course with those leftover firecrackers. Who knew they could do that type of damage? Still LMAO.

Remington stopped reading and ordered the emotions clogging her throat to go away. She glanced around. Her gaze landed on the framed picture of her most recent fake family. Of all the fake family pictures she'd ever slipped into that thrift-store purchased frame, this one looked the most probable.

If the four strangers smiling back were her real family, would they help her find a new job? Let her live with them now that she was on the verge of being evicted? Or would they be all like, "Poor Remington, fired. We always knew she'd be nothing more than a perfume-spraying bathroom attendant in a bar frequented by Spanx and skanks."

Why had Beth lobbied against the one thing Remington wanted most in life? Beth had parents. Why would she not want that for Remington? They could have still been friends. And why had she left this Jonathan kid her half of their memory rocks? What would he get out of a rock that represented the first time she and Beth had skipped school, their first school dance with dates, or their first periods?

Remington glanced at the letter.

Now, to your inheritance.

Her grip crumpled the edges. *An inheritance.* She stood. Paced. The thump of her heartbeat in her ears reminded her of the ominous music played in horror flicks right before someone too stupid to live wanders down a flight of stairs into a dark basement. If not the rocks, then what would she inherit? People with family inherited real stuff. Not orphans. She didn't deserve an inheritance from Beth.

Remington flipped the page.

I've left you my home. It's in Knotty. A couple of streets over from the house I grew up in.

"A home?" Remington swirled the word on her tongue like a sip of wine. It tasted tart and sweet. She gazed out the window at a puffy cloud.

Beth used to say she saw her deceased grandpa sitting on clouds. And they chatted. Had that been true? If so, was becoming a ghost an inherited trait? Was Beth on that cloud? Was it her voice Remington kept hearing?

Remington shook her head to dislodge the stupid thought.

In return for leaving you my furnished house and my life-insurance, I want you to finish a to-do list for me.

"A to-do list?" Remington resumed pacing as a strange feeling grew in the bottom of her stomach.

You're going to laugh when you read the list, but I'm

serious. I want you to live in the house while you complete the to-dos. Once you've finished, if you choose to move, you have my blessings to sell your home and use the money to buy your dream.

P.S. Smile if you love me.

Remington's breath hitched. She pressed the back of her hand to her lips. Beth had never said goodbye. She always said, "Smile if you love me." That's how Beth's mom had always said goodnight.

"Thank you," Remington said the words out loud…just in case Beth could hear.

She waited for a reply.

Nothing.

"I have a freaking home." A sloppy smile spread across Remington's face and imprinted on her heart. She picked up Max, her neurotic wiener dog, and twirled until he growled. "I'm not homeless." Feelings, the good kind, whiplashed through her. She laughed.

"Hell, I'd take a bullet for my own home," she said to her wiggling dog. "And not one of those wimpy types of bullets that catch you in the foot from a Red Rider BB gun. I'd take a real bullet… from a real gun…for a real home."

Max yapped and licked Remington's cheek.

After executing another happy twirl, Remington dropped Max on the couch before turning the page.

Remington Smith's inherited To-Do List

Drum roll please.

Get to know Johnny B—the boy I gave my memory rocks to. He's at the orphanage, and his big blue eyes stole my heart. I need to know he has someone wonderful in his life.

Have a one-night stand with a totally hot guy. (Remington, stop trying to find the elusive Mr. Right and enjoy Mr. Well-Hung.)

Run Knotty's Marathon for Orphans. (You said a million times growing up you'd like to do it someday. So, do it.)

Live in Knotty while you complete the list. (I know you think you want to live in New York where no one will care if you have family roots, but you need roots.)

One more that you will discover later.

If you need help with any of these, ask your neighbor Jason Hart. Just DON'T fall in love with him. Don't. Don't. Don't.

Are you wondering why this list?

When I found out I was dying, I put together my own list of things to do. I wrote about them in my journals. On the days I didn't feel like working on my list, I compiled this one for you to complete. Why? Because imagining you doing some of these things gave me peace and imagining others would make me laugh so hard I'd get the hiccups. I mean really. You...doing what comes later...better than Prozac chased with wine.

Remington, if you choose not to do the list, your inheritance will be given to that lovely family, the Watsons, who kept you for a week and then returned you to the orphanage on Christmas Eve.

Remington recoiled. Her giddiness evaporated. The Watsons had decided she exhibited signs of having Tourette's Syndrome because she'd kept blurting out *damn it*. They didn't feel they were the right couple for a *special needs* child. She'd been four.

At the time, she hadn't understood why they had taken her back to the orphanage. She'd thought they liked her. That, this time, she'd been good enough. Her orphanage bunkmate had told her it was because she was too different, and she belonged on the Island Of Misfit Toys.

Later, she'd learned that Sue, one of the caregivers at the orphanage, had tried to explain to the Watsons about orphans and their coping mechanisms. That some of them sucked their thumbs, some of them carried a blankie, and that Remington had the phrase *damn it*. Whenever she was scared, that's what she would say.

But the Watsons wouldn't take a chance. They weren't convinced she didn't have Tourette's.

I know my terms are harsh, but it's the only way I can be sure you'll finish the to-do list. And all joking aside, it's something I really want you to do.

I trust you won't let those people get my stuff. Remember, we hate them.

Love and hugs,

Smile if you love me,

Beth

P.S. Rumor has it—the town is hexed. I may or may not have had something to do with some of the hexing. Wink. Wink.

Remington chuckled. Hexed? As in a spell? Totally something Beth would believe possible.

"I'll finish your to-do list," Remington said to

the letter as if it were Beth in the flesh. "And not just because I'm jobless and about to get evicted because my loser boyfriend stole the rent money or because the Watsons will get your stuff if I don't."

She nodded as her decision grew two-inch roots gnarlier than black roots on a bleached blonde. "I'll do it because I owe you that much." She would make amends for being a crappy friend.

When her phone rang, she let it go to voicemail.

"Hi, Remington. It's Vivian. Sorry about this morning. Of course, you're not fired. Call me. I have a new costume order. The Rockettes are performing in Branson at Christmas, and I'll need your help. Darling, this could be our ticket to New York City."

CHAPTER TWO

R EMINGTON LEANED FORWARD IN HER vintage Volkswagen Bug and peered through the windshield at the house on 1818 W. Knotty Avenue. Emotions, the horrid sort, swirled in her stomach. "You've got to be kidding me," she said to Beth.

She had decided to talk to Beth as if she could hear. Sort of like how people chat up comatose patients just in case. So far, Beth hadn't responded.

"Don't get me wrong; I'm grateful to inherit a house. But *this* house?" Remington shook her head, and her stomach flipped like a pancake tossed by a master chef. "You left me C–Squared LW's house?" She, the girl afraid of the dark, was expected to spend the night, alone, in this house.

The house stared back at Remington in equal disbelief. Like it was saying, "You're not exactly my dream-owner come true, either."

C–Squared LW hadn't liked children or dogs or happy people. Just cats. Lots and lots of stray cats. Why had Beth purchased the scariest house in the town when she'd moved back to Knotty? Had it been the only house she could afford?

Remington considered backing out of the

driveway and going back to Branson. Vivian, her whacked-out boss, was right. Remington didn't belong in a quaint boutique town. She didn't belong living beside people whose family trees bulged with leafy branches.

Remington's family tree was a spindly Charlie Brown. "I'm the only twig," she muttered to Beth.

Vivian understood Remington. Vivian had no one, either. That's why they both wanted to make it to New York someday. Live in a town that didn't place a high value on who your grandparents were and if they came from good stock.

Max, who'd snuggled behind Remington's back like an oblong pillow, wiggled out. He settled in the passenger seat and gave Remington a look of kingly arrogance. All that was missing was the crown he'd worn with his Halloween costume.

Max had been caged next to a cat during his time at the shelter. As a result, he had a lot of cat-like idiosyncrasies. He'd probably love the vibes in the house.

"You know you're not a cat—right?"

Max didn't deign to respond.

"Maybe I'll one-up C-Squared LW," Remington said to Max. "I'll get myself a bunch of cats and herd them through the town square at midnight during every full moon."

Max whined, laid his head on the seat, and covered his face with his paws.

Remington rubbed the dog's head. "I'm sorry. Am I scaring you?" She didn't need a fat-ass family tree. Or a crazy-cat lady persona. Who gave a

rat's mangy butt if her life-plan didn't include a
cozy small-town home with a husband and two
children and a ruffled apron and a flyswatter? Certainly not Remington Smith of Knotty, Missouri.

She starched her spine and climbed out of the
car. Determination lifted her chin as she breathed
in the fresh country air and listened to the rustle of
the leaves tossed by the late September wind.

"You son-of-a-bitch. I hope you rot in hell," a
female shouted, ripping Remington out of her
trance.

She spun and saw a stomping, steaming redhead
in hooker heels storming from the house next
door, awkwardly rolling a car tire toward a shiny
white Camaro. A red velvet bow hung precariously
around the side of the tire, threatening to fall off
with each wobbly turn.

"For Christ's sake. Can't we at least talk about
this?" asked a man, his voice full of disbelief. Or it
might have been mockery.

Remington glanced back at the house. A shirtless
man holding a pizza box with what looked like a
candle in its center stood on the front porch.

"No, we can*not* talk about what an asshole you
are," shouted the redhead.

The man ran a hand through his hair. "How in
the hell was I supposed to know you thought I was
going to get you a damn ring just because I said
your gift was round?"

The man was an idiot. Of course, that's what the
redhead had assumed. Remington glanced back at
the woman.

The pissed-off redhead struggled to lift the tire into the back end of her car without letting the tire touch her. "Send me the other three." She slammed the trunk.

Remington glanced back at the man. His lips lifted in a look of bemusement. "Do you at least want your birthday pizza?" He held the pizza out in front of him.

Remington whipped her head around to see the woman's reaction. Personally, she would have pulled out Hank—her Smith and Wesson—and shot at a spot about two feet above the guy's head. Just close enough to get her point across but far enough away for safety's sake in case her aim faltered.

The redhead was apparently unarmed, because she went for the less impressive flipping-him-the-bird reaction and peeled away from the curb, Dukes of Hazzard style.

When had Knotty gotten so exciting? Remington now gave all her attention to the guy.

He pulled on his ear, looking like a man who'd been wrongly accused. She softened toward him.

"I take it you're not going to be nominated for boyfriend of the year?" Her tone held more smirk than jerk.

Long and Lanky glanced over at her. Chuckled. "Just as well. If I won two years in a row, my buddies would make me forfeit my kegger-of-the-month membership."

Remington grinned. He had a self-deprecating sense of humor. She liked that in a guy.

He gave her a steady glance. "Why do women always think they can change a man? I told her on our first date I wasn't ever getting married." He sounded truly befuddled.

"We tend to like a good project, and, to be fair to her, you sort of look like a fixer-upper."

He set the pizza down, hopped over the railing of his front porch and strolled, barefoot, to her side of their shared driveway. He didn't stop there. He walked right up to her. Stopping only when he reached the minimum edge of her personal space, causing her breaths to come out in tiny hitches of anticipation. Which was ridiculous. What was she anticipating? That he'd throw her down and kiss her senseless?

Up close, Long and Lanky could be marketed as a living decadence. The dark-haired, dark-eyed man defined wicked-delicious. Not a damn thing needed fixing on him.

"I don't want to be anyone's project."

"Duly noted." She gave him a two-finger salute, careful not to touch him in the process. "You must be the neighbor Beth warned me not to fall in love with." She dropped her hand to her side and quickly added, "Which is so not a problem, because I'm currently taking a hiatus from men." No crazy falling-in-love type here.

He laughed, and his eyes crinkled around the edges. "Since we're being honest, I should tell you, when a woman declares she's on hiatus from men, men take that as a challenge. Like maybe she has something that needs fixing."

Remington's heart sparked and sputtered like a light bulb in the throes of burning out.

Max barked from the driver's seat, interrupting what was surely a moment between them. *Damn dog.* Without tearing her gaze away from the man, Remington blindly reached for the door handle.

"Allow me." He took a step closer, prompting Remington to quickly suck in her stomach.

Staring into her eyes, he leaned around her and opened the door for Max. His shoulder brushed her arm, sending spikes of awareness everywhere.

When he stepped back, she released her stomach muscles and exhaled a lung full of hot need. God, he smelled divine. Like manly spice and bad boy and pepperoni. She wanted to sniff him and lick him. Like Max would. Afraid she might act on her weirdness, she pulled her gaze from his and glanced at her dog.

He stood on the driver's seat, eyeing them. Remington scooped him up.

"Cute beast," the man said.

Max wiggled, trying to scramble out of Remington's arms. "Thanks. He's a pain in the ass, but I love him." She leaned down, let Max loose, and, as she slowly stood back up, she soaked in Long and Lanky's chiseled chest.

He laughed. "Most dogs are. You're Remington, right?"

Remington adored a man with abs and pecs. Such a first-rate masculine package.

"Am I right?"

Remington met his gaze, and she blinked. Had

he said something? "Do I know you?" she asked. "I mean other than you're a bad gift giver." Her voice came out sounding like she'd been inhaling helium. Her cheeks caught fire. *What in the hell is wrong with me?* She'd never had this type of reaction to a man she just met.

His eyes did their crinkly thing again. "Beth told me about you." He motioned over his shoulder with his thumb toward the white, two-story house he'd just exited. "I moved in six months ago to keep an eye on my company's final renovations of Knotty. The name's Jason Hart." He held out his hand.

Visions of him naked with a tool belt buckled low on his hips hip-hopped in front of her eyes. "That would explain why Main Street now looks like something out of Crate and Barrel." She placed her hand in his and pumped up and down like she gripped the handle of a Vegas, penny-slot machine with a fifty-dollar credit begging to be used. She couldn't stop. Just kept on shaking.

"When the renovations are over, if they ever get over, Knotty will be considered a hotspot to live. Complete with coffee bars, upscale shopping, and a five-star restaurant."

Was he high? Knotty didn't draw in the uberchic. "I'll believe that when I see it."

He wrestled his hand out of hers. "Stick around, and you will see."

"Honestly? You think you can get real people to live here?" She couldn't picture that ever happening in Knotty. The town inhaled tired and exhaled old.

His square chin jutted. "If by real people, you mean part of the young techno-crowd, then yes."

"What?" The word popped out like a sprung Jack in the Box toy.

"Think Tank Innovations partnered with me on this project." A little-boy-spark of ornery glee lit up his eyes.

She laughed loudly. "Have you been smoking weed?"

"You wound me with your doubt. TTI has partnered with me on this project."

Remington placed her hands on her hips and gave him a squishy, squinty look meant to convey serious doubt. Knotty didn't even have a Walmart. "What carrot did you dangle to get them to build here?"

"A unique living laboratory for newly recruited employees."

"I'm not following."

"Think Tank Innovations is big on their workplace offering what they like to call spontaneous collision occasions—"

"What's a spontaneous collision occasion?"

He tugged his ear. "It's when employees get together outside of their work environment. When TTI considers new locations, they look for a unique living laboratory that will encourage their employees to be friends outside of office hours."

"Why do they care what they do in their off time?"

"TTI believes the best ideas can't be timetabled."

She nodded. On the surface it sounded logical.

"Florida office has beaches," he said. "Boston has a pub meeting room. Silicon Valley has a sidewalk café."

"And Knotty?" she asked.

"The small-town experience. The employees can play sand-volleyball on the weekends. Barbeque in their backyards—"

"I'd rather have the beach option," Remington said, interrupting him.

He held up a hand. "*Plus*—because the cost of building here is so cheap, the company picks up the cost of their rent. It's a great way for TTI's first year employees to pay off their college loans."

Remington did a full-body shudder. "I'd rather barf for a living in New York than make this town my forever home."

His lips twitched. "They are also encouraging young entrepreneurs to open up new businesses in Knotty by bankrolling their loans. Knotty might be a sleepy town, but it's about to wake up."

Max's tail rubbed Remington's leg. Distracted, she glanced down. She immediately wished she hadn't. Her ego deflated like a crushed whoopee cushion. "Oh God. Oh God. Oh God." Her voice got louder with each *God* she uttered. Where was a sinkhole when you needed one?

Her sweet, neurotic, rescued dog was humping Jason's leg. Like a bottle-of-gin-for-an-hour street hooker.

"Max," Remington squeaked, snagging him up by the collar. "Stop doing men. I mean humping men. I mean, stop doing that. It's not polite."

Max licked her cheek.

A thunderstorm of laughter rumbled out of Jason. "Did you teach him to hump strangers?" His voice was a sexy, suggestive combination of panache and perfection. "I know—don't tell me— that's a pickup routine you've taught him? It's your way to meet men at doggie parks?"

Remington stammered and sidestepped away from him, trying to think of a witty response. "Of course not." *Yeah, that had witty written all over its ass.* She glanced down at Max.

"Relax. I'm teasing." Jason took Max out of her arms and held the dog, scratching him under the chin. "Wait until you meet my dog. Now there's an animal with no manners. He's a farter."

Remington coughed in surprise. "Is that *your* pickup act at doggie parks?" Joking with him left her breathless and caused her heart to slobber like an excited puppy. She told her heart to get a grip and wiped the stupid grin off her face. No one had ever loved her. Not her bio-parents who had dumped her at an orphanage before she turned one. Not the trial parents who had never chosen to adopt her. Certainly not that dickhead Linny who had taken the rent money and disappeared.

Letting her heart get sloppy was asking for pain. Especially with Long and Lanky. Plus, Beth had told her not to fall in love with him.

He smiled. A slow smile that didn't peak quickly. "Touché."

Rattled, Remington glanced at her house. "I

should get inside before it's too dark to see the stepping stones." They were in the shape of cat paws. Big surprise there. She walked to the back of her car, opened the trunk, and pulled out a suitcase and an old dress dummy partially clothed in one of her dress designs.

"Is your moving truck on its way?" Jason inquired, taking the thrift-store suitcase from her.

Remington jerked. "Shit. Do I need furniture? The letter said the house is furnished." She'd sold everything but her sewing machine, dress dummy, and clothes to pay her credit debts. What was left had been enough to buy a hamburger, a bag of chips and a tank of gas.

"It is." The streetlights flickered on, and she had a better view of his short-cut black hair, his strong jaw line, his diamond-studded ear.

Her gaze skimmed slowly down to the nicely creased, dark-washed jeans and his bare feet. Interesting combination of good and bad. Ashley Wilkes and Rhett Butler. Batman and Joker.

She glanced up at his face and found his eyes doing their own survey.

She straightened her shoulders and sucked in her stomach. Damn her belly for not being flat. Of course, considering the tilt of his head, she had the impression it wasn't her belly he was focused on. His gaze appeared to be a few inches higher than that area of her body. Her breathing sped up.

Could he see her nipples *scraping* the thin material of her well-worn *I Heart Sex* T-shirt? One of her first designs. God, she hoped not, he'd think she was no different than her damn dog.

"If you like, I'll come in and light your furnace. Beth could never light her own fire."

Remington stuck her hip out in a flirty manner and plopped her hand on it. "Any woman with the right vibrator can light her own fire," she husked in a Betty Davis voice. Impersonations were Remington's thing. That and quoting lines from old movies. And not having a brain-to-mouth filter. Beth had once called her impressions a gift. As gifts go, it was pretty worthless.

Jason didn't blink. "Any woman with the right man doesn't need a vibrator."

CHAPTER THREE

R EMINGTON'S FIZZLE FIZZLED.
My house.

She stood next to her car, unable to move. Emotions tumbled about inside of her like thrown dice on a casino's craps table. She tried to follow Long and Lanky, who held Max in one arm and her suitcase in the other as he strolled toward her house, but her feet wouldn't obey.

Jason glanced over his shoulder. "Are you coming?" His tone was gentle. Like he understood how hard this was for her.

Remington inhaled a deep breath through her nose and exhaled fear through her mouth. "Right behind you." She took one step and then a second, shifting the dummy from one arm to the other.

With each hesitant step she took, memories surfaced of dead dreams, of dismal disappointments, of depressing disillusionments. Of two families taking her home for a trial run only to return her like a shirt that didn't quite fit.

The universe whispered, "Poser," and she stumbled.

She squared her shoulders and whispered back, "Am not," and then kept going. It was probably just old C-Squared LW trying to scare her away.

At the door, she fumbled the key.

Jason recovered it. "Allow me." A smile curved his lips...and strangely enough, her toes.

She uncurled her toes and watched the door swing open.

"*Welcome*," said a cheerful voice.

Remington about peed herself and shuffled back.

Max barked and wiggled in Jason's arms like he was possessed.

Goosebumps played tag across Remington's skin. "Did you hear that?"

"The dog barking?" Jason let Max down and moved aside.

Remington's goosebumps tripled. He hadn't heard the voice. *Damn it.* Her gaze darted past him into the entry. Not a ghost in sight. Then again, were ghosts ever in sight? "Never mind." For one wild second, she'd thought Beth had spoken to her.

"This is your house, now." His voice held a hint of sadness.

Did he miss Beth?

Remington opened the wood-framed screen door. Max ripped past her, barking. Remington stepped slowly across the threshold. "I have a home." Saying the words out loud made it feel more real. She set down the dress dummy.

Her home didn't come with a mom and dad, *but* it did come with a forever key.

Jason placed a hand on her shoulder and eased past her. He switched on a light and a soft glow flooded the room.

Remington's eyes widened, her heart jerked, her eyes felt funny, and she hiccupped. "Oh, Beth." The happiest moment of her life came at the expense of her friend.

Red, oversized furniture dominated the living room. The walls were a sunny yellow. A picture of a field, drowning in colorful wildflowers, held court over the couch. A huge circular, braided rug anchored the furniture into a setting begging for tea and cookie moments. It didn't look anything like a house C-Squared LW would have lived in.

"Do you like it?" Jason asked.

Remington nodded, unable to speak past the tightness in her throat. She glided through the room, letting her hand trail over the furniture and pillows. She stopped and stared at the painting. "Beth loved wildflowers."

Jason laid his hand on her shoulder and gently squeezed. "When we were painting, Beth said this room reminded her of you. She said your favorite colors were red and yellow."

Remington's pulse skipped. She turned so she could see Jason. The movement caused his hand to fall away, and she missed the warmth.

"Beth had a 50s style yellow sundress and I had a red one. I designed them, and her mom sewed them for us." The memory formed clear in her mind. That had been the year Remington had decided to become a costume designer when she grew up. The career combined her love of old movies with her surprising talent for designing clothes.

Jason didn't respond. Although he was looking at

her, she had the feeling he wasn't seeing her. Had he heard what she'd said? "Jason?"

He shook his head like a dog shakes off bath water. "Yes?"

"Did you love Beth?" Had he been thinking of Beth just now? Had they been a couple? Was that why Beth had told her not to fall in love with him? Had the warning been one of those I-may-be-dead-but-don't-you-dare-touch-my-man messages?

His face softened as if he'd released an imaginary sigh. "Everybody loved Beth."

Remington opened her mouth to ask for clarification and stalled. Did she really want to know? "She was voted most popular our senior year."

His lips lifted into a genuine smile. "That doesn't surprise me."

Of course, he thought the world of Beth. Everybody loved Beth. She dropped her purse on the couch and strode out of the room.

The house had two bedrooms, a kitchen, and a bath and a half. While the living room had been updated, the rest of the house felt old and spooky. Like C-Squared LW still lived there. When Remington walked through the kitchen, the hairs on the back of her neck snapped to attention.

"Everyone knows when you get goosebumps and shiver for no apparent reason, it's because a ghost is nearby." Beth had once explained the supernatural to Remington.

Was a spirit living in her house? Was it sitting in her kitchen? Was it Crazy Cat Lady Witch? Or a friendly spirit? Perhaps Beth. Had Beth stayed behind to kick Remington's ass for being a bad friend? Or to lay claim to Jason?

"A dead girl shouldn't be allowed to place dibs on a man," she mumbled to Beth—just in case it was her. If it was the crazy cat lady, she didn't want to acknowledge her. *If you acknowledge a ghost, they have more power.* That was another thing Beth had taught her about the supernatural.

Remington strolled back into the living room and found Jason lying on his back, lighting the pilot of what looked like an ancient heater-slash-stove. "Is that thing safe?"

"It is if you don't spread your clothes all over the top to dry."

Remington scrunched her nose. "Duly noted. No panties on the heater." Did that mean the house didn't come with a clothes dryer? Crud, she'd been looking forward to doing her laundry at home. Not lugging her undies to a Suds & Duds.

"Have you had dinner?" Jason sounded like he was laughing. He probably was. Words tended to blurt out of her like fat rolls being released from a pair of Spanx.

"Not since last night." Her stomach grumbled.

He slid out from behind the stove. "Great. I have a pizza and a bottle of wine. Come over and share them with me, and I'll tell you all the gossip in the neighborhood." He flashed her a conman's grin. One she was pretty sure he could use to steal any woman's panties.

Remington placed a hand on her hip and ignored

her wobbly legs. "Gossip? You keep up on the gossip?" She really wished she had a definitive reason why Beth had warned her off him.

He chuckled and disappeared behind the heater once again. "I do. You will too if you want to get invited to Ruby Rae's for her famous cinnamon rolls or Sara Ann's for her out-of-this-world potato soup."

Remington sat on the ottoman. "Who are they?" Beth hadn't said anything about one-night stands being off the table with Jason.

"They're a couple of widow ladies who live together. I'm surprised they're not already here pounding on your door, checking you out. Until the renovations are complete, there are less than twenty still living in Knotty. We're a close group."

"Joy," she muttered. Old people liked to talk about two things—what ailed them and kinfolk. Remington had neither.

"Did you say something?" Jason asked.

"I'm not the neighborly sort."

Max walked over to Jason and licked his free hand, causing him to yank it back and reminding Remington of an article she'd read.

"According to a post in *The Millennial Blogger*, the length of a man's fingers is an indicator of the size of his cock." At this level, she had a good view of Jason's digits. Nice and long. "Do you think they were right?"

Linny, her boyfriend until a few mornings ago when she'd woken up and discovered he'd disappeared with her bank account, had been a penis midget.

Jason laughed, low in the throat. "You should definitely believe *everything* you read online." He emphasized the word *everything*. "But you should do your own research. Double check the facts."

Remington analyzed his tone for signs of flirting. Found some. What kind of guy flirts with a new girl right after being dumped? "I hate research." Then again, what kind of friend flirts with the one guy your dead friend says is off limits?

"Well, damn," was all he said. But the way he said it made her tingly.

He might be off-limits, but it felt great to be flirted with by a cute guy. Remington grinned, feeling light and bubbly, like she imagined she would feel if she'd consumed fine champagne. She couldn't remember ever feeling this way. She hoped Beth was haunting her house. They needed to talk about Long and Lanky. Maybe rock, paper, scissors for him.

Remington channeled a test to Beth to make the picture above the couch move. The hanging didn't budge. In the movies, the picture would have fallen off the wall and landed with an ominous thud.

"That's too bad," Jason said.

"What's too bad?" What had they been talking about?

Jason scooted out from behind the stove. "The more you try to go unnoticed in a small town, the more you'll be fodder for gossip."

"I'm twenty-four. I haven't lived long enough to be the source of gossip." Not entirely true, but true enough.

"Ruby Rae and Sara Ann are harmless." He stood, and his height and overly large hands seemed absurd in the small room with its low, papered ceiling.

Remington couldn't help but take a quick peek at his zipper area. *The Millennial Blogger* could be wrong. Jason wasn't sporting a hard-on so she couldn't tell the size of his cock. *Or very right.* Someone should ask them for their data.

"Get rid of him so we can talk," the voice in her house whispered.

Remington did a one-eighty looking for a body to go with the voice. She didn't see anything out of the ordinary.

Max howled.

"Is your dog crazed?" asked Jason from behind her.

She jumped in fright and swirled back around. "Of course not." Remington leaned down and picked up Max. "I'm not planning on getting to know my neighbors." She had to raise her voice to be heard over Max's wailing. "That's one of the reasons I want to eventually move to New York. I won't have to worry about neighbors wanting to chat." Nerves quivered her voice and legs, embarrassing her, because she'd been going for normal. But it was freaking hard to be normal with a voice in her house and curiosity in her veins and a howling canine in her arms.

She walked to the door, set Max outside on the porch to do his howling, and glanced back at Jason.

"We're a tight neighborhood," he said. "We even play cards on Sunday afternoons. Beth taught us Rummy."

"Rummy?" Good God Almighty, her sexy neighbor who had her all in a tizzy played table games with little old ladies. "Thanks for the dinner invitation, but I'm going to pass."

Jason smiled, flashing dimples and dazzle. "Are you sure? I sprung for the expensive wine, and, if you don't like pizza, I make a mean bruschetta."

His deeply delicious voice was so amazingly alphalicious she wanted to nibble on him. To taste him naked. To declare him doable.

She lifted her eyebrows. "Is everyone in this neighborhood famous for a food item?"

"Pretty much. Do you have a specialty?" His eyes added heat to the question, like about a hundred degrees, and more tingling where tingling shouldn't be happening.

"Chocolate-covered strawberries," she blurted, blushing at the lie. Goulash was the correct answer. What in the hell was wrong with her? And why had God given a Knotty citizen smoldering eyes? A strong jawline? A great butt? Long fingers?

Jason stepped closer and tapped her on the tip of the nose. The feel of his hand on her skin was like wind to a fire. "Decadent fruit. Makes me hungry."

"Hard work makes me hungry."

He swallowed, his Adam's apple catching her eye. "*Hard* is an interesting word choice."

"For crying out loud. Go take a cold shower." Remington didn't know if she was talking to him or herself. "I don't know you. You don't know me. We're not going to do you-know-what. I will not be your rebound girl tonight."

He laughed, a rich and happy sound. "If you change your mind, come on over." An ornery grin accompanied his invitation.

She hesitated for just a second. Okay maybe five seconds. Twenty tops. Or perhaps a whole minute. But then she said, "I won't change my mind."

He wiggled his eyebrows. "About dinner or about doing you-know-what?"

"Both." She managed not to smile.

"Harsh. My ego's going to need a Ben Gay rub-down to recover from the bruising."

"Somehow, I think it's used to bruises."

A funny look crossed his face. "You might be right." He reached for the doorknob. "If you change your mind about dinner, there's a gate that connects our two yards. Slip through and come to the back door. It's never locked. The gossips won't see you. And I promise to behave like a perfect gentleman."

She nodded. Despite his apparent flirting flaw, she liked this guy. Really liked him. He was funny and a straight talker and charming…and he belonged to Beth. Or maybe he didn't, and she'd just known his reputation and hadn't wanted Remington to get hurt.

"There's one more thing." The teasing left his tone.

Remington stilled. "What?"

He stood close enough she could smell the mint

CHAPTER FOUR

R EMINGTON BLINKED. RUBBED HER EYES. Blinked slower. And rubbed her eyes really, really hard.

Beth's dead. There's no way in hell's diary she's in my living room wearing a poodle skirt and oxford shoes. She is most definitely not waving at me.

Sure, Remington had been talking to Beth for the last couple of weeks as if she could hear, but that had just been for kicks. Not reality.

Perhaps the ghostly vision was a result of the mushrooms on the hamburger Remington had devoured at the diner. Perhaps the mushrooms had been *psychedelic*. Perhaps the mushrooms had been elephant-on-the-ceiling and ghost-in-your-living-room *psychedelic*. Yes. That could explain…a lot. Sort of like marijuana brownies.

Remington opened her eyes. "Son of a bitch and his mistress." The image remained. "Beth, is that you?" Despite Remington's common sense, the question slipped out of her parched lips.

"How many ghost friends do you have?" Beth asked in a Grade-A-Smartass tone.

Max growled and crawled under the couch.

Remington stood cemented to the spot. Her

heart pounded like she was seeing a ghost. *Oh shit. I am. And she's a talking one.* "Is it really you?"

Beth gave Remington double thumbs up and a goofy grin.

Remington made a noise. Something between a cry for help and a death rattle. She slammed her eyelids shut and turned around. "I don't believe in ghosts, I don't believe in ghosts, I don't believe in ghosts." Keeping her eyes shut, she waited for a response.

Nothing.

Her breathing slipped into neutral. She opened her eyes and saw nothing out of the ordinary. On the verge of relaxing, she heard a throat being cleared.

"It's me. In the ghostly flesh." Beth spoke in a melodic-version of her old voice.

Remington spun so fast her stomach forgot to follow.

Looking quite demure in her vintage duds, Beth floated in front of the window, her feet about two inches off the gray carpet.

Remington screamed. At least she opened her mouth to scream. Sound failed to launch. A chill somersaulted down her arms, taking her courage as it went.

Max bolted from under the couch and over to Remington where he jumped up and down as if wearing springs on his paws.

Remington caught him on one of his high bounces. "You're shaking like a chicken at a plucking. Do you see her?"

Beth clapped her hands together. "Hi doggie," she cooed at Max.

Max whimpered and pawed at Remington, trying to climb on her shoulder and up her head. A ghost sighting would no doubt quadruple the little dog's neurosis. How much did doggie psychologists charge?

"What are you doing here?" Remington's voice cracked on the last word. Or maybe it was her sanity.

Beth shrugged one shoulder. "I have unfinished business." She glided over to the overstuffed chair, perched on its arm, and crossed her legs at the ankles. "I'm living in the second veil until I set something right."

"How did you get from the second veil to this veil?" Remington asked.

"Oh. That's easy. When the tornado went through the town, it caused a crack between the veils. We can come and go as we please."

"We?" Remington croaked.

"Any ghost with unfished business who ever had anything to do with Knotty is able to slip through the town's crack."

"There's more than one of you?"

"Yep."

"I'll be right back." Remington hurried into the kitchen and poured herself a glass of water and drank it in one gulp while maintaining her grip on a wiggling Max. "You're not going anywhere. If I have to deal with a ghost, so do you."

She walked back into the living room and stared

at Beth from the doorway.

Beth still looked like Beth. Translucent, but the same. Big blue eyes, shoulder-length blonde hair, cute button nose.

Her childhood friend motioned her to come into the room. "I don't bite, you know. I'm not a vampire. You don't believe in vampires, do you? You always were so gullible."

Remington swallowed and took a few steps into the room. The only thing she'd ever been gullible about was her hope her parents would come back. "What kind of unfinished business?" She sort of wanted to hold out her arms for a hug. But what if they came up empty? What if they didn't? And why was Beth wearing clothes from the fifties?

"The ghostly kind."

The ghostly kind sounded menacing to Remington's ears. She stuck her hand out behind her and tentatively backed up to the couch, careful not to take her eyes off her visitor. Using her fingers as a guide, she scooched to the furthest point from Beth and wrapped her arms around Max. "Could you expand on that?"

Beth tapped a finger against her makeup-free cheek. "That's the tricky part. I'm not sure what my business is. 'They'"—she did air quotes around *they*— "don't tell you. You've got to figure it out for yourself. I thought I'd start with you."

"Why'd you buy Crazy Cat Lady Witch's house?"

Beth looked at her blankly. "The who's house?"

Remington held out a hand, palm up. "C-Squared LW—remember, the lady who never left her house?"

Beth's brows pearled together.

"The one with a gazillion cats?" Remington prompted. "And on Halloween, she'd stake a sign in her yard that said anyone caught trespassing would be hexed?" That woman had scared the pee-water out of the town's kids.

"Do you believe in hexes?" Beth asked, looking amused at the idea.

"You said in my inheritance letter you might have hexed the town."

"I did?"

What in the hell was wrong with Beth? "You really don't remember any of this? Does amnesia come with death?"

Beth shook her head. "Not that I've been told, but I did miss one of the mandatory meetings."

"You have meetings?"

"I'm in the second veil, not heaven. There are rules, and jobs, and drama. Oh God, the drama. Just like on earth. Anyway, I'm sure if I think about it hard enough, my memory will come back."

Remington chewed on her bottom lip. "I'm sorry I was a bad friend."

Beth's eyes shined. "I don't know what you're talking about." She slid into the chair and leaned forward. "Let's talk about your to-do list. Your one-night stand." Beth picked up a pillow and hugged it like a teenager about to play truth or dare.

"*That* you remember?" Nerves cha-cha-cha'd in Remington's stomach.

"Oh, for crying out loud, would you stop looking at me like that? I'm here. I'm real. Accept it. You know you want to talk about this one-night stand. So, let's talk."

"I do. But…" As much as she'd oohed and ahhed over Jason, the last thing she needed was to get herself goofy over a guy. She didn't trust her judgment in men.

Beth shot Remington a hard look. "Don't worry. I'm not asking you to get all goofy over a guy."

Remington gasped. Shit. Shit. Shit. "Can you read my mind?" Embarrassment flooded her body until she thought she was going to drown.

Beth shrugged, looking not at all sheepish. "I guess so."

"Do you realize how tripping-unnerving that is?" Remington shrilled. Max escaped her grasp and darted from the room.

"What can I say? Ghostly privilege." Beth gave her a get-over-it look. "You need to find a guy for impromptu sex."

"Why did you want me to have a one-night stand?" Remington tried to erase her thoughts.

Beth's face softened. "Casual sex is liberating." She gave Remington a look of pity. "You've always been so hung up with the fear of getting pregnant out of wedlock that I bet you haven't even allowed yourself to enjoy your body. Are you still a virgin?"

"I've had sex," Remington said like a starchy butler.

"Did you enjoy it?"

Remington tasted the implication in Beth's words. Sour like the lemons life always slammed her with. "According to Linny, I suck at sex." Those weren't his exact words, but the meaning had been clear.

Beth threw the pillow at Remington, hitting her in the head. "Any man who would tell a woman that is the scum of hell. Besides, this isn't about a man and his experience. This is about you and your experience."

Remington tossed the pillow back. "That's how unwanted babies are conceived." She couldn't help the preachiness in her voice. Remington had obviously been an unwanted baby, and that's why her parents had dumped her on the steps of an orphanage.

Beth caught the pillow and hugged it to her chest. "That's why I left you a supply of super-duty condoms in the medicine cabinet. Practice putting them on zucchinis until you can roll them like a pro and then use them. I'm telling you, you need a night of wild passion. Mind-blowing pleasure. Mindless orgasms."

Remington tried to envision herself rolling a condom on a vegetable and not think about orgasms. "I don't know any men who want to take me to bed. And getting one there on my own hasn't exactly been my cup of luck."

"Honey…you have a single man living right next door. And if you didn't notice, Jason's as cute as the devil and horny as hell."

Remington's toes curled. That he was. "I'm—"

"Not that I think he's right for you. Something tells me he may not be. I just can't remember why."

"You told me not to fall in love with him." Remington tried to visualize herself rolling a condom on the hard cock of a man with impressively long fingers. She probably should practice on a massive zucchini.

Beth gave her an I-just-read-your-thoughts look.

"Get out of my head." Remington grabbed her head with both of her hands, causing Beth to burst into laughter.

Once her giggles subsided, Beth said, "I don't remember why I told you not to fall in love with him, but I'm sure I had a good reason."

"Does it still count as a good reason if you can't remember it?"

Beth nodded. "He's out of the lineup for now. But he has friends. Kevin would be a tasty one-night stand. And he's funny. Or there's Tom, who could be a Playgirl model. Or Maverick—he is bad all the way down to the boner he woke up with yesterday morning which I saw when I popped into his house by mistake."

"By mistake?" Remington shook her head. "How do you pop into a man's house by mistake?"

Beth ran her tongue along the inside of her cheek. "He lives near Ruby Rae and Sara Ann. That's where I meant to land."

A bell rung. Obnoxiously loud. Remington's nerves screeched into a new gear, and her body jumped six inches off the couch. "Is that the freaking death bell?" Her uneventful life whipped before her eyes. "You're the Grim Reaper, aren't you!" Her liver cowered. "You've come to reap me." Beth wasn't a ghost. "Oh God, I'm going—"

Beth cut her off with the flick of a hand. "That's my next appointment." She floated into a standing position.

"Wait. Can I hug you? Can you hug me?"

Beth shook her head. "I'm still mastering the ability to manipulate inanimate objects. Things with a pulse are a whole different level of skill. I've been told that one can take weeks, maybe centuries, to conquer."

Remington watched in fascination as Beth's feet disappeared. And then her legs. And then her torso. Until all that was left of Beth was her mouth and eyes hanging in mid-air. "Ta-ta for now." And then she was gone.

Remington frowned. Beth hadn't said, "Smile if you love me." Why not? Had she forgotten her exit line? Or was she an imposter? Was she C-Squared LW pretending to be Beth?

CHAPTER FIVE

R EMINGTON WOKE TO A STRANGE sound.
She tensed. Listened.

Thump. Thump. Rata-tat-tat. Boom.

Not a threatening noise, just as annoying as for-
ty-nine shades of dingy-white. She opened one eye
and pushed curls out of her face. Damn it, thumping shouldn't be allowed when the sun slept. When
she slept.

When she'd been dream-dishing with a ghost.
With Beth. Had it been a dream?

Thump. Thump. Rata-tat-tat. Boom.

She dragged a pillow over her head. She despised
mornings. "Stop." The word sounded more like a
plea than a command.

Had she talked with a dead Beth?

Thump. Thump. Rata-tat-tat. Boom.

"Where in the freak is the racket coming from?"
Remington lifted the pillow and took a deep
breath. "I'm going to shoot whoever you are." No
sense leaving Hank lying around unfired when she
had a textbook reason to discharge the bad boy. No
jury of her peers would convict her for shooting
someone who woke her before dawn on a Saturday. Especially if her lawyer stacked the jury with

night owls. They'd understand her defense.

Thump. Thump.

The sound originated from outside. She shoved the covers down.

Rata-tat-tat.

She untangled her legs from the body pillow.

Boom.

The sound was coming from her front door. As in front porch door. Her target was within-shooting-range. "Prepare to die," she said in a sleepy impersonation of Arnold Schwarzenegger.

She shook off the final remnants of sleep and blindly grabbed for Hank on the night-table. Her fingers collided with nothing. Well, maybe a little dust. She flattened them and groped for metal. Nothing. Nope. Not true. She touched an envelope. An envelope with her name written in orange on the front of it. She'd found it last night under her bed when she'd checked there for other ghosts. She'd immediately decided she wouldn't read whatever was in it until Beth came back. Maybe it told her what the *other* thing was she'd been assigned on the to-do list.

Max poked his head out from under the quilt. He gave Remington a look that clearly said, "And *why* have you woken me?"

"I left Hank in the car," Remington explained as if the dog would understand.

Without so much as a snort of support, Max flashed Remington his butt and tunneled back under the covers.

"Dumb dog."

Max growled.

"Don't think I don't know you just called me a dumb gun owner in dog-speak."

Thump. Thump. Rata-tat tat. Boom.

Remington threw her legs over the side of the bed. Only one person knew she'd arrived. What did he want? How big of a hole would Hank have blown in him? Not that she would have used her weapon on Long and Lanky. Or at least she didn't think so. Mornings weren't good for her. She tended to have drama-queen brain until noon. She should probably sell Hank before she found herself using it on a sleep-deprived whim.

"I'm coming." She slipped on her piggy house shoes and shuffled to the door wearing her *Any time. Any place.* night-shirt. Another Remington original. Crud, it was cold.

She pasted on her what-in-the-hell-do-you-want scowl—she didn't want to appear eager to see Jason—and opened the door with a yank.

It wasn't Jason. Disappointment scraped her heart. The feeling was about as pleasant as having her teeth cleaned by a gorilla. Her scowl became genuine.

A five-foot-nothing female stood on Remington's porch. The woman wore purple tights, purple shorts, and a purple short-sleeve shirt. Her hair even had a purple tint.

The Purple People Eater scanned Remington, then arched an over-plucked eyebrow until the peak resembled the tip of a sharpened pencil. "Aren't you just as pretty as a freckle on an angel's face?"

The compliment faded some of Remington's anger. "May I help you?" Did angels have freckles?

The elderly woman smiled, causing her wrinkles to shift. "I was jogging by, saw your car, saw the light, thought I'd introduce myself. The name's Ruby Rae. You can call me Ruby Rae. I live in the two-story house across from the Old Hammer's Store. Welcome back to Knotty."

Had they met? "For real? You jog?" The questions were meant to be spoken silently. But they popped out of Remington's mouth, disbelief hanging on them like frozen icicles. She searched for words to soften their insultiness.

Ruby Rae lifted both brows, scanned Remington from head-to-toe, spending an extra few seconds on Remington's stomach, which wasn't sucked in. "You obviously don't. Bless your heart."

Remington stopped searching for words of apology. *I've just been handed my ass by a senior citizen.* She nodded in approval. The woman had game. "The light was on because I'm not fond of sleeping in the dark."

That type of fear happens when at the age of nine someone tries to abduct you, and no one believes you when you tell them the story. Add to that the fact she was sleeping in a house that used to belong to a witch, plus had at least one ghost, and well...

"Oh honey, I don't blame you. I think it's terribly brave of you to move in."

Remington stilled. "Why do you say that?"

A look of triumph crossed Ruby Rae's face,

making Remington think she really was an old bat, and why did Jason like her so much?

"Didn't Beth's lawyer tell you that Old Lady Zinger died in this house?"

Remington's right leg wanted to shake, but she forced it not to move. "Who?"

"The lady who lived here for years. The one who adopted all the town's stray cats. Her body wasn't found until after the tornado."

"After?"

"Bless her heart. The authorities went door-to-door, checking on everyone and found her. The coroner guessed she'd been dead for months."

"Ewww." C-Squared LW had died here. Remington's right leg led her body in a wiggly dance. "Which room did they find her in?"

"This one. The living room. That's why Beth had this room completely redone. She did a good job of getting the odors out, don't you think?"

Remington grabbed the door for support. "If I'd known, I wouldn't have moved in."

Ruby Rae leaned toward her. "If the rumor is true that Old Lady Zinger hexed the town before she died, no one would blame you for moving right out."

Remington laughed. A nervous laugh. "You believe in hexes?"

"You don't? Well, you should. No one's found happy love in this town since she died. That's why so many of those who survived the tornado moved. They were miserable here."

Remington knew all about unhappy love. That's

the kind where one loves, and the other doesn't. If there was an unhappy love hex on the town, it would be drawn to her like steel to a magnet. She decided it was time to change the subject before she had a heart-attack and became the third dead owner of the house at 1616 W. Knotty Avenue. "Are you the potato soup aficionado?" She wasn't great at guessing ages, but she'd say Ruby Rae was on the graveyard-side of old.

Ruby Rae snorted. "Not hardly. Anyone, and I do mean anyone, can make potato soup. I'm known for my cinnamon rolls. You won't find a gooier, stickier, nuttier roll this side of the Mississippi." She pointed to herself with both thumbs. "Five County Fair, blue-ribbon winner. Cinnabon didn't even place."

Remington yawned. "Jason mentioned a neighbor who made great cinnamon rolls."

Ruby Rae swatted the air with her hand. "Oh, that young man. He's such a mess. I keep telling him I'm too old for him, but he's not having any of that argument. I hope he didn't bore you too much with my virtues."

Remington laughed. Perhaps becoming semi-friendly with the neighbors wouldn't be disagreeable. Especially if they were all like this old bat with brain-to-mouth filters that didn't work either.

Ruby Rae didn't laugh. Her pressed lips held a touch of challenge. Or maybe speculation? Or maybe female conniving? Or—

"Is there something you needed?" Remington

opened the screen door and sniffed the air for hidden cinnamon rolls. None. Damn it.

"I'm meeting a group for a run, and I'm a bit early. I thought you could get dressed and run with us."

Remington winced. "Run? Before the freaking sun's up? I'm not a runner." She leaned against the doorframe, her brain begging her to go back to bed.

"Fart blossom." Ruby Rae balanced on one leg and stretched the other behind her.

"Did you just call me a fart?" She'd been called worse, but that wasn't the point.

Ruby Rae changed legs. "I called you a blooming fart which is completely beside the point. The point is you can't participate in the Orphan's marathon if you don't run."

Remington's stomach dipped so close to her toes it could have given them a pedicure if only she'd thought to swallow a bottle of nail polish with yesterday's hamburger. "How did you—"

"Know you plan to run a marathon? Missy, easy, I know everything. Beth and I talk."

Remington's ears sucked in those last three words and held tight. "Do you believe in ghosts?"

"What's that, dearie?"

"You said talk, like you still talk to Beth. As in, you're still having conversations with her now that she's dead." Thank you, God. Hallelujah, and cancel the counseling sessions. She wasn't crazy. There was someone else talking to Beth's ghost.

Ruby Rae's eyes lit up. "Honey, do *you* believe

in ghosts?" She leaned forward, inspecting Remington's face. "Ever since the tornado, when eighty-five people died, Knotty has been rumored to be haunted." She sounded like a nightly news reporter.

Were all the folks who had died the ones currently coming in and out of the crack in the town? The ones Beth mentioned. "I'm not sure if I believe in ghosts. Or hexes." No way would she admit to a damn thing until Ruby Rae admitted to it first.

Ruby Rae nodded like a school teacher trying to find the right in a child's wrong answer. Then she bent down and touched her fingers to the tops of her fluorescent orange shoes, which were laced with fluorescent green strings. "Well then—"

"Goooooooood morrrrrrrrning."

Remington squinted into the predawn dark. She spotted a woman running down the street toward them. Tall and slender.

Ruby Rae muttered something that sounded like a curse word. She wrenched up and around. "Fiddlesticks. Sara Ann must have found her Garmin."

"What in the hell is a Garmin?"

"It's a fancy runner's toy. It tells us how far we've run and how fast we're going."

"Who would want something like that?"

Ruby Rae gave her a look of exasperation. "A runner."

"Oh."

Ruby Rae shook her head. "I've got to get going or Sara Ann will be the first to the Elm. The witch beat me yesterday."

"Is she a witch?"

Ruby Rae looked at her like she'd lost her marbles. "No."

"You said witch," Remington said in her defense.

"I was going to say *bitch* but thought that might make me look bad in your eyes. Anyway honey, I don't plan on cooking dinner tonight. I'll see you, sweet britches." Ruby Rae threw the words over her shoulder and sprinted away, disappearing down the sidewalk like an apparition.

Sara Ann jogged in place underneath a street-light in front of Remington's house, apparently not as concerned about who got to the Elm first. "Hi Remington. Glad you've finally moved in."

Remington gave a tentative wave. "Hello." Did everyone know who she was? She didn't remember knowing either of these ladies when she'd lived in the orphanage.

Sara Ann gave her a princess wave back. "I have to go. I need to appear to chase Ruby Rae. Between you and me, her cooking isn't much of a prize. I lose on purpose most of the time."

Jason's two-year-old bulldog, Scotch, barked.

Jason dragged his attention from the computer screen. "Are they out there?" He glanced out the window in time to see Ruby Rae flipping Sara Ann the bird. He chuckled. They were two of the more vibrant residents of Knotty.

"They're early this morning," he said to Scotch.

The Knotty Ridge Runners weren't scheduled

to meet for another forty minutes. Time enough for Jason to respond to a business proposition he'd received from the local university.

The university wanted to reserve all the living units of the orphanage. An orphanage he'd planned to demolish once it belonged to him. The decaying building sat on the outer edges of the town like a dirty welcoming mat to visitors.

According to the university, the rooms would be used as housing for college seniors minoring in The Cognitive Structure of the Supernatural. Seniors willing to pay extra to have boots on the ground in a haunted town.

Word had leaked concerning Knotty's unique state of affairs. Mostly because two construction crews had quit after their work sites had been vandalized by beings who didn't show up on security cameras.

Thankfully, the powers that be at TTI weren't concerned about the rumors. In fact, they viewed it as a fun element for their workers to bond over.

Jason's fingers hovered over the keyboard while he considered his reply. *I'd be interested in sitting down with you and discussing your proposition.* No harm in hearing their offer. He hit send.

If he leased to the university, between their students and TTI's first-year employees, he would be essentially turning Knotty into a singles town.

He logged off, grabbed his jacket, and slipped on his running watch. Much more useful than the Rolexes his father had given him for his birthday this year, last year, and the year before.

"Scotch, do you want to go for a run?"

Scotch farted and dragged his leash to his hiding spot behind the couch.

Jason grimaced. "I'll take that as a hell no." Scotch liked to run about as much as Beth had. Which was little to none.

He missed her. Missed the camaraderie.

Beth had been everything he wasn't. She was a romantic, an optimist, a do-gooder. He was a wolf, a realist, and a shark. They'd argued a lot about the myth of love. She believed. He didn't. Being abandoned by his mom to be raised by his father—a man his mom had known was a cold-hearted bastard—had squelched Jason's belief in the happy-ever-after fairytale.

Sometimes Jason thought he could hear Beth laughing in his kitchen when he tried a new recipe. Which was ridiculous. He didn't believe in ghosts. Beth, of course, had. She'd said Knotty was the home of several who'd been released via a crack caused by the tornado.

Jason stepped out on his porch and rubbed his arms. Once he started running, he'd warm up. Out of habit, he glanced at Beth's house. *Remington's* house. A light was on. Was everything okay? The wild-haired beauty didn't strike him as an early riser. Had her pilot light gone out over night? He should check. Knotty was experiencing a cold spell.

Jason took the shortcut through the yard, hopped onto Remington's front porch, took two steps toward the door, and froze so quickly his brain slammed into his skull.

He ordered himself not to stare. To about-face and go home. Neither happened.

Remington's door stood open, giving him an unspoiled view through her screen door. She lay curled on her couch, pink panties playing peek-a-boo. Heat stormed his body like a Navy Seal attack.

He gulped, reminding himself Beth had asked him to not get in a romantic relationship with Remington. Reminding himself he owed her an apology after yesterday's bad behavior. Still, his gaze swept down the silky length of her curvaceous legs and roved all the long way back up, leaving him feeling like he'd just run a speed interval around killer curves.

The same attraction that had plowed him in the gut last night did so again, coming damn close to dropping him with its unexpected jab.

He wanted her. Pure and simple. He shook his head to clear the desire. There wasn't anything pure or simple about having Remington Smith. He'd made a promise to Beth. Women had called him a bastard many times in his life, especially lately, but never because he hadn't kept a promise.

He assessed his options. A silent retreat would be the smart thing to do. "Good morning."

After a three-second delay, Remington squealed, jumped up, and pulled at the hem of her shirt. Her long hair, a riot of curls, tumbled into her face. "God, I'm going to get a sign that says beware of crazy gun lady bitch."

He swallowed, incoherence scrambling his thoughts, desire stroking his cock. Sweet Jesus.

The display of cleavage Remington had unwittingly flashed while tugging on her v-neck T-shirt caused his mouth to unhinge. Without him consciously telling them to, his legs carried him to her front door for a closer view. "Good morning... neighbor." The last word barely escaped his dry throat.

Her jaw hardened, and her eyes iced over. "Do you *know* what time it is?"

He shook his head, trying to dislodge the fog engulfing his brain. "Time to take a neighbor to bed?" he teased in a piss-poor attempt to elicit a smile out of her.

Remington stopped pulling at her T-shirt and rolled her green eyes. "Don't tell me you're at my house at *five* in the morning just so you can practice a cheesy-ass pickup line."

He tried to look wounded while standing neck-deep in the frost she blew at him. "Cheesy-ass?" He flattened his right hand across his heart. "That was one of my better ones." He might have continued with his you've-wounded-me speech, but the sight of her T-shirt hugging her assets, outlining her full breasts dissolved his ability to speak.

Damn if his hands didn't ache to follow the line, to feel the soft cotton, to skim the lace of her panties.

Her gaze narrowed and traveled down his body. "What do you want?" She spoke in an adorably grouchy voice. "And stop staring at me like you want to eat me."

He coughed sharply into his hand to keep a vulgar response from slipping out of his mouth. He'd obviously been spending too much time around the construction crews.

A blush flooded her face, highlighting the smattering of freckles on her cheeks. "Don't be crude. That is not what I meant."

He also wanted to individually kiss each of her freckles. "Actually, I was watching for Ruby Rae and Sara Ann to run by, and I noticed your light on. I came over to check and make sure things are okay." Remington was everything he got a hard-on for in a woman. Curves and personality. He should have questioned Beth on her request for him not to pursue Remington instead of saying yes without clarification as to why. But when a dying woman asks for a promise, you give it.

Remington pressed her lips together and made a noise of disbelief. "As you can see, I'm fine."

He nodded. That was his cue to say goodbye. He really should go. "Would you like to join us for a run?" Beth *had* asked him to help Remington train for the marathon.

Car lights flickered somewhere behind him.

Remington picked up a pillow from the couch and held it in front of her. "Get in here before you and I become Knotty's new gossip." Without waiting to see if he complied, she plopped down on the couch and folded her feet beneath her.

This was a terrible idea, he knew it, but he wasn't able to stop his forward movement. Jason opened the screen and stepped inside.

"What makes you think I'm a runner?"

He took a seat at the opposite end of the couch. "Beth mentioned she asked you to run the Orphan's marathon."

Remington ran her fingers through her tangled hair. When she let go, the black strands fell to her shoulders in a mass of crazy curls. They framed her high cheekbones, giving her a fresh out-of-bed look. Which was exactly what it was. "What do you know about the hex on this town?" she asked.

Jason clasped his hands behind his head and settled into the corner of the couch. "Who filled you in on that little nugget of information?"

"Ruby Rae."

He watched as Remington shifted and stretched her legs. The thought of her wearing running shorts, her legs spread wide in stride, caused his heart rate to increase faster than the speed of normal lust. He forced himself to replace the image with thoughts of the town's hex. "If you believe in that nonsense, Old Lady Zinger was found with a spell book, and the book was opened to a love spell. There are those who think the town is destined to never know love."

Remington glanced at him through lowered lashes. "Do you believe in hexes?"

"Beth did. She tried to convince me she'd accidentally placed a hex on me."

Remington leaned forward. "What kind of hex?"

He ran a hand through his hair. "I don't know. I never asked."

Remington grimaced. "Who doesn't ask *that* when someone tells them they've been hexed?"

The look she gave him made him worry he'd grown three heads and four noses and the tongue of a lizard. Max ran out of the bedroom and jumped on Remington's lap, causing her nightshirt to ride up her legs, robbing Jason of the ability to think.

"Men are so stupid." She emphasized *stupid*.

Jason pulled himself out of his fog of lust and grinned. "I'm not going to argue with you." He patted his leg for the dog to come to him.

Instead of coming to Jason, Max jumped off Remington's lap and ran to the front door.

"Good. Because you would have lost."

What was it with all the women in his life turning against him?

His thoughts must have shown on his face, because she said, "I'm sorry. I don't do nice before noon."

Did that take morning sex off the table? "Are you going to train for the marathon?"

"When is it?"

"You sound like someone asking if they are getting a life sentence or the death penalty." Jason got up and let Max out. "Six months."

"That soon?"

He glanced back at Remington. The look of horror on her face caused him to smile. "Plenty of time for you to train." He sat down and reached behind him to turn on a small table lamp.

"I wouldn't be so sure."

"Last night you said you were on a hiatus from men. Care to tell me why?"

Why had he asked such a personal question? It wasn't like he cared.

She glanced down at her clasped hands. "Not particularly. Are you a marathon runner?"

He reached out and tilted her chin up, wanting to read her face. "I've run a few." Four freckles crossed the bridge of her nose. He'd never been a freckle type of guy, but on her they were enchanting.

Her eyes were puffy as if sleep hadn't found her until the wee hours of the morning. "Have you ever trained someone to run a marathon?"

"Would you like me to train you?"

She made a *pfting* noise. "That's not going to happen. Remember, I'm on a hiatus from men."

"I didn't realize your break included activities outside of dating."

"It doesn't but—"

"We could agree that our relationship is strictly about running. As it turns out, I happen to be on a hiatus from women. Last night's fiasco broke this guy's game."

Her smile took on a swagger, catching him off guard because he'd been expecting another soul-burning scowl. "Actually, that would work. My hiatus does have a built-in loophole."

"What would that be?"

"I'm only on hiatus from men I might want to *do*."

Her words flattened his ego and engaged his male pride. Leaning forward, he brushed a lock of hair back from her face. "Are you trying to say you haven't considered us having sex?" Hell. His first thought of having sex with her had been when she'd climbed out of her car.

"You're my neighbor, and I don't do neighbors."

Call him fourteen, but the testosterone in him demanded he take her up on the challenge she had unwittingly, or quite wittingly, tossed at his feet. "I—"

She held up a finger and stopped him. "Nor do I give blowjobs to men who think that's not the same as having sex." The words were delivered straight-faced. No sign of a blush.

It took his brain a second to replay them. To make sure he'd heard what he thought he'd heard. When he was sure he had, it was his jaw that dropped as he envisioned her on her knees, her luscious lips surrounding him.

There was no telling what might come out of her mouth at any given time. And he liked that. He was tired of women who never said what they meant. "May I kiss—"

The old-fashion trill of a phone ringtone stalled the proposition he'd been about to make. "Ignore it," he ordered.

"I should get it."

He placed the palm of his hand on her cheek and turned her head, so she looked at him and not toward the phone. "Don't."

"It could be…" Her words trailed off as if she'd been about to say something she didn't want anyone to hear.

"Who?"

She reached out and grabbed her cell phone.

"Hello?" The smile playing with her lips fell away. "Linny?" Her body stiffened. "You good-for-a-punching-bag thief."

Jason stiffened, and his hands clenched into fists. Who was Linny? Where did he live? What had he stolen from Remington?

She waved a hand in the air. "No. I won't tell you where I am. I can't believe I gave you my—" She stopped mid-sentence and glanced toward Jason. "Just leave my money with the landlord. She'll send it."

What? Jason wanted to know what Remington had given Linny. He cut off his thoughts. It wasn't any of his business. She wasn't any of his business. What in the hell was he doing?

Remington ended the call with a few curse words that continued after she had disconnected. She paced back and forth, muttering to herself. Then she stopped in front of him.

"A friend?" The question was meant to lighten the heavy shadow surrounding her and loosen his desire to beat Linny senseless.

"Wrong number."

He pinched the bridge of his nose. "You okay?"

She bit her upper lip as if trying to keep it from trembling. "I've been better."

The admission kicked him in the stomach. He instinctively knew she wasn't the type to admit to not being okay. According to Beth, Remington's heart was as calloused as his. He stood and took a step toward her.

She took a step back.

"Who did you hope was calling?"

Her shoulders jerked up as if the kindness in his voice undid her. "My mom." The low, tortured tone cut at him.

"Has she ever called?" He stepped forward and ran the pad of his thumb down the side of her face.

Her lips tightened, and she jerked away from his hand. "No. But who's to say she won't try to find me some day? It could happen. Especially while I'm living in Knotty. She might come to the orphanage looking for me, and here I'd be. And I know saying all of that makes me sound like I'm ten, but I can't help it. Some hopes don't die."

A desire to pull her in his arms and offer comfort left him uneasy. He needed to get out of here before he did or said something stupid. "You're right." He made a point of glancing at his watch. "I should go. Our run starts in ten minutes."

She opened her mouth. Shut it. Opened it again. "Sure."

"One more thing." He wanted to leave her with a smile. Wanted to leave her with the feeling he was shallow. As long as she thought that, he wouldn't have to worry about her falling in love with him and him hurting her. He just wasn't capable of love. Even now, despite the fact he'd bed her in a hot minute and found her quirky and fun, his heart was cold. Sure, it kicked up at the idea of sex, but that's it.

She lifted her chin and looked him in the eyes. "What?"

"You totally want to have sex with me."
The lights flickered.

CHAPTER SIX

"YOU'RE LATE," RUBY RAE SAID to Jason when he joined the running group. She sounded like a drill sergeant talking to an undisciplined recruit.

"Sorry." He bent and tied his shoe before she could get a good look at his eyes and read something there he wasn't ready to acknowledge.

"Sorry." Ruby Rae echoed loud enough to wake the dead in the supposedly haunted graveyard across town. She leaned down, tilted her head, and made eye contact with him, her glasses sliding down her nose. "God blessed us with this beautiful fifty-degree morning, and you couldn't be bothered to get your ass out of bed on time?"

He shrugged and stood.

Ruby Rae stood and stepped into his space. She placed her index finger on her glasses and executed sharp, tiny pushes until they were back in place. "Don't you shrug that shoulder at me, young man."

He took a step back and swallowed the truth on the tip of his tongue. "How about—I'm really sorry." Better the group think he'd slept in than to know he'd been flirting with his new neighbor.

Ruby Rae poked him in the chest. "You don't

look sorry, let alone really sorry. You look like a boy with a new toy." She rubbed the material of his shirt between her thumb and forefinger. "And you're a little sweaty."

This must be what it felt like to be interrogated by a mother when you came home late from a date. He pressed his lips together and did his best to look contrite. "I'm sweating because I sprinted from the house so I could clear my head." He turned away from her but not before he saw a glimmer of triumph in her eyes. He shouldn't have mentioned the need to clear his head. Damn. Almost kissing Remington had been a mistake that had left him fuzzy. His mission was to transform Knotty into a hip community, not shag all the singles as they moved in.

"You're sure there's not more to it?" Ruby Rae dropped to the ground and executed a quad stretch.

Jason looked around for help. For someone to jump in and save him. The other runners looked at him with varying degrees of speculation in their eyes...not a savior among them. He'd have to rescue himself. "You're feeling feisty today." He simply needed to place the attention back on her. "Which usually means you have some juicy gossip you're dying to relay?"

All gazes skidded from him to Ruby Rae. He repressed a smirk and leaned his head to the left, then the right to release tension.

She eyeballed the crowd. "I do not gossip." Her wrinkles waved in the slight breeze. "I did, however, meet that tart living next door to you."

Kevin Livingston, a member of his design team, punched him in the arm. "Tart? You have a new tart?" He gave Jason a charged look. "I thought you'd sworn off tarts."

He and Kevin locked eyes.

"She's not a tart." Jason shoved Kevin back and, for the ears listening, corrected, "We have a new resident in Knotty. Her name's Remington, and she's…" He struggled for the right word. "Kind." What a puny-ass description.

Ruby Rae snorted. "I'm telling you she's a tart. You should see what she sleeps in. A T-shirt that says *any time any place*. Don't tell me that's not some sexual mumbo jumbo." Ruby Rae popped up and bent over, then flattened her palms to the ground, her bones cracking. According to Ruby Rae, her years of doing yoga kept her sprite. He wondered if her bones agreed.

"How exactly do you know what she sleeps in? Have you been playing with your crystal ball again?" teased Maverick, another key member of his team.

"You liked my crystal ball when I saw a tall red-head in your…" Ruby Rae's words trailed off. She glanced past Jason. A victorious smile stretched her lips so far her dentures were in jeopardy of falling out. "Lord have mercy, someone bring in the cows, I do believe that's our new tart coming down the street now."

Remington walked, because there's no sense

running before one has to run, toward the meet-up spot for the runners. Not because she wanted to, but because she'd committed to finishing a to-do list. Plus, her new translucent friend had popped in within seconds of Jason's departure and told her to get her ass out the door and train for the marathon. Hell, her Casper with a vagina even had running gear stashed in the closet for Remington.

What kind of person dies prepared to haunt her best friend?

One that believes in ghosts and witches.

The only other reason Remington allowed herself to be bullied by her mouthy spirit buddy was it kept her from thinking about the kiss that hadn't happened.

That, and how does one stand up to a corpse wearing a tiara, a siren-red ball gown, and a pair of scuffed army boots before noon?

"I know what your unfinished business is." Since Beth could read her mind, Remington just thought the words to Beth instead of speaking them.

"You do?" Beth appeared in front of Remington, did an about-face, and flew backward which allowed them to make eye contact as they talked. "What is it?"

"You placed a hex on Jason before you died," Remington said. "You need to undo it." Too late, she remembered she should be thinking her questions instead of speaking them. Practice now would prevent an embarrassing slip up in front of the living.

Beth squealed. Stopped flying, and Remington

jogged through her.

Remington shivered, the coldness making the morning air feel tropical.

"Oh my God," Beth said from behind Remington. She sounded excited.

"Oh my God, what?" The streets were peaceful this time of the morning, as if they also refused to wake up before sunrise.

Beth reappeared with the backward flying thing. "I remember now."

"You do?" Remington hadn't expected Beth to remember. *"What did you hex him with?"* Dear God, were witches real? Was she living in a former witch's house? Was Crazy Cat's spirit still in the house? Was that why the lights kept flickering this morning? Because Crazy Cat didn't like the new owner? Would she try to scare Remington out of the house? That wouldn't take much effort.

Beth's smile drooped. "I flicked the lights. You two were about to get gross."

Remington frowned. They needed to set ground rules about when Beth could and couldn't be all up in Remington's business. Like when Jason was in the house, Beth couldn't be within hearing distance. And no listening into her thoughts when she wasn't speaking directly to her. *"Tell me about the hex."*

"What hex?"

Remington rolled her eyes. *"The hex."*

Beth shrugged. "I don't know nothing about no hex."

Remington remembered the envelope. Maybe it

contained information about the hex.

"What envelope?" Beth asked.

"Stop reading my mind and go get the envelope on my nightstand." She turned a corner and could see the runners standing under a big tree, so she fell into a really slow jog. *"Hurry,"* she urged Beth.

Beth disappeared and then reappeared with the envelope.

"Open it and read it to me."

"You're so bossy." Beth opened the envelope and pulled out a sheet of stationery.

Dear Remington,

I knew you'd find this under the bed because you always check under the bed before going to sleep. I need your help. You see, my sources tell me there's going to be a murder. The murderer will be a Knotty resident. If the killing occurs, two ghosts will be released from their confinement in the second veil. These are not the kind of ghosts you want roaming Knotty. They create mayhem wherever they go. Please stop the murder from happening.

Beth

P.S. Smile if you love me.

P.S.S. This is not your other thing on the to-do list.

CHAPTER SEVEN

BY THE TIME REMINGTON GOT to the running group, her legs wobbled her body like a cheap bobble-head toy and her brain had murder and mayhem playing on repeat.

Gasping, she leaned over, grabbed her knees, and tried to breathe. "Hi." She spoke the greeting to a bunch of kneecaps.

"Everyone, this is Remington," Jason said.

Remington glanced up into his slightly horrified, slightly amused eyes. You'd think they'd never seen an out-of-shape runner.

"Yep, that's me." She shuffled around so her butt wasn't all that everyone saw of her. She raised a hand, gave a little happy-to-meet-you-at-six-in-the-freakin-morning wave.

Jason touched Remington's arm.

The touch prompted her heart to giggle like a love-sick teenager who'd just been bumped into by the school jock in the middle of a crowded hallway. Ugh. She didn't know what it was about this guy that had her so I've-fallen-in-love-at-first-sight gushy. Not once, in all her time with Linny, had she mused mushy meanderings.

If she wasn't careful, this man would jeopardize

her promise to herself. The one where she swore she'd never fall in love with someone who wasn't at a high likelihood of loving her back. She'd thought Linny met the high-likelihood rule. She'd been wrong. Which meant she had to be uber-careful with her future choices.

"Remington-badass-Smith has turned into an emotional wimp." Beth's words dripped with a thick syrup of disgust.

The old nickname, spoken by her overdressed, under-shod specter, jabbed Remington's pride. *"Shut up."*

"You okay?" Jason asked.

Remington glanced into his eyes. "Sure." She tried to sound nonchalant. "I'm just a little out of shape." Instead, she sounded like a heavy breathing phone prankster.

A shaggy blond male stepped forward and elbowed Jason out of the way. "Hi, I'm Kevin Livingston. I'm the normal one in the group."

She took a calming breath. "Normal's good." She took note of the mischief living in his eyes. He had I-live-for-a-good-time practically stamped on his forehead and engraved in his grin.

Ruby Rae muttered something. Remington thought she heard the word *tart*.

"Toodle-loo," said a tall, slender female wearing black tights, a pink Nike shirt, and a black jog jacket. Her face was Botox perfect. But not rubbery perfect. Just perfect.

Remington recognized her. Ruby Rae's roommate.

"I'm Sara Ann. No wonder Rube has her bloomers in a wad. You're beautiful."

Remington felt a blush sting her cheeks. Her hand came up, and she wiped the sweat off her nose. She resisted an urge to hug Sara Ann and ask her if she'd like to be BFFs. No one had ever told her she was beautiful. Not even Linny on the day he'd taken her virginity. "Thanks."

"I'll have you know, Miss Priss, I'd have to be wearing bloomers before I could have them all in a wad." Ruby Rae's sharp voice carried clearly in the morning air.

Everyone laughed and made comments about too much information.

"I hope you guys don't mind my crashing your running group?"

A decadently handsome man stepped forward. "Hi, I'm Tom. I live next door to the post office. I'll let you discover on your own what I'm good at." He ended his introduction with a debauchery-loaded wink.

Jason coughed into his hand and said, "Bullshit."

"How far are we running?" Remington liked the camaraderie among all of them.

"Seven, but you just do what you can," Jason said.

Remington nodded. "Seven blocks? I can do that." Would the three she'd run to get here count as part of the seven? She wanted to get this run over so she could get back to Beth and learn more about the murder note.

Everyone laughed. Louder than they had laughed at Ruby Rae's no-bloomers comment. Like what

Remington just said was more colorful than running commando. They looked at one another, shaking their heads.

She was pretty sure they were shaking them about her. But why?

She watched them slip ear buds in their ears, and in unison start running, each of them pushing buttons on their watches as they took off. Like gazelles. Super-fast gazelles. "What the hell—no one counted to three and said go," she complained.

Jason laughed and touched her arm. "We all start together, but that's it. Everyone runs at their own pace."

"Oh." Remington fell into a slow jog. "Why did they laugh?" Jason ran at her pace. So thoughtful of him.

"They're all doing seven miles."

Remington stumbled, and Jason held out a hand to steady her. "Crap. They're going to think I'm an idiot."

"Not an idiot. Just a cute recruit."

Remington shook off his hand. "Seven. Freaking. Miles. Who in the hell does seven miles at this hideous hour?" She picked up her pace and continued ranting. "Or any hour?" Irritability bubbled in her veins.

"Some days we do more. Depends on what the training program calls for." He led them around a corner.

Remington's gaze ripped away from Jason and soaked in the view. Her jaw dropped, and she was pretty sure her eyes were rolling around in the back of her head like a slot machine on the verge of dinging a winner. "It looks like…a rainbow puked on the ground." All the old houses lining both sides of Farmer Street wore coats of colorful paint. Purples, pinks, yellows, greens.

"It is bright," Jason agreed.

"Does anyone working for TTI live in them yet?" There weren't any signs of occupancy. No cars. No trashcans. No curtains in the windows.

"Not yet."

The next several streets had also received facelifts. The view made running a little easier. It was so unlike the drab orphanage she'd grown up in or the low-rent apartment she'd been living in before coming here.

Then came an area demolished by the tornado. The spot her old school had once sat upon now held a partially built condo. "Why is that area not renovated yet? I would have thought you'd want to clear up all the damage before renovating any of it."

"Every time I hire a crew to start on the old school, they quit. Say it's haunted."

At one time, like two weeks ago, Remington would have laughed at the idea of grownups quitting a job because they thought their worksite had the haunts. "What happens to cause them to think it's disturbed?" Beth had mentioned other ghosts floating in and out of Knotty.

"Their work is undone overnight. Or they see movement in debris where there shouldn't be movement."

"You don't sound like you believe them. Do you think they're making it up?"

"I think hoodlums are messing with them. Who knows why. Could be someone else who wanted to buy the land is pissed because I purchased it and they are trying to sabotage my plan by setting up these pranks."

"Or they could be right. It could be haunted." She'd have to ask Beth.

"You sound like Beth. She insisted they were telling the truth."

Had Beth known there were ghosts before she died? Of course, she had.

"Were you living here when the tornado hit?" she asked Jason.

"I was in Seattle."

"Is that where you're from?"

"Yes."

She waited for him to say more, but the single syllable was all he offered.

With the conversation stalling, she started thinking about running again. How much it hurt. She'd never really liked running, but she did like the way it made her ass look in jeans. "Have we gone two miles yet?"

When her running partner didn't answer, she glanced his way.

The corners of his lips twitched.

"What?" What had she said wrong this time?

"We're not quite to two miles. More like half a mile."

"A half a damn mile." When had she gotten so

out of shape? She stopped and turned around. "Are you sure? It seems a lot farther."

"Positive. But you can stop."

"You all woke me up so damn early my sensors are skewed." She continued to run.

"Almost kissing you skewed me." His deep voice made the words feel like a caress, and she melted just a little.

"It's a good thing we didn't. I'm sure I'd be too hot for you to handle." Talking and running was getting harder.

"While we're talking about being skewed, do you always wear pink panties with the words, I-heart-good-tongue across their ass?"

Remington glanced down. Thanks to sweat, her shorts—shorts given to her by Beth—were now transparent. "What can I say? I believe in letting a man know what I want." The panties had been a gag gift from last year's office Christmas party. Before coming to Knotty, she'd burned every pair of panties she'd ever worn around Linny and replaced them with granny panties. These were the only fun ones she still owned.

Jason laughed. "And I believe in giving a woman exactly what she wants."

She gulped, imagining the scene in vivid detail. "Touché."

"You're not going to just take my word for it, are you?" He turned around and jogged backward, his gaze fastened on her.

The guy could run backward faster than she could run forward. "What other choice do I have?"

She should shove him on his ass.

His eyes lit with humor. "Darling…we're in the show-me state. You could demand… I prove my mastery of giving good tongue."

The guy was incorrigible. "You really think I'm going to ask someone I barely know to prove he's good with his mouth?" An image of him proving he gave good tongue popped into her head. She had to bite her lip to keep a groan from escaping.

"Why not?" He turned back around and ran forward, giving her a good look at his butt and his legs. "You wouldn't be the first to ask me to prove it."

His words wiped away her smile. Why was she flirting with him? He probably had more women than Ruby Rae had secrets. He was way out of her likelihood league. Way-way-out. "I'm on a hiatus." She spoke the words as much for herself as for him.

They turned a corner and ran along the side of the town's only cemetery. Somewhere out there was Beth's tombstone. Was that where Beth slept at night? Did Beth sleep? Remington thought she saw movement, but nothing materialized. Were ghosts watching them run?

In an attempt to catch her breath and slow down her thoughts, Remington stopped and pretended to retie her shoe. *I'm going to die training for a marathon while being haunted by ghosts.*

As soon as she let go of her shoestring, Jason slapped her on the butt. "Let's go."

"Hey…hands off the merchandise." She straightened and threw her meanest eye-daggers at him.

The look used to stop bullies in their tracks.

His eyes widened and a hint of red stained his cheeks. "I am so…fuck. I don't know why I did that. It's like… Of course, it's not okay."

Her death stare blinked. He sounded truly mortified. Which made her wonder if a ghost hadn't controlled his hand. Then again, it wasn't like they hadn't both been thinking about doing the dirty this morning.

"Just don't let it happen again." She fell into a forward motion that forced her to either run or commit to an asphalt face-plant. She tried to ignore the prickling sensation his slap had produced.

Glancing around, she realized they'd made it to the town's square. Everything was a riot of colors. Like a box of crayons had fallen into the hands of a painter.

Two of the storefronts had new signs. CUP OF SPIRITS and TATTLE TALES. "What other businesses are coming to town?"

"I have a lot of applications but haven't chosen the others yet."

"Do you need a break?" she asked him.

"Why?"

"Because your answers are losing length."

He grinned. "Running is not the problem."

She didn't believe him. "Right. No really, we can totally walk or whatever for a while if you want?" He was just too macho to admit he might be tired.

He made a weird sound deep in his throat, grabbed her arm and spun her around. "I'll take you up on the—*whatever I want.*" Before she could sidestep his intentions, he slipped a hand around the back of her head and yanked her against him.

Remington barely had enough time to gasp in surprise before his lips were on hers. It wasn't a soft kiss. It demanded surrender. And she did, like a servant to a king, until she finally managed the strength of mind to pull away. Barely away, but away.

What the hell? She stepped back, putting air between them. "That is *not* what I meant by whatever."

He ran his hand through his hair. "I'm sorry." A stupid grin accompanied the apology.

"I've run far enough for one day." Her voice shook. "I'll see you tomorrow morning."

Jason reached out to touch her.

She took another step back.

He let his hand drop back to his side. "Tomorrow, don't wear those panties."

She scrunched her eyebrows. "You want me to run pantiless?" The question was out before she could pull it back in. God, she wished Walmart sold mouth filters.

He made some weird animalistic noise. "Remington, my self-restraint is only so strong."

"Go home and take a cold shower." She bent down to pick up a rock on the side of the road, looked it over, and stuck it in her jacket pocket. "It was nice of you to run with me." She walked over to a tree and leaned against it, gazing off down the road.

He took the hint and started running.

She watched until he turned the corner.

Beth immediately appeared in front of her. "Stop thinking about having sex with him." She wore a green hospital gown.

Remington stomped her foot. "Stop reading my mind unless I know you're reading it."

Beth laughed. "It saves us time."

"Stop it anyway, or I'm going to report you to whoever your higher ups are." Remington turned and walked in the opposite direction of Beth. She didn't have to put up with a mouthy translucent friend.

Beth appeared in front of her, causing Remington to stop. "I know. I'm bad." She stuck her fingers in her ears. "See, I'll do this, and then I can't hear your thoughts."

Remington wasn't ready to forgive. "What do you want?"

"I have something I want to show you."

"The answer to 'who is the town's future murderer?'"

"What murderer?"

CHAPTER EIGHT

A GRAVEYARD AT 7:00 ON A Saturday morning sucks. Even if the tombstone you're sitting by sparkles like polished diamonds. Especially if it's your best friend's final resting site.

Not that Beth appeared to do much resting at this site.

Luckily, Beth conjured coffee to lessen the suckiness of the moment, and a jacket to keep Remington warm.

"Okay—what did you want to show me?" Remington asked. Obviously, the note from Beth had been written while she was high on pain medicines. No way could she have actually forgotten about a future murder if it had been for real.

Beth held out a massive leather-bound book. An intricately carved symbol adorned the cover, looking like a fancy-ass O with lots of embellishments. Remington tried to read the book's title, but the words faded in and out too quickly to catch. Combine that with the strange magenta glow off the edges of the pages, and she knew, just like Dorothy in *The Wizard of Oz*, she wasn't in Kansas anymore.

Remington shivered. "What in the hell is that?" She took a sip of hot coffee.

"My witchery manual." Beth thumbed through the pages, causing dust particles to float and twinkle in the morning's dew.

Remington managed to read the title of the book. *Hexes and O's.* "How did you know to look for it?"

"Common sense says if I cast spells while alive, I must have had a spell book." Beth sat down. "Finding it jogged my memory about C-Squared LW." She patted the ground for Remington to join her.

Remington reluctantly did so. "Do you remember why you bought her house?"

"If my memory's true, I was walking by it one afternoon, and a cold chill blew my hair, and I had this sudden certainty it was the house I had to buy."

She leaned her back against Beth's headstone. "Do you sleep here?"

"Sometimes."

Remington pulled the collar to her jacket up around her neck. Call her hysterical, but it felt like ghost breaths were slithering down her spine one at a time. Like maybe all the ghosts in Knotty were gathered around. Remington shook off the chill.

"Are you cold?" Beth asked.

"A little."

Beth flipped to a page in the book. "Cold and chill are for ghosties. Warm and cozy keep Remington toasty." She flicked her hand as if tossing something at her headstone. "Is that better?" she asked Remington.

Remington suddenly felt as if she were leaning against an electric blanket. "Much. There's a truly a spell in there for warming someone?"

"There's a spell for almost everything."

"You know…I've been called weird more times than I can count in my life, but now it's official. I'm talking to a ghost—with a witch's book—in a graveyard. I'm weird with a capital W."

"Normal's overrated." Beth continued to thumb through the pages of the spell book. "Besides, you should try being me. I'm the witch-ghost…" Her words trailed off, and she squinted at a page in the book. "Here it is." A smile took over her face. "The spell I did on Jason. There's even an orange asterisk by it."

Remington scooted closer so she could read. "A Spell…To Block Love…From Finding A Person." She pulled back. "You cast a spell on him to keep him from falling in love? Isn't that the spell Knotty is already under?"

"Not exactly. The spell on Knotty is that in every relationship, one person *will* fall in love and the other *will not*. So every relationship that gets its start *in Knotty* ends with a broken heart and sparks. The spell I cast on Jason ensures that he is the one who *never* falls in love in a relationship that starts in Knotty. The other person *always will*. Not him."

That explained Remington's unnerving attraction toward Jason. It was Beth's hex at work. If he couldn't fall in love, then it would have to be Remington. That is, if they started a relationship. Did bone-melting sexual attraction count as the start of a relationship? "Why did you do that?"

"If I recall correctly, he was dating a woman who

claimed to be head-over-giant-rack in love with him. But she wasn't. With the spell on Knotty and her love being fake, Jason was doomed to be the one to fall in love. Unless I did something about it."

Remington bumped Beth's shoulder with her own. "How do you know she wasn't in love with him? My senses tell me he's a loveable sort."

Beth shook her head sadly. "I confronted her." Her voice took on a growl. "She said she didn't love him but there wasn't a damn thing the poor little cancer girl could do about it."

"Did you set her straight? Tell her you were a Capricorn?"

Beth giggled. "I've missed having a friend who could make me laugh."

"I've missed having a friend," Remington said softly. "I'm sorry I shut you down after high school."

"I don't remember that, but why did you stop wanting to be my friend?"

Remington sighed. "I flunked out of cosmetology school. I was allergic to all things perm-ish. It embarrassed me because you were at Harvard, and I couldn't even graduate from beauty school. Then I convinced myself it was your fault."

"How's that?"

"I told myself you were a bad friend for leaving me all alone. If you'd stayed and gone to school here, I wouldn't have failed. I decided I didn't need you or anyone else. I made plans to reinvent myself. Family and all. And then I was going to call you and rub it in your face. And you'd feel bad, and then we'd make up, and we'd be friends again."

Beth frowned. "You did a good job of disappearing."

"It's not hard to disappear when you're a nobody to begin with." Remington gave Beth a tight smile, still embarrassed that she was a beauty school dropout. "So, Jason has money?"

Beth looked like maybe she wasn't going to let Remington change the topic. Like perhaps she was going to call bullshit. "A lot of money," she said instead. "There was no way I could die knowing Jason was bound to fall in love with such a bitch."

"What was her name? I'll look her up and kick her ass. Nobody messes with my friends."

Beth scowled. "I don't remember."

"Your memory sucks rubber duckies." Remington reached for the book, curious about the words fading in and out on the pages.

When their hands touched, static electricity zapped them. Sparks bounced off Beth's tombstone, and her hair flew out straight while Remington's curls tightened.

"Ouch," they said in unison, locking gazes.

Beth swallowed hard.

All of a sudden, Remington saw the ghosts she'd sensed were breathing down her neck. They stared at her as if trying to determine if she was friend or foe. She looked away and noticed faces on the trees in the cemetery. The trees were talking to one another. Remington flexed her fingers. They tingled. Something cosmic had just happened. Her heart rate flipped to high speed. "Can I read the spell?"

"Yes, but…" Beth looked down, "…don't insert a name when you read the spell, or you'll cast a spell on someone as well," she said all in one breath. Then she patted her hair back into place, her hands shaking, still not looking at Remington.

Can a mortal cast a spell? "'All great witches that there be, from light, dark, dead and healthy, assign no true love to insert-name's heart.'" She glanced up at Beth and waited until Beth looked her in the eyes. "That's it?"

Beth nodded.

"That wasn't much of a spell. What makes you think this thing worked?"

Beth scooted until she laid on the mound of burial dirt. She propped her feet on her tombstone, causing her wardrobe to malfunction.

Remington smacked her hands over her eyes. "Whoa, don't hike your legs up there like that without giving a girl some warning. You're wearing a hospital gown."

Beth giggled. "I'm wearing underwear." She exhaled hard and gave Remington a big smile. "I know the spell worked because within minutes of my chanting the spell, I heard yelling in his driveway, and when I looked out the window, the bitch was walking to her car and screaming she didn't want to ever lay eyes on him again. Later, he told me they'd decided they weren't meant to be."

Remington mimicked Beth's position. "That's funny because I witnessed a similar scenario with a redhead and him when I got to town yesterday."

Beth glanced sideways at her. "Since he's not capable of falling in love, C-Squared LW's spell causes every girl he dates to instantly fall in love with him. He went through at least three more women while I lived. They all ended with a driveway scene."

"No wonder you warned me about him. If I get into a relationship with him, I'm doomed to have my heart broken for my efforts."

Beth reached out and touched her hand. "You have to avoid having a relationship with him at all costs."

Remington recrossed her legs at the ankles. "Why didn't you undo the spell once the bitch left?"

Beth crossed her legs at the ankles. "There's no undo-spell in the book."

"Then why not cast a falling in love spell on him to counter the not being able to fall in love spell?"

"If I did, he might reconnect with the bimbo from hell. I couldn't risk that. You need to find the anti-spell to what I cast, and then you need to not fall in love with him and let him fall in love with you. Then when the spell on Knotty is over, I'm sure you'll fall in love with him. I mean—what's not to love? Am I right or what? And then he'll end up with someone worthy of him, and you'll end up with someone worthy of you."

Remington jerked into a sitting position. "Have you lost your wits? I mean, I know you're dead and all…" She paused. A swirly attacked her brain, and she couldn't think straight. "And besides, I'm not a witch. I can't cast a spell on him."

Beth took Remington's hands and held them between hers. "You kind of are."

"Kind of are what?" Remington asked even though her gut and eyes had already told her it was a bad question. One she didn't want to know the answer to.

"When a witch dies, whoever picks up her spell book becomes the next witch."

"Ha, ha. Very funny."

"I'm serious. When I handed you the book just now, and we were zapped, that was a sign of you becoming the new witch of Knotty. Didn't you have a veil lifted? See things, know things you didn't know before?"

Remington jumped to her feet. "You tricked me into becoming a witch?" She walked circles around Beth. "I can't believe you did that." She'd been hoodwinked by her best friend. "You should have asked me first."

"It had to be you. I couldn't risk you saying no. You're the only one who can see me. If the hex is my unfinished business and, if you can undo the spell, I can cross over to the third veil."

Remington glanced at the spell on the opposite page. A spell titled: Make Them Stumble. "Why would a witch want to make someone stumble?"

Beth grinned. "I love that spell. Used it on Jason's fraud of a girlfriend every chance I got."

Remington read the spell. "Do all spells have rhyming words?

"No. Now, let's talk witch's etiquette."

"Etiquette?"

"Well, not so much etiquette as survival 101."

The swirly in Remington's brain screeched to a stop. "Survival?" The ability to take a full breath ceased.

"When you cast a spell, be sure no one hears you."

"Why?" she squeaked.

"Witches are supposed to maintain a low profile. Otherwise, people start burning them at the stake and or tossing them into padded rooms with locks on the outside of the door."

Remington shuddered. "I don't want to be a witch. I'm enough of a freak being an orphan no one ever adopted."

"You are not a freak. And even if, for the sake of argument, you are, you're now a damn powerful freak."

"Not funny." Remington stomped toward the road. She was pissed at her friend, and she didn't like being pissed at her friend. Especially since her friend was dead. And she definitely didn't like the parade of ghosts leading her down the road.

One turned, waved at Remington, and then gave a *follow us* motion with his index finger.

"Where are you going?" Beth called out.

"I don't know." Too many things had happened since Ruby Rae's predawn visit. Hell. Remington hadn't even had a chance to properly process Jason's kiss. Or Linny's phone call. Or the note.

Beth floated in front of her and stopped, forcing Remington to halt or walk through her.

The other ghosts didn't wait. They kept dancing their way down the road, one of them carrying an ancient boombox on his shoulder. Good. She didn't want to follow them.

"You forgot your witch's manual," Beth said.

"I don't want it. I want to be left alone."

Beth's smile slipped. "Fine. I'll drop it off at the house. But in return, would you mind going to see Johnny B when you're done being alone? He's having a downer day."

Remington's chest tightened. She had a bad feeling about meeting Johnny B. "Out of all the orphans, why him?"

"He sleeps in your old room. Your old bed."

CHAPTER NINE

REMINGTON STOOD IN FRONT OF the Knotty Orphanage. Unable to move. Unable to breathe. Unable to leave.

Who knew seeing her old quarters again would hurt? Obviously not her.

Make her sad, probably. But hurt? She hadn't been prepared for hurt. She hadn't been prepared for her heart to squeeze tighter than it had when she'd watched *A Star Is Born*.

Overwhelmed by the emotions engulfing her, she pulled her gaze away from the orphanage and glanced toward the playground. Small children: round, skinny, short, tall, were climbing, swinging, sliding, hiding on the same equipment she'd once played on. To the casual observer, they were normal.

But she wasn't casual, and they weren't normal.

She didn't need to be a doctor to know if you took an x-ray of their young bodies, you'd see loneliness lining the inside of their laughter and caution patrolling the outside of their hearts.

You'd see trash bags full of rotting hope at the bottom of their bellies. And on broken-down shelves…you'd see old tattered bags of self-esteem.

You'd see the hardened souls of the older orphans, tattooed with name-calling graffiti. Words like *unloved, unwelcomed, unliked, unwanted* permanently etched in pain.

And you'd see their memories of the families who came looking for a child and didn't choose them… and didn't choose them…and didn't choose them.

And that's not all you'd see.

You'd see—

The thump of a ball, plowing into the side of Remington's neck, caused her to stumble sideways and almost fall. "Ouch." She jerked out of her hellish thoughts and into the present, a fresh layer of sweat coating her skin.

"Hey, lady, throw us the ball."

Remington picked up the dirty kickball and tossed it toward a group of children who cheered and waved. Beside them were the dancing ghosts. They were now playing kickball. They waved at Remington. A couple of them gave her a thumbs up. Had they known all along this was where she would come?

She gave a half-hearted wave to the children, not the ghosts, peeled her eyes off them, and managed a shallow breath. She should leave before she got sucked back into the orphan's vortex of optimism, disappointment, optimism, disappointment.

She turned her right foot outward, ready to pivot and run.

Only she didn't go anywhere.

Who was she kidding? She couldn't leave. Beth had asked her to meet Johnny B. And Beth was the nearest thing to family she'd ever had. She'd do anything for Beth. Even become a witch so Beth could cross over.

Remington took a deep breath and said, "Excuse me," to the gatekeeper, whose back was turned to her. The two words weren't loud or solid, but they sealed her commitment to stay. She was going to do this. When she left Knotty, left the orphanage, she'd promised herself she'd never come back. That she would forget her past and build herself a bright future.

The woman didn't turn. Apparently, her job description didn't allow her to look away from the orphans. Either that or she couldn't hear.

"Um, excuse me," Remington said a bit louder.

"How may I help you?" the woman asked in a dreary tone, not bothering to twist her head in Remington's direction.

"Could you tell me which one of those boys is Johnny B?"

The woman pointed a plump finger. "He's the one sitting over there by himself."

A small, dark-headed boy sat huddled under a pine tree, rolling a car in the dirt.

"Is he in trouble?"

"He prefers to play alone."

"Beth asked me to keep an eye on Johnny B while I'm in Knotty."

The woman swirled a half-circle. "Beth?" A child-drawn smile lit up her face. Child-drawn because it was a smile that went beyond the normal areas for a smile. One that touched every part of her face—scribbled both inside and outside of the lines of her lips. One that could strip Mona Lisa of her fame. One that clearly said how much she thought of Beth.

Remington nodded.

"You must be Remington. Beth told me *so* much about your friendship. Johnny B's been waiting for you." The words toppled out in a fast blast of giddiness. She opened the gate and motioned for Remington to walk through. "Johnny B," she shouted.

The woman's gushiness made Remington feel special. She straightened, did a little shoulder roll of importance, and forced her legs to move inside the courtyard. She could do this. She was an adult. She was not afraid of ghosts or orphans.

The sound of the gate clanging shut froze Remington's bravado. She broke out in yet another sweat. The ground in front of her spun.

She grabbed for the fence and held tight to a post. The coolness of the metal helped her regain her senses. The gate was shut to keep the children safe. Not to keep her from leaving. If she wanted to, she could bolt. She wasn't stuck here forever. She was a visitor. An adult. No need to panic.

"Johnny B," the woman called out sharper when Johnny B didn't respond.

Johnny B rose slowly and plodded over to them. "Yes, Mum?"

"Johnny B, this is Remington. She's the one Beth yapped about."

Johnny B's mouth fell open showing a gap where

two front teeth should be. "I didn't think you'd come."

Remington licked her dry lips. Damn, *adorable* didn't begin to describe him. Why hadn't he been adopted? What was wrong with him? The horrid thought bitch-slapped her. Hell. When had she become that person? "Of course, I came. It is so nice to meet you."

The little boy rocked from one foot to the other, wringing his hands. "Are you going to die, too?"

Remington's stomach twisted into a pretzel. "Not that I'm aware of." She could have simply said no, but then what if she did? He'd think she'd lied. She would never lie to an orphan. Never. And lord knew if she ran a marathon, she just might die from the experience. Maybe she could cast an adoption spell on him.

"Beth died." His bottom lip trembled.

"I bet you miss her."

The gatekeeper cleared her throat. "Why don't the two of you go sit under the tree and get to know each other?"

Johnny B grabbed Remington's hand. "Beth liked to play pretend. Do you?"

His hand felt small and warm, and he held on tight.

"What did you play?"

He smiled up at her, showing Remington the dimple Beth had mentioned in her letter. "We played adoption day. She was the mom who came to adopt me."

Remington tripped. The air whooshed out of

her lungs, and her heart shriveled like an old man's cock about to get a sponge bath from the meanest nurse at the senior-citizen home. Remington gasped at the pain.

She and Beth used to play adoption day.

She dropped Johnny B's hand. "Why don't we get to know one another a little better first and then we can play...something?"

A look of disappointment brewed on his face. "Okay." He sat on the bench, pulled his legs up until his knees touched his chin, and then hugged them with his bare arms. "What do you want to play?"

Remington sat beside him and mimicked his pose. "What's your favorite thing to eat?" Maybe she could bring him his favorite candy bar next time.

He opened his mouth and then shut it. He rubbed his eyes with the back of his grubby hands and sighed. "Meatloaf."

"Meatloaf!" She couldn't stand meatloaf at his age. "Why?"

Johnny B laughed. He crawled up on his knees and grabbed her shoulders in his pudgy hands. "Because Jason likes meatloaf. Do you know him?" His whispered words tickled her ear.

Instead of sitting back down, Johnny B hugged her around the neck and sniffed audibly.

Remington inhaled the scent of little boy. Sweat... soap... dirt. "I do know him. He's my neighbor."

He sat back in his spot. "Can I come see you

when I visit him?"

A chorus of *nos* screamed in Remington's head. Her mission was to find Johnny B a buddy, not become his buddy. She planned on exiting his life without having done any damage to his tender heart.

She tapped his freckled nose with the tip of her finger. "Of course." She tried to suck the words back in. *Crap.* The wrong response had come out. How had that happened? Who'd just controlled her mouth? What in the hell was going on? She glanced around for Beth. Didn't see her. Had one of those other damn ghosts just used her as a ventriloquist dummy?

Johnny B beamed. "You smell pretty."

Remington grunted. She was pretty sure she smelled like dried sweat.

Stop it. She sent the stern thought to whichever ghost was at fault. "Is Jason's meatloaf any good?"

Johnny B studied her for a minute digging in his ear with a finger. "Nah, but he likes me because I like his meatloaf. So, don't tell him."

"You happen to be looking at an expert secret-keeper."

"Beth and me used to have a secret."

The mention of Beth and a secret caused Remington to remember Beth's letter. Beth's secret. Beth praying Remington would never get parents. "Your turn. What do you want to ask me?" She didn't want to examine how she felt about Beth's betrayal.

"Can you do this?" Johnny B puffed out his

freckled cheeks and then collapsed them with his hands, producing a farting noise.

Remington grinned. "Nope."

"How about this?" This time he put his hand under his armpit and strenuously pumped his other arm up and down until he produced another fart.

"No."

Johnny B and Jason's farting dog probably made a great team.

Johnny B tilted his head sideways and took on a serious look. "Do you have orphans?"

"I do not."

His little body leaned toward her. "Do you want orphans?" He stared straight into her eyes waiting for her answer. Shimmering hope filled their blue orbs.

Remington swallowed and didn't try to scrutinize the weird sensation in the bottom of her stomach. "I don't know. Maybe…when I'm married." Her tongue tangled on the ragtag team of words.

He leaned even closer and placed his palms on her cheeks. "Would you want a *boy* or a girl?"

A shadow touched her mind, and she pulled back out of his plump hands. Dear God, he was sizing her up as a potential mom. He still felt hope. How old had she been when the last of her hope of being adopted had leaked out?

Eighteen.

"That's a fine question, Johnny B," said a voice behind them.

Remington whipped around, thrilled to be

interrupted.

"Jason!" Johnny B squealed. He ran to Jason and leaped like a tree frog into his open arms.

Jason lifted him over his head and twirled him up and down and around, causing giggles to spill from the flying Johnny B.

One of the kickball-playing ghosts hopped on Johnny B's back and enjoyed the ride as well.

The sight of Johnny B having fun, not the ghost, caused Remington's heart to ache. Ache for something she'd never known. A dad.

Would her dad have twirled her in the air until all of her giggles evaporated? Did he even know of her existence? What kind of person was her dad?

Was there a spell for Dad-finding? Mom-finding?

"What are you doing here?" she asked Jason, sounding more abrupt than she meant to.

CHAPTER TEN

JASON'S GAZE RAKED DOWN REMINGTON, looking for clues to what it was about her that made him act like he hadn't been laid in a decade. That made his heart beat a little too fast for comfort.

Even when he'd erroneously thought himself in love with Bernadette, he hadn't reacted with so much naked abandonment. Luckily, he'd had a wake-up call where Bernadette was concerned. He still didn't understand why he'd ever thought himself in love with her. She wasn't anything like the type of woman he'd want to spend the rest of his life with. If it didn't sound so crazy, he'd swear he'd been drugged and brainwashed.

Anyway, he'd do well to remember that his heart was not to be trusted. The damn thing could be manipulated by a woman.

He shook the thought off and lowered the still-laughing Johnny B to his feet. He gave him a conspiratorial wink. "Do you want to tell her, or should I?"

Johnny B collapsed on the ground, hands, and legs sprawled. "You."

Jason placed a foot in the middle of Johnny B's

stomach sending them both into a round of giggles. "Johnny B. keeps me company on my cool-down walks. He says he likes walking with me, but I think he's really searching for fairies in the forest."

"Am not, you are," Johnny B exclaimed. "Can Remington go?"

Jason held out a hand and tugged Johnny B off the ground. "She's a girl, you know. I thought you said girls have cooties?"

"Ms. Sue says old girls don't have cooties."

Jason assessed Remington's body, lingering on the parts below the neck. "She is old."

Remington pursed her lips at the two boys.

He tried not to notice her nipples. "Remington, would you like to go with us?"

Remington shook her head. "I've had my quota of exercise for one day."

Jason glanced at Johnny B. The little boy's bottom lip trembled like an earthquake. He glimpsed sideways at Remington and pointed at the boy's face. "How can you say no to this?"

Remington peered down at the top of her Nikes. "I'll come by and see you tomorrow, Johnny B."

"I want you to come now." The disappointment was tangible in the child's voice.

Remington gave Jason a silent look of something, but he couldn't interpret what she was trying to tell him. It was as if she was afraid to spend time with the kid. What was there to be scared of? He was hopelessly cute.

As much as Jason didn't understand why this was such a big decision for her, the look of panic on her face told him it was monumental. "Do you think she's trustworthy?" he asked Johnny B. Jason resisted the urge to pull Remington in his arms and ask her what bothered her about spending time with a little boy.

"Beth said she was," Johnny B said, digging a hole in the ground with the toe of his shoe.

Jason smiled. A smile he used often to get his way. "Maybe we could talk her into going with us if we tell her our secret."

Johnny B stopped digging and gave Jason a wide-eyed look. He cupped his hands around his mouth and whispered. "We can't. Then it won't be a secret."

Jason placed his hands around his mouth and whispered back. "It'll still be a secret, but three of us will know instead of two."

Johnny B thought about it for a moment. "You can do that?"

Jason's heart melted a little. "Absolutely." One of these days the kid was going to get adopted, and Jason would miss him. Beth had introduced them the first week he'd moved to Knotty and asked him if he knew of anyone who might want to adopt. He'd put out some feelers and came up with a family who lived in Seattle who'd been trying to adopt. They were going to come and visit Johnny B in December.

"Okay," Johnny B whispered.

Jason turned to Remington. "If you walk with us, we'll tell you our secret."

Remington twirled a strand of hair around her

finger. "You two have a secret?"

Jason shrugged. Johnny B was a collector of secrets. Jason didn't know if this was normal of all boys his age or if it was an orphan thing. Maybe Remington could answer that for him. Jason spent a lot of time with Johnny B. They took walks and talked about secrets…and life…and girl germs. Jason tried to spend time with the other orphans as well. The older boys usually talked him into a game of baseball.

"Yup," Johnny B said, nodding hard, causing a lock of hair to fall over his face.

Remington dug the toe of her shoe in the ground, mirroring Johnny B's actions. "Is it a good secret?"

"Better than best," Johnny B assured her.

Remington glanced from Johnny B to Jason. "How far of a walk are we talking?"

"About a mile." He smiled, thinking about her seven-block run quip.

"I think—"

Her reply stalled. Jason waited.

She bit her lip and closed her eyes. Then they opened slowly as if attached to a weary sigh. "Okay." She gave him a dull smile. "What's the secret?"

Realization hit Jason between the eyes. She was fearful of being hurt. She was terrified to care about Johnny B. That's why she was reluctant to spend time with him. He cleared his throat of the emotions trying to form. "First…we walk."

Beth's childhood friend, the one who had no fil-ter on her mouth, the one who acted tough when pushed against the wall, had a heart that could be melted by a child. "We wouldn't want her to listen and run," he said to Johnny B. To himself he said, *stop trying to put the Remington Smith puzzle together.*

Remington shot him a wounded look. "I don't—"

"This way," Johnny B shouted.

Jason held out a hand to Remington.

She ignored the invitation and trotted off in the direction of Johnny B.

They took a zagging trail through the woods that originated behind the orphanage and continued to the outskirts of town. As soon as they were out of sight of the other orphans and the gatekeeper, Remington stopped. "Okay, what's the secret?"

Johnny B motioned for Remington to bend down so he could whisper in her ear. "This is a secret. You can't tell nobody."

She crossed her heart with her index finger. "I won't."

"Promise?"

She gave him a you-can-trust-me smile. "Promise."

Johnny B glanced over his shoulder at Jason. "Should I make her spit and shake hands on it?"

"She'd probably scream and bring everyone running."

Johnny B put his lips right up against her ear. "Down there where the big tree used to be"—he pointed to an opening in the forest where the tornado had taken out a lot of trees—"Jason's building a new orphanage. With girl tree houses and boy tree houses."

Remington pulled back. "What's wrong with the orphanage you have now?" She glanced at Jason.

Jason pulled his gaze from Remington and glanced at Johnny B, who'd made a strangled noise.

The child's eyes were wide and filled with tears.

"Are you going to talk him out of it?" the little boy asked Remington. His voice whisper quiet.

Remington shook her head.

Jason bumped Johnny B's shoulder with his fist. "I told you man. She's a girl. They don't like change unless it's their idea."

Remington frowned his direction. She gave Johnny B a wide smile. "Don't worry sweetie, I'm not going to change his mind. It's a grand idea. It just startled me for a second."

Johnny B glanced at Jason. "Do you still promise to build it?"

"Of course." He resisted the urge to walk over to Remington and hug her.

Remington looked him square in the eyes. "It's not okay to break a promise to an orphan. So, you'd better build it."

Jason raised her finger to his lips and kissed the tip. "It's not okay to break a promise to anyone." He pulled her next to him and placed his hand in the small of her back.

Remington sidestepped his hand. "Why are you spending money on building a new orphanage?"

"Because I can." It was the right thing to do. The whole town was getting a facelift. The orphanage should, too. If there were college seniors eager to move in and try their hand at conjuring ghosts, who was he to say no. "Join us in the creek," he said to Remington. "The water feels great on tired feet."

She shrugged a shoulder and gave him a smile that barely tilted her lips. "No thanks."

He battled the urge to pry. To say anything that would build a bond between them. "You're no fun."

Remington blinked hard. "That's what Linny said when I refused to let him tie me up during sex."

A desire to beat the shit out of the asshole, Linny, slammed Jason in the ribs.

"Come on," Johnny B yelled. He'd already run to the creek.

Remington turned her head to glance at Johnny B, and Jason took advantage of the moment to lighten the mood. He swooped down and bit her earlobe.

She yelped and rubbed her ear. "Why did you do that?"

"Don't ever let a man tie you up…unless it's me."

While they played at the creek, Remington walked over to the area where the big tree used to be. That tree had been famous with the orphans because it was the tree Trevor Johnson had climbed and refused to come down from. Those in charge had to call the fire department for help. Unfortunately, Trevor had fallen to his death before they could get to him. After that, the orphans were no longer allowed to play in the wooded area.

Now, with ninety percent of the trees downed by the tornado, the area was drenched in sunlight. As if a memorial to Trevor. The spot where he fell even appeared to have its own sunlight beam. Like the sun was going above and beyond to make sure his location of death would never be forgotten.

Remington walked to that spot, hoping to warm up. Instead, when she stepped into the sunbeam, she shivered. She glanced around for ghosts. Had she stepped through one by accident? None were around. She took a few steps to the right and found warmth. The ghost must have vanished the moment she'd stepped into it. The brightness of the sun probably kept her from seeing it. Remington took a seat and waited on the boys.

Thirty minutes later, Jason and Remington left a reluctant Johnny B at the orphanage for his daily routine. One Remington knew by heart. She and Jason walked to the parking lot. Remington thinking about spells, Jason whistling the *Andy Griffith* tune—poorly.

Remington stopped in the parking lot to retie her shoe. "Why are you really building a new orphanage?" Why would he bother?

"Have breakfast with me and I'll tell you."

"No thanks." The guy was a serial flirt. "Hiatus and all that jazz." At least the ghosts hadn't tagged along on their walk. They were still in the yard playing ball. Exactly where she'd told them to stay but hadn't expected them to listen. She heard a few of them arguing but couldn't decipher what they were saying. One was probably upset over a called out.

"You're hungry, aren't you?" Jason asked.

"You're on a hiatus too, remember?" The guy was a heartbreaker.

"I'm only offering to cook your breakfast. Nothing more. We can talk about Beth. She knew all about my plans for the orphanage. She helped me design them."

Remington caved. "What are you fixing?" Sure, she could ask Beth, but knowing Beth, she'd already forgotten she'd turned Remington into a witch.

Jason gave her a cocky smile. A smile that made her wish for a heart that could never be hurt or a town that wasn't cursed to lead her down that path. "Frosted Flakes."

She laughed. Her heart was surely safe with a Frosted Flake kind of guy. "Fine, but only because I don't have any breakfast food in the house. And, I'm really attached to the orphanage." As long as she remembered he couldn't fall in love with her, she should be able to keep herself from falling in love with him. Only a fool would fall in love with a man who'd been hexed not to love you back.

Only a freaking fool. Then again, she already had the freak part established, which made her fifty percent there.

It would help if he weren't so damn charismatic. Maybe she could find a spell to cast on him that would strip him of his charisma. Maybe make him fart every time he smiled.

"Great. I'm going to stop by Maverick's and then I'll be home. Just come over when you're ready. If I don't answer the door, come on in." He leaned in, stole a kiss. "I might be in the shower. In fact, if I'm in the shower, feel free to join me."

Remington touched her lips. Yep. Definitely needed a charm-be-gone spell. "Why would I do that?"

"You wouldn't. But it would have been rude of me not to ask."

Before she could remove his ego with a sharp-edged retort, or an off-the-top-of-her-head hex, a shiny red Mazda Miata whipped into the parking lot with its top down, stopping inches from them, successfully zapping the moment of its electricity.

A Taylor Swift lookalike sat behind the wheel, her blonde hair protected behind a silk scarf, her blouse unbuttoned all the way to Cleveland. "Where have you been all my life?" she asked Jason. She sounded as gnat-brained as a 1-900 phone sex operator.

"He just got out of prison," Remington answered before Jason could reply. "Six years of hard time." She glanced at Jason. A pulse ticced in his forehead.

"Oh, you poor thing." The empty-headed bimbo wagged eyelash extensions at him. "Were you doing time for embezzlement?"

Embezzlement my ass. "Panty thief," Remington replied. That was a much more likely crime for him to have committed. She playfully ran the back of her hand down his cheek. "I feel like I'm at risk of losing mine every time I'm around him." She did not like the blonde in the red car.

Jason shook his head. "She's right." He tapped Remington's nose. And then turned a full-wattage smile on the blonde. "You should keep an eye on your panties around me."

A burst of jealousy splattered somewhere inside of Remington, leaving a rotten egg taste in her mouth. She hadn't meant to give him an opening to flirt with the stranger.

"Why are you here?" he asked the woman.

The wind picked up, and a cloud went across the sun, perfectly matching Remington's current state of mind.

"I'm here to adopt a child."

He jerked, as if startled anyone would come to Knotty to adopt a child.

"I'm going to be a single mom," Gnat-Brain continued. "I don't suppose you'd be a dear and walk with me inside. I'm a quivering mess of nerves." She held out a hand that shook for proof. "The name's Bernadette."

Jason appeared to have lost his tan, but his devil-may-care grin didn't falter. "I'd be happy to."

"Darling, I promise to repay your kindness." The blonde got out of her car, gave Remington a saccharine smile, looped her arm through Jason's, and turned him in the direction of the orphanage.

"Jason?" Remington waited for Jason to turn around. Tell her he'd just be a moment. He didn't. Instead, he bent his head low and listened to the blonde.

Remington frowned. His easy dismissal was hurtful. She resisted an urge to throw a temper tantrum on the sidewalk. Call him an ass. Tell him never to contact her.

All the ghosts blew over to stand beside her.

"Cast a spell," the oldest one ordered. He had gray hair and wore a pink shirt and gray tie. And baseball pants. His shirt sleeves were rolled up at the elbow.

Of course. Yes. That's what she should do. What's the good in being a witch if you couldn't use it at times like this? She recited the stumble spell.

Rocks, rocks,
Big and small,
Trip the bimbo,
And make her fall.

Gnat-Brain tripped.

Remington smirked.

Jason caught the bimbo in his arms. "Some things never change."

Remington cocked her head so that her left ear was closer to them. *Some things never change.* What did that mean?

"My hero," Gnat-Brain said in a breathy voice.

"Damn it," muttered Remington. She glared at the congress of ghosts. "That was a bad idea. Go away."

"I told you she wasn't going to be on our side," said a ghost carrying a magnifying glass in one hand and a cigar in the other. He was also wearing baseball pants.

Had he been a detective in a former life? And

what did he mean, she wouldn't be on their side?

Before Remington could ask for clarification, they all poofed.

CHAPTER ELEVEN

FIFTEEN MINUTES LATER, REMINGTON STEPPED inside her home. Things were not as she had left them. Every light blinked. The clocks were running backward at a sprint. All the water faucets were spewing water at full capacity. And Max wore a tuxedo jacket and top hat.

He pounced on her the moment she got through the door.

"Oh, my." Max's little body shook in her arms like a trampoline under the feet of a group of teenagers. "What happened?"

Max didn't reply.

She took the hat and the coat off him and then set him outside on the porch where things were normal. And then stepped back inside the house and closed the door. "Beth, can you hear me?"

She glanced out at Max. The tuxedo and hat were back. *Damn it.*

"At your service." Beth appeared on the front porch, scaring the pee out of Max.

Remington held open the screen door. "Get in here and tell me what the hell is going on with my house and dog."

Beth floated inside. Glanced around. "It's just

rewiring itself for a new witch owner."

"Rewiring?"

"Hmmm hmmm."

"And just how long does rewiring take?"

"I don't remember."

"That's not helpful. Try to remember." Remington heard a fluttering noise in her bedroom. She tentatively opened the door and glanced inside the room. The witch's manual sat on her bed, its pages flipping and flapping.

"I remember," Beth said. "You have to find the anti-spells and cast them to get things to stop. It helps you to get in the groove of casting spells."

Remington glanced over her shoulder at her friend. "You're a witch. Can't you stop them?"

"Now that you're the official witch of Knotty, you have to officially stop them."

Remington grabbed the book and looked in the front for an index. She found a spell for anti-running water. "Do I just repeat the words?"

"What level?"

"One."

"Then yes. That's all you have to do."

Two hours later, Remington's house once again resembled normal. Or as normal as a witch's house could ever be. All the furniture kept rearranging itself.

"Nicely done." Beth laid down the magazine she'd been thumbing through and patted the couch for Remington to come and sit.

Remington first walked to the door and opened it for Max. He ran behind an empty platter and hid. "Max's going to need therapy."

"Where's Jason?" Beth asked.

Remington glanced out the window at Jason's house. His truck was in the driveway but no lights were on. "The last I saw him he was with some bimbo."

"That's good," Beth said.

Remington turned and glared at her. "Why is that good?"

"Because he can be in a relationship with her while you're working on finding an undo spell."

"I'm not following?"

"He's the type who can only be in one relationship at a time. We know we don't want it to be with you. So, it will have to be with another woman."

"Why does it have to be with anyone?"

"Honey, a guy like him is not going to stay unattached."

"Oh." That sucked. If he was in another relationship, his flirting with Remington would stop, and she'd been enjoying being flirted with. It felt great to be admired. "Is there an alternative?"

"When you're a witch, there's always an alternative." Beth picked up the spell book and scrolled through the pages. She stopped on several, read them, and then kept going. On the last page, she made a noise of delight. "This one. This should do the job."

Remington grabbed the book and read the title of the spell. "You want me to cast a go away spell on him?"

"It's perfect," Beth said. "As long as he's not in

Knotty, you're not at risk of falling for him."

"But he has work here. Won't his business adventures suffer if he's not around to supervise them?"

"I'm sure he'll manage."

"I don't know. That seems a little extreme."

"Whatever. It's up to you. Maybe once him and this new woman implode, then you'll reconsider."

The idea of watching Jason and Gnat-Brain get chummy churned Remington's stomach. "I guess a little time outside of Knotty's perimeters wouldn't hurt him."

Beth clapped her hands. "What level is the spell?"

"A five."

Beth's enthusiasm dwindled. "Oh. You probably shouldn't try a five."

"Why not?"

"They're more difficult. You have to hold your intention in your brain while you cast the spell. Any variance and the whole spell could get fuddled."

"That doesn't sound so hard. I want him to leave Knotty until it's heart-safe for him to come back."

"It doesn't sound hard, but trust me, it can be hard to hold the intent while reciting a spell."

Remington shrugged. "If it doesn't work, we'll undo it."

"You're the witch. Give it a go."

Remington sat up straight. With the intent of what she wanted to accomplish firmly at the front of her brain, she recited the spell. "Away, away. Go away. Only come back when I say you may."

"Now wind up and pretend you're throwing a

baseball," Beth said. "That's how you toss the spell into the world."

Remington did. When she released the pretend baseball, a streak of light flew out of her hands, through her door, and out into the world.

"Oh, and always have your intent in your brain when you toss the ball."

Remington jerked in dismay. "You should have told me that before I tossed the ball."

"Sorry. You know I'm forgetful."

Did I have the intent in my brain on release? Maybe. "How do I know if it worked?"

"If he doesn't come back, you know it worked."

"And if I didn't hold the intent, will it evaporate into thin air?"

"Probably."

"Probably?" Remington quickly thumbed through the book. "Elaborate." She didn't like the sound of *probably*.

"Sometimes, not often," Beth said, "hexes, free of intent, go catawampus."

The air whooshed out of Remington and her hand jerked and she got a paper-cut. "What?" She dabbed a thick drop of blood onto the bottom of a blank page.

"You know, wonky. Off-kilter. Three-degrees shy of perfect."

Remington wasn't a perfectionist by nature, but this seemed an appropriate time to strive for the gold standard. She found the index and ran her throbbing finger down the categories. She glanced at Beth. "Why isn't there a section on reversing the go away spell?"

Beth's eyes brightened. "That's it. I forgot about this part of being a witch. If you cast a level five spell, you have to create the undo spell on your own. When you successfully undo ten level-five spells, you're an official witch and no longer an apprentice."

Shit. "How long did it take you to become an official witch?"

Beth tilted her head. "I'm not sure. I can't remember ever actually undoing any level-five spells. I remember trying, and man, if you get them wrong, the consequences are fierce."

"Fierce? Fierce how?"

"I think C-Squared LW had something to do with the tornado that swept through the town while she had been trying to undo a level-five spell."

CHAPTER TWELVE

REMINGTON'S FIRST FULL DAY IN Knotty set the routine for the next two-and-a-half months. Minus Jason. Her go-away spell had worked in a glitchy catawampus way.

According to Kevin, who was taking care of Scotch, Jason had received a call saying his father was in the hospital in Seattle. He'd rushed from the orphanage to the airport. This had happened on the same day Remington cast the spell on him, which totally freaked Remington out. Beth should have told her to have a reason for him to be away as part of her intent instead of leaving it up to the universe to come up with one.

Ruby Rae stopped every morning at 5:30 and woke her. Remington groggily made her way to the Elm for a run with the group. Then she'd go for a walk with Johnny B.

Beth never joined her for the walks with Johnny B, but two of the *other ghosts* always did. Not that they spoke to Remington. Instead, they whispered a lot. She thought of them as bad spies. Bad as in she knew they were watching her every move, but for what she hadn't a clue.

From 10:00 to noon, she'd sit in her kitchen and

design new costume patterns for the Rockettes. She'd worked out a deal with her old boss to work from Knotty.

From 1:00 p.m. to 3:00 p.m., Remington practiced witchery. So far, she hadn't gotten up the nerve to try to undo the level five spell she'd placed on Jason.

When time allowed, she studied her weekly Tantric sex lesson. Yes. The study of sex had been the surprise part of Beth's to-do list. Although, when questioned, Beth couldn't remember why she'd added that.

Not that Remington minded. Much. Except, Tantric was hard. She'd actually failed the first online assignment. Who fails an online, open-book assignment? Someone not good at sex was the only answer she'd been able to come up with. Which meant Linny had been telling her the truth.

Witchery was fun but not easy. So far, using level two spells, she'd blown up the tree in her backyard, caused Max to meow instead of bark, and turned one annoying ghost a lovely shade of robin-egg blue. That one she wasn't sorry about. He had a habit of waking her up every night at two a.m. by touching her to see if she was dead.

She'd tried one level-five spell to bring the mail from her mailbox to her front door. Instead, the spell caused all the mailboxes on her street to open and the mail to fly out and blow every which way in the neighborhood.

Then, she'd tried to cast another level four spell to make herself run faster. Instead, everyone else ran slower. Luckily, that particular spell only held for two days. The mail spell still wasn't right. Every day at noon, the mailbox lids flew open.

After the mailbox debacle, she'd decided she needed a beginner's guide to witchery. She'd ordered a witchcraft book off of eBay, but the $5.99 paperback turned out to be a fake. The spells in it wouldn't even brew a decent cup of coffee.

Once a week, she played cards with the Knotty Card Sharks.

Beth popped in and out on a regular basis, her memory sketchy on most things. But one thing was for sure, the mere act of handing off the witch's bible to Remington hadn't been Beth's unfinished business.

The sound of knocking at her front door interrupted Remington's brooding thoughts. She tossed her dishrag in the sink and hurried into the living room. Sara Ann, Ruby Rae, Kevin, Maverick and Tom all stood on the other side of her screen. "It's about time you guys got here."

"Are we late?" Sara Ann asked.

They all single-filed into her kitchen. "No." Remington tossed their coats on the couch, grimaced at the spy ghosts sitting there, and then followed the living. "But I am sick to death of my own company." Beth called them *outlook ghosts*. If Remington did anything to try to discover their secret, they were to stop her and then report the problem to the head ghost. The head ghost, according to Beth, was the detective wannabe.

The spy ghosts wouldn't confide in Beth what

their secret was because she was a witch ghost, and they didn't trust witches. And since Beth couldn't find a ghost witchery manual, she couldn't cast spells on them to find out.

"What's your game of choice tonight?" Kevin asked Remington.

The person hosting game night got to choose the game. "Yahtzee."

"Kevin, that was boyfriend-sweet of you to check on Remington after our run this morning," Ruby Rae said.

All eyes went to Kevin. Even Remington's.

"Is there something going on with you two?" Maverick asked.

"No," Remington said.

"Yes," Kevin said.

The fact their responses didn't match entertained everyone. Even Remington.

Her lips twitched. "Tell them the truth."

While Kevin was not a serial flirt like Jason, he did have an ornery streak.

"Sweetie." His voice oozed sugar. "What's the big deal? I'm hot for you, and you're hot for me."

Remington snorted. "In your deepest dreams." She placed cups of hot chocolate on a tray and brought them to the table. She handed a cup to each person and then went back to the counter to grab the Baileys.

Tom came up behind her and laid his chin on top of her head. "If you two want to swap spit, that's fine, but you really shouldn't miss your training runs." Tom was the most serious of the group. Not old enough to be a father figure—more like an older brother figure. "They're important if you're going to run the marathon." He rubbed the top of Remington's head with the back of his hand and then took his seat at the table.

"I'm sorry I missed this morning's run. I had a splitting headache." Remington placed the liqueur on the table. "Bouncing down the road would have been pure torture." The truth was, she'd tried casting a spell on her shoes so they wouldn't come untied when she ran. The level three spell tied her shoes before she put them on, and try as she might, she couldn't get them untied. So, when she'd gone to town to buy the game, she had to buy a new pair of running shoes.

"I heard something interesting today." Sara Ann poured a healthy dollop of Baileys into her hot chocolate.

"Let the gossiping begin," Beth said to Remington. Beth sat on the counter. She never missed game night. On the nights they played rummy, Beth would cheat and tell Remington their cards.

Anyway, gossiping was what game night was really about. Remington had found this out seven weeks ago when they'd all showed up at her house to play games and to quiz her over her and Jason's seven-block run together. They'd been disappointed to learn nothing had happened.

"What did you hear?" Tom asked.

"Well, I went into the city to have lunch with my niece," Sara Ann said. "You boys should join me someday. She's quite beautiful."

"If she takes after her aunt, I bet she is stunning," Maverick said. The guy was smooth with the elderly.

Ruby Rae harrumphed. "If you want to meet a beauty, you need to meet my granddaughter. She's not only beautiful, but she has a great personality to go with her looks."

"Are you saying my niece doesn't have a personality?" Sara Ann asked.

"I wouldn't have any way of knowing that. Since she never comes to visit."

"But that's what you were trying to imply, wasn't it?"

"Don't get so flabbergasted," Ruby Rae said. "It makes your face look more rubbery than normal."

"Fruit, anyone?" Remington jumped up, went to the refrigerator, and retrieved the store-bought tray. If Knotty was the host of a future murderer, Remington was pretty sure it would be one of the two ladies, and the other would be the dead person.

That thought kept Remington on her toes. She'd also been doing background searches on all the other living residents of Knotty. There weren't many. And she'd met them all. None appeared violent. And so far, none had murder in their background.

Which lead Remington to hope she'd been right with her original thought that the note had been written while Beth was high on pain meds.

"Sara Ann, what did you hear from your niece?" Tom asked. He helped himself to a cluster of grapes and passed the tray to Ruby Rae.

"I heard Jason has bigger plans for our little town than he's told all of us."

"What kind of bigger plans?" Kevin asked. He sounded hesitant—as if afraid of what the answer might be.

"Well, I probably shouldn't tell, but my niece never said I couldn't. So, I guess I can, but to be on the safe side, you all must agree not to tell anyone else."

Ruby Rae made a noise of exasperation. "The only reason you want us to agree to that is that you want to be the one who gets to tell everyone what you know. You are such a serial gossip."

Almost everyone laughed.

Sara Ann looked hurt.

"Please do tell me the gossip. I'm just dying to hear." Remington liked Sara Ann. The dear had been trying to teach her to knit, but Remington was quite the hopeless cause.

"Well, she's a senior partner in an advertising firm in Chicago. She's landed a big account. A really big account."

"Isn't she the one who was supposed to get married last year, and when it was time to say I do, she said I don't?" asked Ruby Rae.

Sara Ann's nostrils flared. "Moments before going down the aisle, the girl found out her fiancée cheated on her. What else could she do?"

"You were never fortunate in love either, were you dear?" Ruby Rae said. "Perhaps it runs in the family."

"As I was saying, she's landed a large account. It is an account that has to do with Knotty." Sara Ann paused and made a production of eating a grape. Then taking a sip of her drink. Finally, she continued. "She had the winning slogan."

"What was her slogan?" Remington asked.

"*Knotty Town Is About to Get a Whole Lot Naughtier.*" Sara Ann whispered the words.

The guys at the table did fist bumps.

Sara Ann gave them a fond smile. "Her advertising plan is to market Knotty as a singles town to potential retailers."

"Retailers only?" Remington asked.

"According to my niece, most of the housing has already been leased to individuals who are single. Knotty residents own the rest of the housing. Like us," Sara Ann said. "No need to advertise the singles-only housing."

Remington opened up the Yahtzee game and passed around a score sheet to each of the players along with a tiny sharpened pencil. "Is that legal?" Wasn't there a quota of married people who had to live in every town?

"Perfectly legal," said Tom. "Jason's not saying married couples can't live here, but the majority of TTI's first-year employees who will be moving here are single. And the college has leased the orphanage for seniors studying creepy crawly things."

"What kind of creepy crawly things?" Remington asked. When had this happened? Why hadn't Jason mentioned it that day at the orphanage?

"They're studying goblins and witches and ghosts." Tom's smile clearly said he didn't believe in such nonsense.

Sparks of electricity zapped Remington's upper arms, wrapping their way down to her fingers. Her curtains flew open.

Beth hurriedly shut them before anyone noticed.

"I guess it's not that farfetched." Remington took a sip of her hot chocolate. Perhaps she would offer to teach a class at the university. "There are already condominiums that are for singles only. Vacation resorts that are for singles only. Why not a whole town?" She smiled at the table's occupants. "Shall we roll the dice to see who goes first?" Perhaps one of the seniors studying the preternatural could take over the role of town witch.

"The only way for a new person to be assigned the job of witch is if you die," Beth said. Tonight, she wore a tiny red bikini, flip flops, and a beach hat.

Stop reading my mind.

"How else will I know what you're thinking?"

Maverick rolled a two.

Ruby Rae rolled a five.

Tom rolled a one.

Kevin rolled a two.

Remington rolled a five.

Sara Ann rolled a six. She smiled in modest victory. "Oh good. I get to go first. I did beat you didn't I, Ruby Rae? You just rolled a five...right?"

"Bite me," Ruby Rae said.

Sara Ann placed the dice in the cup, shook them,

and rolled them onto the table. She kept the two threes, placed the rest of the dice back in the cup and rolled again. She got one more three. She filled out her card and handed the cup and dice to Kevin, who sat to her right.

"What else did your niece say?" Maverick asked.

"That was it. She thinks the account is going to be a big one for her. And…she's going to move here to oversee it."

A new series of sparks shocked Remington. Her hot chocolate cup levitated. She quickly grabbed it before anyone noticed.

What was happening? Were some of her flopped spells about to activate themselves?

CHAPTER THIRTEEN

A MIDST A WINTER STORM DURING the first week of December, thunder-snow sent quarter-sized snowflakes whipping through the air like out-of-control bottle rockets. The sight gave Remington heartburn.

Jason Hart was to blame. They reminded her of the Frosted Flakes he'd offered her for breakfast nine weeks ago. The ones she'd never gotten to eat.

"Stop thinking about him," she ordered herself for the tenth time in thirty minutes, times twenty-four hours in a day, minus eight hours of sleep a day, times seven days a week, times nine weeks, minus a few hours here and there when other things occupied her mind. Things like *Hexes and O's.*

Max's tail thumped so fast and hard it sounded like automatic gunfire. The sound pulled Remington out of her mathematical equation. The phobic dog had begun doing this lately every time he heard Remington's voice. Which was often. Remington had taken up the habit of talking to the ghosts. Some of them would talk back. Some would not. The ones who spoke wouldn't tell her why the others wouldn't. Very frustrating.

She rubbed Max's back with the toe of her piggy slippers. "Don't worry. I'm not going to step on you again."

Max whimpered.

"But, dammit to hell, don't you think any man who gets all tangled up in a woman's brain without her permission should be shot twice...once in each of his hairy balls?" How many women had fallen in love with him since he'd left? Was he falling in love with any of them since he wasn't in Knotty? Was that allowed? Hell. She and Beth hadn't thought about that possibility when they'd vanished him from the town.

Max meowed.

Remington banged her forehead against the windowpane. "Stupid, stupid, stupid." Why couldn't she stop thinking about Jason? She'd never had a man invade her brain so completely. It had to be the hex. The few interactions they shared must have counted as a relationship.

Max ran a circle around Remington before flopping down on his back, offering up his belly for some more slipper attention.

Remington obediently rubbed. "It would help if you could talk." She should look in the book for a dog-talking spell. It might be fun, having a talking dog. Not that she needed the dog to tell her what was wrong with her.

That answer was clearer than daylight on a cloudless day. She was in hex-love.

"You know he can't read your mind like I can."

Max hissed and ran out of the room.

Remington whipped around. "You scared the crap out of me."

Beth smiled, all charm-and-smarm and a touch of no-foul-no-harm.

Remington wasn't impressed. She amped the wattage of her scowl. "Start knocking like a normal person."

Beth's smile didn't dip. "You're really an embarrassment to the witch population." She wore a red raincoat and matching rubber boots. A blue umbrella finished the ensemble. "You should be scaring small children, not getting scared yourself."

"If I could hex you right now, I would."

Her death-on-a-stick friend held up a hand, palm facing out. "Don't get your granny panties in a wad; I'm here."

Remington knocked her knees together and crossed her hands in front of her legs. "Can you see my underwear?" *Damn it.* Her granny panties were her business, no one else's.

Beth giggled. "Want to know what I did today?"

"No."

"I got a call from the big guy. He gave me my assignment." Beth slid on a pair of dark glasses. "I'm going to be an undercover ghost agent. It's going to be a hoot. I get to pack heat."

Remington straightened. Her brain spun like the wheel of fortune whirled by a sumo wrestler, and she waited for it to stop to see which topic she would focus on first. Would it be: *Who is the big guy when you were dead but not in heaven or hell?* Or: *Did Beth say 'packing heat'?*

When it was apparent her brain wasn't going to stop spinning anytime soon, Remington said, "I thought you had a job. Wicked Witch of the Dead."

"Being a witch isn't my ghost career. That's just the career I brought into the second veil. As a ghost, I have to pick a new career."

"Why?"

"Because it keeps us occupied. With too much time on our hands, we can get a little out of control, and then we get sent to ghost jail, and a murder has to happen before we're released."

Mention of murder soured Remington's stomach. As much as she told herself a murderer didn't live among them, her fears whispered that maybe Beth had written that note while completely lucid. "Do you have a gun?"

"Absolutely."

Could Beth be the future murderer of Knotty?

"Nope."

"Stop reading my mind."

"I can only shoot at other ghosts. Which sucks, because do you know how hard it is to kill a ghost?" She opened her raincoat and showed Remington the gun she had holstered on her hip.

"Do you have an assignment to kill one? Is that why the big guy wanted to see you?"

Beth tilted her head to the right and then to the left, her neck popping. "No and yes."

"Spill."

"I'm not supposed to," Beth said. "But since you're my best friend and not a ghost, I'll make an exception. A dead man wants my help finding his killer. Cool, huh?"

"That doesn't sound too hard."

"It wouldn't be if the ghost could talk to me, but he can't. When you die via murder, you're not allowed to talk to other ghosts until your murder is solved. There are so many stuffy rules in the second veil."

Remington glanced around at the ghosts in the room. There were none. They'd all disappeared the minute Beth showed up. Damn. Were the mute ones mute because they'd been murdered?

"So…how are *you* going to get the job done if he can't tell you who killed him?"

"A séance is what the big guy suggested." Beth perched on the countertop and glanced at her nails.

Remington pulled her hair back in a pony-tail. "Sane people don't believe in the validity of séances."

Beth gave her nails one last look and then rolled her eyes at Remington. "They do if they trust their medium."

"Good luck finding a medium you can trust." She reached out to touch Beth. Her hand sank through her. Damn. She'd asked Beth once why a ghost could touch a human, but a human couldn't touch a ghost. Her response had been a shrug. Nothing about the ghost realm made sense. The rules were all willy-nilly nonsense.

Beth leaned forward and flipped Remington on the forehead with her thumb and index finger.

Remington flinched. "Ouch. Why'd you do that?"

"I don't need to find a medium. I've got you, babe."

Remington rubbed her head. The words to Cher and Sonny Bono's theme song played in Remington's mind. She remembered her and Beth belting out the tune in Beth's bedroom one summer after Beth had received a karaoke machine for her birthday. "I'm not a medium." They'd spent the summer learning the words to a bunch of old songs.

"You're talking to me, aren't you? That's what a medium does. Talks to ghosts and relays their messages. You and I are going to be the Sherlock Holmes and Watson of the undead world."

"What?"

"You're going to stay in Knotty and help me solve murders."

Remington tried flicking Beth on the forehead. The experience gave new meaning to the term *airhead*. "Your plan has a flaw."

"What's that?"

"I'm afraid of the dark."

Beth leaned back on her hands. "I don't remember you being such a wimp when we were young."

"You don't remember much of anything." Remington quit trying to touch Beth. Instead, she stood, walked to the table, and plopped down in a kitchen chair, pushing her textbook out of her way. "Did you know you can't study past chapter four to be a Tantric Sex Instructor without a man to practice your homework on? I need a guinea pig. A very sexy guinea pig." An image of Jason flashed in her brain. "Any suggestions?"

Beth didn't answer immediately. "Ask Jason."

"Earth to Beth, he's gone. Did you forget?"

Beth floated into a chair across from hers. "Where'd he go?" She picked up an apple and stared at it. "Has he been gone long?" She tossed the apple from one hand to the other and glanced at Remington.

Remington sighed. "Nine weeks. His dad had some sort of health scare. I might be the reason."

Beth stopped playing with the apple and stared wide-eyed at Remington. "How's that?"

"I cast a go away spell on Jason. Then his father got sick."

"Oh yeah. Now I remember. You know what, if he died, don't sweat it. Every witch, at one time or another, accidentally kills someone. Carnage can't be helped. Spells have a steep learning curve."

"That's not funny. I didn't say anything about him being dead." Oh God. If he died, that would make her Knotty's murderer.

"Stop worrying. I'm sure he's alive."

Relief wrapped around Remington's heart. "Why are you sure?" She didn't think she could handle being the reason someone died.

"If his father was dead, I would have met him at one of the ANWD meetings." Beth picked up three apples and juggled them.

"A what meeting?" Remington asked.

"ANWD...And Now We're Dead meetings. A twelve-step program to help restless spirits to get to the other veil. Unless he came to the one I missed."

Thump. Thump. Thump. Someone pounded at

Remington's front door. Was it a human coming to see her or a spirit coming to see Beth?

"Who is it?" she asked Beth. God, she was glad her friend hadn't yet crossed over. She didn't want Beth to ever cross over. She paused that thought, rewound it, and listened to it again. That was exactly how Beth had felt as a child about Remington getting adopted. The realization brought her peace.

Beth wiggled her eyebrows. "Maybe it's the Tantric Practice Man you asked the universe for a minute ago."

"I didn't ask for a Tantric man." Had she asked for a Tantric man?

"You said you needed a guinea pig—same thing. You are a witch, you know? When you ask for things, things happen."

"Whatever," Remington muttered. It was probably Kevin. She'd invited him to stop by each day for coffee or hot chocolate after he took care of Scotch. She enjoyed his brotherly company.

"I think I'll just skip over to the ANWD meeting," Beth said, "and give you and your sex-dummy some privacy." She waved and then disappeared, starting with her feet and ending with her eyes.

Remington walked into the living room. Her furniture had moved…again. "You're early today." She swung the door open in anticipation of some lively conversation with the town's clown. Kevin could always make her laugh with his stories of practical jokes. Last week, he'd gotten Maverick good—

Remington's thoughts crashed, ass-in-the-air, to

the ground.

It wasn't Kevin.

It was Jason. All haggard, hair mussed up, six-sexy-foot of him.

"Hi," she squeaked.

CHAPTER FOURTEEN

THE MOMENT THE NEWLY PAINTED, lime-green door swung open and Jason saw Remington standing in front of him wearing the ugliest orange robe and the loudest pink animal slippers he'd ever seen on a woman, he became apprehensive. His palms grew sweaty, and his heart tried to escape its frozen cage. And not because she was obviously color blind. But because of the sexual desire the sight produced.

He tried to swallow but wasn't successful.

He'd convinced himself while he was gone that he hadn't felt anything but lust for her. He'd been wrong.

The way his muscles tightened and his breathing sped up and his fingers tingled wasn't just about lust. And he knew he shouldn't have stopped at her house.

But he'd missed her. And he had to see her. It had been a hell of a few months. "Hi," he drawled. As one day had slipped into the next, his thoughts of her had multiplied. No woman had ever affected him this way.

"Do I know you?" She asked the question in her trademark smart-ass tone capable of reducing a man's height by several inches, but she ruined its punch by licking her lips in an adorable gesture that sent his fantasies down another rabbit hole.

"I hope so." His thoughts had strayed to her during the most inappropriate of times over the past few weeks.

He'd been jealous as hell when he'd spoken to his team and learned Kevin had been hanging around her. He'd toyed with the idea of having Kevin come back to Seattle to get him away from Remington.

He'd thought of what he wanted to do with Remington when he got back to Knotty. None of which were doable considering his promise to Beth.

"So," Remington said, pulling a tie out of her hair and letting it fall softly around her shoulders.

"So," he echoed, wanting to touch his lips to her neck.

Good thing his past had gotten in the way that morning at the orphanage, or he would have broken that promise to Beth. He'd been stunned when Bernadette had shown up and acted like a stranger ready to adopt. He'd had no choice but to follow her act. See what in the hell game she was playing. And with Bernadette, it was always a game.

As it turned out, she thought if she adopted Johnny B, Jason would reconsider his view of their relationship. Would want to try again for the sake of the child. She'd been wrong, which had quickly ended her desire to adopt Johnny B.

Not all bad came out of her self-serving scheme.

Before she'd known it would fail, she'd told several of her friends of her plan to adopt. They decided to also check into adoption. As it turned out, being a green parent—having a recycled child makes one a green parent—appeared to be the latest fad among the rich and famous.

Which brought him back to Remington. The seductress. What else could he call her? Any woman who could turn a man on while wearing that wardrobe malfunction had to be a seductress.

Or a witch.

The thought made him smile. Beth, on her deathbed, had told him she was a witch and had cursed him. Of course, she'd been doped on pain-killers.

"Did you want something?" A soft smile tugged at her lips, completely at odds with the grumpy tone of her voice.

"May I come in?"

She nodded and shuffled back like a starchy English butler.

The sight of oversized fur-balls on a woman's feet should turn a man's engines off, not on. Not do funny things to his heart and his blood pressure. He reached for the screen door's handle and tugged. "It's locked."

He understood his desire to ravish her. She was gorgeous and built like an old-time movie star. But he didn't understand the way looking at her tugged at his heart. He wasn't the fall-in-love type. Hence the past four failed relationships he'd been in. "You're even more beautiful than you've been in my dreams."

She clutched the opening of her robe together. "Don't flirt with me."

"Why not?" The thing had holes in the elbows and down one side, he noted.

"I am *not* very happy with you." Her stormy green eyes shot him with lightning bolts.

He winced. Damn, those bolts felt real. "You're not?" He caught a flash of naked skin and gulped. Loose threads stuck out everywhere around the seam of the robe. One tug on any of them and the whole thing would probably disintegrate around her cute little ankles. Just how naked was she beneath it?

Hell, Beth was dead. She'd never know if he and Remington hooked up.

Would she?

"You flirted with another woman right in front of me."

Without telling her more than he was ready to reveal, he wasn't sure how to defend himself. He chose to remain silent. He'd been putting on the bad boy act for so long he sometimes forgot to turn it off and be sincere.

She pointed a finger at him. "One moment you were asking me over for Frosted Flakes, the next your eyes were all over Ms. Boobs and Ass." She plopped her hands on her hips in that way he loved, giving him a good view of the round curve of her pale breasts.

"I'm—"

"And now you show up and think you can

schmooze your way onto my good side? You're not even carrying flowers or chocolates, or the deed to a condo as a peace offering."

He'd wanted to call but didn't. He kept visualizing Beth, and his promise to her to take care of Remington. And somehow, he didn't think Beth would approve of his intentions that morning.

"I'll have you know, Jason Hart, you might have more pickup lines than a drunken sailor, but I wasn't born yesterday. Well, actually I was. You missed my birthday. But even if you didn't hurt my feelings, and you did, I wouldn't fall for that rookie-ass line." She crossed her arms and gave him a look that clearly said, "And now you may grovel."

"Unlock the door, and I'll make it all up to you." Beth had told him lots of stories about Remington, but he didn't remember her ever mentioning a temper. He found the sparks erotic.

Remington made a *pfting* noise. "Stop looking at me like that."

"Like how?" Had the running group had a birthday party for her? He hoped so.

"Like your eyes are massaging me."

He gulped, and his fingers begged to do what she suggested his eyes were already doing. "Does the thought of my hands roaming intimately over your body bother you?" The thought of his fingers caressing her naked skin bothered the hell out of him. As much as he wanted to be the good Boy Scout and stay away from Remington, he knew his willpower was on a slippery slope.

Her top lip lifted, causing her nose to twitch like

the cute little witch he kept imagining her to be. "You…wish."

His ego might have died as a result of her ability to make those two words sound like a defensive lineman's insult, but her eyes weren't quite as indifferent, and his ego expanded.

She flipped the lock on the screen door. "Come in before you freeze your dumb…your cute derriere off."

He glanced over his shoulder at his butt. "So, you think it's cute?"

"I only said cute derriere because I'm too polite to say dumbass. Which you are."

He chuckled, hung his coat on the hook next to the door, followed her through the living room—which felt very cold—regretfully past the bedroom, and to the kitchen. "I don't care what terms you use, as long as your mind is on my ass."

He inhaled the aroma of cinnamon. Had Ruby Rae been by with rolls?

Remington sat down at her kitchen table and crossed her eyes. "I really am irritated with you. And I know I probably shouldn't be because it's not like you *chose* to leave, but you could have reached out and let me know you didn't find me totally forgettable."

Shit. He should have told her he was leaving. It would have been the neighborly thing to do. But when he'd received the call saying his father was dying, all he could feel was anger. Anger at his dad for dying. Anger at his mom for not being around to be there for him. Anger that had carried him to the airport, to Seattle, to the funeral, through all of his father's things, and back to Remington. "I'm sorry."

She uncrossed her eyes. "How's your dad?"

He considered lying. It would be easier. But he didn't want to lie to Remington. He wanted to be a better man than that. "He's dead." He'd said those words plenty over the last few weeks, but they still tasted bitter.

A flash of lightning and then a boom of thunder crashed outside.

"Dead?" Remington shot out of her chair, causing the salt and pepper shakers to fall off the table. "You should have told me." She glanced around as if afraid the ghost of his dad would appear at any moment.

"I should have?" The bastard had died without telling him how to find Mom. Even on his deathbed, when Jason asked him, he'd said Jason was better off without her in his life. Said he was doing him a favor.

Tears brimmed Remington's eyes. Her footsteps stalled, and she blinked.

"Why would you want me to tell you about my father? You and I barely know one another." As mysterious as they were, her tears were touching. No one at the funeral had cried. But tears for his old man weren't necessary.

"We're neighbors. I could have sent flowers. How did he die?"

"A sudden heart attack."

She held out a hand and touched his face. "I'm

sorry." A tear rolled down her cheek, causing his heart to ache. "Why didn't Kevin tell me?"

Why would she shed tears for a man she'd never know? Jason turned and walked to the window, saving him from the moment. "I told him not to. Don't be sad about my dad. He was a dick."

He heard a sharp intake of breath from behind him.

He sensed her stepping up to him. Felt her slip her arms through his and hug him from behind. "That's an awful thing to say about your dad."

He stiffened, pulled away, and turned. The last woman who had tried to comfort him had been his mother. And that ended very badly for them. "I'm not good at receiving comfort."

Her lips trembled.

He sighed and held open his arms. "Come here."

She walked into his arms, once again molding her body against his. "Why aren't you good at receiving comfort?"

"I grew up without a mom and with a dad who thought comfort was for poor children." He couldn't keep the sharpness out of his tone. He'd never spoken about this to anyone.

"I don't understand."

He cupped a hand along the side of her face. The silkiness of her skin left him rattled. Should he give her the long version or the short? He decided for something in the middle. Untangling himself from her arms, he said, "One day, Dad came home and discovered Mom had bought me a teddy bear to sleep with because I'd been having nightmares. He accused her of undermining his desire for me to grow up strong and manly. He gave her one hour to pack and get out. And she did. She left me."

Remington shook her head. "There had to be more to it than that."

"I'm sure there was. But if she loved me, she would have never left me behind."

"Was she afraid of him?"

"Everyone was afraid of him. Including me." Jason brought his other hand up and cupped both cheeks. "He gave her cash. Bought her airline tickets and told her if she ever stepped foot in the state of Washington again, he'd make sure she died a horrible death. I was hiding under the bed. I heard everything."

Remington gulped. "Would he have done that? Would he have killed her?"

"I don't know." For some reason, the admission of what he'd heard lifted a massive weight off his shoulders. He'd never repeated any of that to anyone. He took a step closer, their bodies brushing one another, his hands settling on her hips. "That's why I don't care that he's dead. He's never been one to give much stock to someone's life, so why should anyone give much thought to his death?"

Remington worried the bottom of her lip with her tiny white teeth. "I'm sorry…about all of it."

He didn't want her to feel sorry for him, so he leaned down to lightly touch her lips with his. "Don't be. I've grown up in the lap of luxury." He definitely didn't want to talk about Dad.

What he wanted was to nibble all over Remington. And he could tell by her body language she wanted that too. "I need to go check on Scotch. Come with me. Help me forget." He'd never asked that of a woman before. Never felt like there was a woman who could ease his emotional pain. Never felt like there was a woman he could trust. Never felt an actual ache in his heart.

She placed her palms on his chest, hesitated. "I better not."

Her rejection was like whiskey on an open wound. One he thought he had sealed off from further pain. Anger flared in his gut, and he suppressed it.

When she stepped out of his arms, he let her. "I…have homework." She walked to the kitchen table.

Emotions cut off the oxygen to his heart. He'd allowed himself to be vulnerable in a woman's presence and she'd been unmoved. More worried about her own needs than his. Like his mother. Was Remington like his mother? "I shouldn't have asked," he said in a tone of forced indifference.

"Don't be like that." She reached for the chair behind her and sank, not looking him in the eyes.

He walked to the table. "Homework for what?" He'd be damned if he'd leave with his tail between his legs. He pulled up a chair and sat across from her. Their knees touching.

"I'm studying Tantric sex."

He jerked and laughed. He'd been expecting something else. Not sure what. Maybe college algebra. But definitely not Tantric sex. The two words were a blast from his past.

He cocked his head, gave her a quizzical look, and tried to process her words. Did she know? Was she playing him? He'd told Beth, but Beth had never spoken to Remington. She couldn't have told her. Maybe Remington had found Beth's diary and Beth had written about it.

Or maybe this was pure coincidence. Did it matter? "My first sexual experience, outside of backseats, was with a Tantric instructor." He leaned back in his chair.

Her eyes dilated. "Right." She drew the word out in a tone of disbelief, as if he'd just told her he was Santa Claus.

"If you don't believe me, come home with me, and I'll demonstrate my mastery of the technique. I know all about a woman's Yoni." His heart tripped at the idea of doing anything with Remington's Yoni.

Remington's eyes widened. "You know about the Yoni?"

"For starters." He imagined Remington in the nude. "I'd love to give great tongue to your Yoni."

"Where did you meet her?" Her cheeks were rosy.

"Dad and I spent a year living in Vegas. Moon was the sexy older woman who lived upstairs in the condo we rented." He paused in thought. If it hadn't been for Moon, there's no telling what might have happened to him. At that time in his life, he'd been on a path of destruction. Ready to do anything to embarrass Dad. Disappoint him. Cause him pain. Moon had tamed his inner demon. "At seventeen, I immediately noticed her and noticed she had visitors in and out of her home all day. I was curious. One day, she caught me lurking around and invited me in. She told me she was a Tantric instructor and offered me a free lesson. The free lessons continued until I left for college."

Remington moistened her lips. "Are you any good?"

"Definitely." Taking her hands, he tugged her out of her chair and carefully yanked her against him. "But don't take my word for it."

CHAPTER FIFTEEN

REMINGTON TRIED TO THINK STRAIGHT. Beth's prediction had happened. A murderer did indeed live in Knotty. The actual death hadn't occurred in Knotty, but the killer had done the deed while standing in Knotty. Remington had killed Jason's father by sending a wonky hex out into the Universe.

Had the earlier boom of thunder and strike of lightning represented the release of the two mayhem ghosts?

Of course, that's what it meant. Now, it would be her job to keep them from creating mayhem in Knotty.

And Jason just asked her if she wanted to have sex. Not a good idea. But not a bad one either. And it would take her mind off of being an accidental murderer.

"Does your silence mean yes?" Jason asked.

Remington's knees sagged along with her willpower. What good is willpower if it bends like a Gumby doll at the first administration of pressure? If it murmurs, "Why exactly do you need to resist Jason?" in a soothing voice, while you're trying to remember the reason.

Remington wanted to learn Tantric sex. Jason knew the technique first hand. To turn down this opportunity would be an insult to the universe. Cause the cosmos to lob more lemons at her. Besides, Beth had invited her to use him for just this thing. And if she failed another assignment, they might kick her out of the program.

The problem was, around him, her heart was hex-melty. Which would leave a sloppy mess, and her holding the mop when the affair ended. God, how she hated mopping. And cleaning toilets—but that was beside the point.

Of course, Jason couldn't hurt her if she didn't let him. She was the master of her own heart. Not the other way around. All she had to do was keep her brain engaged during their relationship. And keep her defrosting heart from any future thawing. And remind herself a million times a day that he was cursed to never know love. And the supposed love she felt was nothing but a hex. *And*, and, and, and, she'd killed his dad. When he discovered that piece of information, he probably wouldn't even want to be her friend.

She placed her hands on Jason's chest and pushed out of his embrace. With those parameters solidly in place, having sex with him wasn't out of the question. In fact, as long as she engaged in emotionless sex (sex between a teacher and a student—sex meant only for educational purposes) the answer to the question could be an easy yes. Yes.

Yes meant she could use Jason to learn the Tantric techniques. She'd get her certification. Move to New York and design for the stars. *No* meant she might fail the course, not finish the to-do list, and the Watsons would get her inheritance. And she'd be homeless again. And surely, Beth had meant for this to happen all along. Why else would she have asked Remington to learn about Tantric sex? Unless she'd wanted her to learn the skill to use it as a source of income in New York City while looking for work as a seamstress.

"I have no intentions of ever falling in love or getting married. As soon as I have finished Beth's to-do list, I plan to move to New York," she stated in her most professional, no-nonsense tone. "And open up a Tantric studio," she added for good measure. "I just thought you should know that up front."

"Duly recorded."

She took a deep breath. A guy who doesn't even blink when you tell him you're going to open up a Tantric studio is categorically not harboring any feelings for you. Damn hex. "How about you? Any rules you want to set?" She needed to make this a professional involvement. Not an emotional one. For her sake.

He drew his brows in until they touched, giving him an irresistible look of confusion. "Rules?"

"Rules," she affirmed.

"Are we entering a business proposition?" He pinched the bridge of his nose. A tell of uncertainty she'd learned from Linny when he'd taught her how to play poker.

"We're not doing this for pleasure."

He laughed. "Oh, I'm definitely doing this for pleasure." He picked her up and set her on the kitchen counter. "But your plan, not to fall in love, is a relief. The last four women I've dated have fallen in love with me."

"That's because you date airheaded bimbos." *And you're hexed.*

Jason laughed and pulled back. "You don't think real women, women with brains, would fall in love with me if I dated them?"

"You don't see me falling in love with you…do you?"

He frowned. "If we do this, we're going against Beth's last wishes."

"Beth didn't ask me not to have sex with you, just not fall in love with you. I can't see *that* being a problem."

He smiled, but his eyes didn't. "She told me not to hurt you. But you're so tough, I can't see anyone being able to hurt you."

"Absolutely. I'm unhurtable."

His mouth found hers. Taking. Plundering. Owning.

When he pulled back, Remington said, "You are an excellent kisser."

He laughed. "You are so different from any woman I've ever been with. I actually thought about you and your mouth while I was gone."

He'd been thinking of her mouth. What did that mean? Had he begun falling in love with her while he was away? And now that he was back, the hex was preventing the rest of the falling? "How am I different?"

"I could tell you, but that would go against the rules. This is strictly business. Personal conversations are not part of the bargain." His warm breath slid across her cheek. "Besides, I don't want to waste time talking, I have so much I want to teach you." He led them from the kitchen and into the living room toward the bedroom.

He stopped at the doorway, placed his hands on the wall and leaned in and kissed her again. "I'm not sure—"

Remington trembled. But not from desire. She trembled because the hairs on the back of her neck rose. And someone—or something—yanked them. *Ouch.* Had Beth done it? Was she pissed they were kissing? Remington jerked back and looked around for Beth. No sighting. If not Beth, who?

She refused to think it might be one of the mayhem ghosts. If you don't acknowledge a ghost, they can't bother you. Someone, or something, tugged her hair again.

"This is a bad idea." Her words came out in a gush, sticking together like Velcro babies.

Jason covered her hands with his big, strong warm ones and squeezed comfortingly. "Hasn't anyone ever told you bad ideas make the best stories?"

She opened her mouth to reply, and he leaned in and caught her lips in another kiss. Warm skin against warm skin. Lips open. Tongues entangled. The feel of his hands, stroking her back through the cover of her robe, robbed her of a desire to be smart. "No," she answered.

"They do. Just get me drunk some night and ask me about the stories of my life. Live on the edge with me, Remington. Let's have some fun."

Go away. Go away. Come again another day. She mentally cast the spell on whatever ghost was yanking her hair. The yanking stopped. "Okay," she said to Jason. He wasn't going to fall in love with her. She just had to keep reminding herself of that.

His reply was another kiss.

When their lips parted, she added, "I'm going to mark you off my to-do list as my one-night-stand man."

"If I'm you're one-night-stand man, we'd better be sure and do the experience justice."

"Right. Because even if we go more than one night, this relationship is definitely a fling-type of relationship."

"I'm liking the way you're thinking. Keep going."

"Right. It's not going to be a staying type of relationship." Her nerves were causing her to ramble. She told herself to shut up.

He chuckled. "Perfect. We can be neighbors with benefits. If you want to date others you can, and so can I."

Fuck that. "Right. Kevin's kind of cute. I could date him as a—"

Jason's grip tightened. "Wrong. Forget that asshole." His hands jerked open the top half of her robe, and one hand slipped through to cup her bare breast. "I've been wondering ever since I saw you in the doorway if you were naked under this ugly thing."

Ugly? Remington froze. *Crap.* "I'm not." If he thought her robe ugly, wait until he got a peek at her granny panties. She took a step away, out of his embrace, intent on making a mad dash to her panty drawer. Their first time together couldn't begin with ugly panties.

"Not what?" he asked.

"Not naked."

Jason's normally tanned skinned turned white. Whiter than Beth.

"Are you o—"

"Beth—" he whispered.

Remington flinched feeling like he'd just back-handed her. Her heart jerked against her ribs. He'd said *Beth*? She stumbled and grabbed for the coffee table. Her ears buzzed as if a train went through her living room.

Had he really called her Beth?

Pain, the horrible kind, like a paper-cut-to-the-heart horrible kind, swept through her. Was Beth who he'd been thinking of while he kissed her? "The name's Remington." With hands that shook, she tightened the belt of her robe.

Had he and Beth been an item? *Neighbors with benefits?* Those three words had rolled off his tongue quite easily. God, did he do all of his neighbors? Had it all started with the Tantric instructor? And now it was a psychological flaw. One he couldn't control. Like the *Fifty Shades of Gray* dude who liked to spank?

Jason rubbed his eyes with his thumb and forefinger, glanced around the room, and then his gaze met hers.

She stood mute. Afraid to open her mouth. Afraid of what might come out.

"What?" He rubbed his chin, still pale, and a pulse ticced in his right cheek.

"You called me Beth." She said the words with careful blandness.

Jason ran a hand through his hair, leaving the strands standing on ends. "I did?"

I did? For a smooth operator, he had some jagged edges.

She crossed her arms, tapped her foot, counted to three. "Yes." The declaration came out low, normal, nothing shouty. Perfectly disguised.

He whistled, shaking his head. "I'm sorry."

Her calm evaporated. "Sorry?" Sarcasm sprayed from the word like a skunk unleashing its perfume. Was that all he had? Well shut the fridge and call in a repairman, she'd sort of expected more excessive begging for forgiveness. After all, he wanted in her panties. Granny or thong. Son of a bastard.

"Yes." He pulled at the collar of his shirt, swallowing hard.

She leaned against the couch and ran her tongue over her upper teeth, damping her desire to explode. Which wasn't easy. He'd been imagining *her* best friend while his tongue had been stuck down Remington's throat. And he was sorry. She shook her head slowly.

She took a breath and blew it out hard. Sorry should be enough. They were to be neighbors with benefits, not emotions.

So why did she feel hurt?

Fuck. "Okay. But you've totally ruined the mood." She didn't shout the words.

"Okay."

"Go home."

"That's not what I want." He sounded sincere. Of course, he did. She was nothing but sex to him.

"Too bad." He could teach her about Tantric another day.

She waited until she heard the door shut before she added, "Asshole." Then she ran into the bathroom and slammed the door.

"Beth, are you here?" Remington shouted. Jason didn't owe her anything, but dammit, Beth did. The least she could have done was warn her they'd been a couple.

Nothing.

"Beth, I want to talk to you."

Still nothing.

"You should have told me," Remington said on a strangled sob.

Inky nothingness.

She stumbled into the bedroom, collapsed onto the bed, and piled the pillows around her, making a fortress. "Remington Smith you are an idiot, Remington Smith you are an idiot, Remington Smith you are an idiot." She chanted the words into her pillow until she fell into a fitful sleep.

Memories of wanting to be loved while growing up but never getting it haunted her dreams. No matter how good she'd tried to be at the orphanage, no one had found it in them to love her.

Jason let himself into his house. Why had he let Remington believe he'd been thinking about Beth while kissing her? Why had he sabotaged what would have surely been great sex? And why had he thought he'd seen Beth standing behind Remington?

Beth seemed so real floating there giving him *the look*. He could even swear he heard her say to not hurt Remington. Hell. Was he losing it? Had the death of his father affected his brain?

CHAPTER SIXTEEN

J ASON STARED OUT HIS KITCHEN window at Remington's house. The small white structure, built over one hundred years ago, had something the home he'd grown up in never had—character. From here, he could see a small round window in the attic and what appeared to be a person looking back at him.

He sighed and ran a hand through his hair. There wasn't anyone looking at him. Just his imagination— a result of last night's vision. He hoped Remington wouldn't push for an explanation. How could he explain he'd thought he'd seen Beth?

Of course, there were those who believed a house could be haunted by its previous owners, Beth included. His subconscious had probably conjured her up because he felt guilty for getting involved with Remington, Beth's BFF, who was living in Beth's house.

He wiped the condensation from his window with his shirtsleeve and peered harder at the attic window. He'd always wanted an attic with a slanted roof-line to play in as a boy. A place he could hide out from the servants and spy on the strangers who visited his house at all hours.

Shaking his head at the ancient thought, he walked to the counter, poured himself a cup of coffee, and wondered what time Remington would wake. The light was on in her living room, but there'd been no sign of movement in her kitchen. Or at least he didn't think there'd been any movement. She must have gone back to sleep after Ruby Rae had called to cancel their morning run. He wasn't sure when Ruby Rae had taken over the leadership of the group. Not that it mattered.

The heavy snow, blowing around frantically in the blustery wind, was the reason their run had been canceled. So heavy, that at times, the weather people were comparing it to a mountain blizzard. Part of him wanted to bundle up and run, anyway. He needed the activity to clear his head. But that would be foolish. If he slipped and broke his leg, he'd be laid up for weeks.

Perhaps later when the snow calmed, he'd go outside and brave the elements. The scenery would be beautiful. By then, Tom would have had a chance to plow the streets. A duty he'd taken on, of his own free will, while Jason had been gone. Or that was Ruby Rae's story. Jason was pretty sure Tom's own-free-will had been manipulated by Ruby Rae and Sara Ann.

Jason didn't mind the snow, although he preferred beaches and bikini-clad women. He just didn't enjoy the holidays that came with the white stuff. Thanksgiving and Christmas. His least favorite time of the year.

He'd never enjoyed the winter holidays. Mostly because he'd spent them with a variety of nannies while his dad had jetted off on vacation with one woman after another.

Of course, gifts were never a problem. Anything he could possibly want showed up under the professionally decorated trees. All from Dad. God forbid he'd been allowed to believe in Santa.

Once he'd moved out of the awkward Hart-Mansion and started his own life, the tradition of spending Christmas alone hadn't changed. This year would be no different. Unless he invited Remington to spend the day with him.

Her memories of Christmas were probably more dismal than his. Christmas in an orphanage couldn't be much fun. The two of them could get drunk together, strip out of their clothes, and make ass-cheek angels in the snow. Thumb their noses at tradition.

He chuckled, causing Scotch to glance his way. Jason didn't get the impression Remington allowed herself to have much fun. Everything she did was for a reason. Like agreeing to have sex with him.

That had been Beth's motive behind the to-do list. She'd wanted Remington to do things that didn't have anything to do with the outcome. She'd wanted Remington to live in Knotty and live her life for herself. Make friends. Realize family didn't have to be blood.

Beth had asked Jason to help her help Remington discover these things. But Jason had declined the invitation. He wasn't exactly a poster boy for the well-adjusted. But he had promised to keep an eye out for her.

The pounding of a fist against a screen door scattered his thoughts. Remington must have finally woken up and wanted a freshly brewed cup of coffee.

Smiling like a silly schoolboy, glad she wasn't the type to hold a grudge, he swung open the door. He'd make last night's slip of the tongue up to her. Hopefully with his tongue.

His smile straightened. It wasn't Remington.

A tall man wearing a black overcoat and black mirrored glasses stood on his porch.

"Mr. Hart?" The man's voice held an edge. An edge of power and arrogance.

Jason opened the screen door. "Who's asking?"

The stranger pulled a badge out of his coat pocket and flashed it. "FBI. The name's Meek. Agent Meek."

Jason's blood ran cold. He'd always suspected his father of being involved with unsavory characters. So many rough-looking guys visiting his dad late at night. "Is there a problem?" Jason stepped back and motioned for the agent to come inside. What kind of illegal activity had his dad been a part of?

The man thumped the snow off his shoes and walked inside.

Jason took his coat and motioned for him to take a seat on the couch. "That's some weather we're having out there." Hung his coat in the closet. "Would you like a cup of coffee?"

"No, thank you. Unfortunately, my bosses don't

care if the weather sucks. The job comes first."

"What brings you to my house?" Jason asked, not one to beat around the subject.

Agent Meek nodded and opened a tattered briefcase. "I'm sure you understand I'm here on official government business."

"I figured as much."

Meek pulled out a document. "This is a contract to purchase the orphanage here in Knotty. Is that your signature?" The agent handed Jason the papers.

Jason took the papers and flipped through them. They were a contract between him and the owner of the orphanage. "It's not a forgery, if that's what brought you here."

Agent Meek lifted an eyebrow. "I see."

Jason took a seat across from the agent. He didn't reply. There hadn't been a question.

"May I ask, what is your purpose in buying the orphanage?" Meek asked.

Jason thought about telling him it was none of his fucking business. But then, why piss off the government? One never knew when they might come in handy in a business dealing. "I've purchased most of the property in Knotty, and I'm transforming the land into a singles-only town. It's all perfectly legal. I've done my research. I already have the orphanage leased. I'm going to build a new orphanage for the orphans on the southeast side."

The agent nodded. "The man who signed the contract isn't in a position to sell the property."

Jason stilled. His muscles tensed. "Does he know that?"

"He does now."

Jason leaned forward, alarm bells ringing in his ears. "Are you saying this contract is fraudulent?" Shit.

"Not exactly. He owns the property." The agent uncrossed and recrossed his legs in the opposite direction. "He's just not free to sell the land without meeting a set of stipulations."

Jason resisted the urge to curse. "What type of stipulations?"

"Mr. Smith inherited the orphanage from his great grandfather. In the inheritance, there was a stipulation that if at any time he decided to sell the orphanage, the FBI had to approve of the new owner."

Jason's mind raced. "Why would he have that in his will, and why would the FBI approve of that stipulation?"

The agent looked straight into Jason's eyes. "Because Mr. Smith's great-grandfather used to be an agent. When he retired, he opened the orphanage as a way of doing something good in the world after all the horrible things he'd seen in the field."

Jason shifted in his chair. "Okay. What do I have to do to be approved as the new buyer of the land?"

"First of all, you mention this conversation to no one. If we learn you've discussed our dealings with anyone, we'll shut down all efforts you make at getting permits for anything you try to build or open. Your town will never happen."

Blackmail. "Done. What else?"

The agent cleared his throat. "You're not going to build a new orphanage. You need to make sure this is handled in a diplomatic fashion that does not stir up any controversy. Nothing can be reported in the news about this orphanage."

Jason's hands tightened into fists. "I've promised a young child a new orphanage."

"Did your father raise you to believe we live in a fair world?"

A flare of adrenaline fired through Jason. "Of course not."

Agent Meek gave him a pensive expression. "Then you understand fairness has nothing to do with this condition. If you want the property, your job is to make sure it's done."

"What will happen to the orphans? Where will they go? Some of them are currently being considered for adoption."

The agent raised a dismissive hand. "That will not be of any concern to you."

Jason pressed his lips together. "Is that it? I have to keep my mouth shut and not build a new orphanage?"

"There's one more thing. If anyone comes to Knotty and asks about the current orphans or any of the former orphans, there is to be no information given. If there's a leak, and that information is told, then the government will come in and shut your town down. Do we make ourselves very clear?"

"What if I back out of the deal? Don't buy the

orphanage? Can the orphans stay?"

"That's no longer a possibility."

Jason leaned forward, his chest tightening. "Are they in danger? Has there been a threat?"

"Mr. Hart, you are an intelligent man. If the news got out the previous owner was FBI, an agent whose undercover work helped bring down infamous criminals—criminals with family who declared war on him for generations to come— descendants of those family members might decide to kill an orphan as revenge for their family name."

Okay. That could happen. But it sounded far-fetched. And unnecessarily cruel. Even for the tight-knit crime families of the world. "I get the feeling there's something you're not telling me. What is it?"

"You are speculating. Speculation is a dangerous game. I would advise you to leave the mysteries to those of us who make a living at solving them."

Jason crossed his arms. "There is one orphan whom I've grown fond of. Will you let me know where he ends up? I want to keep in contact with him." How would he explain to Johnny B that he wasn't going to keep his promise?

"I'm afraid that will not be possible. None of the current orphans will ever be adopted."

"Why the fuck not?"

"Safety." He closed his briefcase and stood. "I will see my way out."

"Am I allowed to adopt one?"

"Mr. Hart, I imagine your town will have an appeal to many. None of them will want children in a singles town. Good luck with your adventure. It will be bigger than anything your father ever did."

CHAPTER SEVENTEEN

REMINGTON WOKE TO THE SOUND of a car door slamming and her heart hammering. *Thank God I'm awake.* She popped up, threw off the covers, and scurried out of bed. Bizarre dreams had dominated her sleep. The kind of dreams where anger and spells mixed, lightning and thunder collided, and love and pain squared off.

She exhaled hard and shook her head to clear the cobwebs.

Max poked his head out from under the pillow next to the one Remington used. He looked at Remington with criticism, whimpered, and then tunneled back under the pillow.

Remington pushed her hair out of her face and glanced around her room. Her heartbeat tripled. "Damn it, damn it, damn it." Her dress dummy laid prostrate on the floor and pins stuck out of it everywhere. Her granny panties hung from the ceiling fan, the doorknob, and both ends of the curtain rods.

Oh God, had any of her dream spells worked? Was Jason still alive?

She grabbed her robe, slipped on her boots, and drudged through the knee-deep snow to Jason's house. What if she'd cast a dead spell on him just because he'd said Beth's name in the middle of their moment? Could she cast an undead spell? Was there such a thing as an undead spell?

A dark Sedan was parked along the street in front of Jason's house. Its black tinted windows did nothing to squelch her nerves. Who visited in the middle of a snowstorm? A cop who'd been tipped off that something unearthly had taken place in Knotty overnight? Or a coroner?

She crossed the fingers of her left hand and knocked on the door with her right hand. "God, please don't let me have killed Jason."

She heard Scotch bark and then the front door opened. "You're alive," she blurted.

Jason cocked his head. "Did you think I died?"

"I—" Remington snapped her mouth closed. Behind Jason, she saw a serious-looking dude closing a briefcase. She bit her lip and shook her head.

Jason raised his eyebrows, obviously waiting for her to expound.

Remington didn't know what all damage she'd done in her dreams, but at least Jason was alive. "I just thought I'd come over and tell you our run was canceled this morning in case you didn't get the call."

Jason glanced at his watch. "That was three hours ago."

Remington nodded. "Right. Okay. Sorry to bother you. Just trying to be neighborly." She turned and walked as fast as she could back to her house, feeling like a moron of massive magnitude.

And no doubt looking like one as well. "Damn it."

Max met her at the front door. Remington scooped him up and set him outside to do his business. As she did so, she noticed her congress of ghosts standing on Jason's porch high-fiving. Weird.

She closed the door and glanced around. "Okay, so the dead spell didn't take. I wonder if any of the other spells did?"

Max meowed and she let him back inside.

Remington started the coffee and grabbed a pen and paper. She needed to make a list of the spells she remembered.

At the top of the paper she wrote, *An Angry Witch Is a Dangerous Witch.*

Then, starting with the number one, she wrote the spells she remembered chanting in her dreams.

1. *Fiddle Dee*
   Fiddle Dum
   The Spell on Jason
   Be undone

2. *Granny panties far and near*
   Never again grace my rear.

3. *Men who are pigs*
   Make them humble
   They'll crawl on their knees
   And hear me rumble

4. *Fool me once*
   And get your comeuppance

Fool me twice
And lose your existence.

Remington stopped writing. That was the one. The spell she'd cast on Jason in her sleep. That's why he wasn't dead yet. She'd given him a second chance in her spell. Thank God.

She poured herself a cup of coffee and added a generous portion of Baileys. This witch stuff was dangerous.

She needed to tell Jason she was a witch. Tell him he'd die if he ever lied to her again? What would he say? Would he laugh?

Of course, he'd laugh.

She should leave Knotty before she caused the man real harm. But if she didn't finish her to-do list, the Watsons would get her inheritance. She'd be homeless again.

"Beth?" Remington took a sip of coffee and waited for Beth to appear. They needed to renegotiate her inheritance.

Beth didn't appear. Hell. Had she cast a go-away spell on Beth? She tried winging an undo spell. "Oh Beth, Oh Beth, you are my dear friend, please come back and spend time with me again."

Beth appeared.

"Damn it, Remington, that wasn't funny. Don't send me away." Beth wore a wedding gown.

So, it had been Beth pulling on her hair last night and not a mayhem ghost. That was a good thing. "Sorry about that." Remington pointed to her list of spells. "Look at these. Do you think they worked if I cast them while I slept?"

Beth groaned. "Of course, they work. Why would you do an undo spell on him while you slept?" Beth read the rest of the list. "Oh. My. Death. You cast a kill spell on him! You're going to be a double-murderer."

CHAPTER EIGHTTEEN

THE NEXT MORNING, THE GROUP'S long run wasn't canceled. The sun shone, the snow had stopped, the roads were plowed, and the temperature was above freezing. Jason couldn't wait to see Remington. She'd never shown back up the day before, and he'd left her alone.

At precisely six a.m., all the Knotty Ridge Runners glanced at their watches.

Ruby Rae cleared her throat. "You jackrabbits ready?"

Jason glanced up the street. "Shouldn't we wait on Remington?"

There was a chorus of nos.

"Why not?" Jason asked.

"She signed the running prenup. On time or you run alone," Sara Ann said. "Don't worry. It's not like there are bad guys in Knotty waiting to grab her from behind the bushes."

All the runners pushed their tracking buttons and started running. Including Jason. It was, after all, their rule. "Did anyone hear from her this morning?"

"She didn't answer when I knocked," Ruby Rae said. "But sometimes she doesn't hear me because she sleeps with earphones, listening to music."

"She knows the rules. Show up on time or run by yourself," Maverick said, before turning and talking to a cute blonde. They must have recruited her while Jason was gone. A few of the employees from Think Tank Innovations were starting to move in. His town was coming together.

Ruby Rae matched her pace to Jason's as some of the others lengthened theirs and began to separate from the group. "We've missed you while you were gone. Are you going to tell us where you've been?"

Jason hadn't run for over a month. His calf muscles weren't happy with him starting again this morning. "I had to deal with a family crisis. My father died." There'd been plenty of opportunities to run, but his motivation had disappeared.

"Oh darling, you should have told us. We'd have been there for you," said Sara Ann, flanking him on the other side, touching his arm in support.

He shrugged off her hand. "Not a big deal. We didn't like one another," Jason said, uncomfortable with their concern. "Has Remington been running with you while I've been gone?"

"Like clockwork," said Ruby Rae.

"Yes, like clockwork," agreed Sara Ann. "She's pretty good. She's a natural. And she's got good speed."

"She's beginning to grow on me. Not as much a tart as I thought," Ruby Rae said. "Tom and Kevin and she have *really* had a good time trying to outdo each other with their practical jokes."

Jason's senses sharpened. His team was bonding with Remington. For some reason, he didn't like it. As soon as her to-do list was complete, she would leave to go to New York. He didn't want anyone encouraging her to stay here. He couldn't shake the feeling Agent Meek left out a significant component of his story. Something that warranted drastic actions concerning the orphans. And she was technically still an orphan. Beth would want him to protect Remington, even if it meant pushing her out of Knotty.

"Speaking of Kevin, why isn't he here this morning?" The question came out sharper than he'd intended.

The ladies giggled.

"Who knows with him? He misses more runs than he makes," said Ruby Rae. "Too many late night, hot dates. Although he never brings anyone home with him. I admire that in the boy."

Jason assured himself the niggling in the pit of his stomach was a result of his concern for Remington after yesterday's FBI visit.

He should have checked on her before meeting the other runners. Damn. Why hadn't he checked on her? *What if…* "I just realized I forgot to let Scotch out this morning. My routine is messed up." He made a quick U-turn. "You guys go on. I'm going to go back and let him out." He didn't wait for a reply.

Jason sprinted toward Farmer Street. Now that the thought had taken residence that something bad might have happened to her, he had to make sure she was okay. He rounded the corner to their street and skidded to a halt.

Kevin's truck sat squarely in the middle of Remington's driveway.

Jason's heart sagged, and the grinding tension in his temples eased. She was okay. Nothing sinister had happened. She was with Kevin.

Ignoring the new emotion churning his gut, Jason went home, showered and tried to concentrate on work. Unable to do that, he called Bernadette. He might as well get this conversation over with. Let her know her friends were not going to be able to adopt any of the children from Knotty. Her answering machine picked up on the third ring.

"Hey Bernie, I have some bad news. Give me a call."

Twenty minutes later, when he'd accomplished nothing—unless you count walking to the window to see if Remington was home alone—Jason knew what he had to do.

He slipped on his boots, traipsed through the snow, past Kevin's truck, and up the steps to her house. The youngest member of his team needed to grow up and stop notching his belt with every good-looking woman he met. Someone was going to get hurt.

Remington surprised him by opening the door before he could knock, robbing him of the opportunity to put on his game face.

"Hi." The scowl on her face probably matched the one he wore.

He tried to erase his. "I didn't knock yet."

"I saw you through the kitchen window." She wore running gear. So why hadn't she met the group for their run? "What do you want?"

"May I come in?" he asked, unable to keep the anger out of his tone. Or was it jealousy?

She motioned him inside.

Jason stomped the snow off his boots and followed Remington into the kitchen. A cozy arrangement of two cups of cocoa set next to each other on the table. He tripped. "Am I interrupting something?" He draped his coat over a chair.

Kevin smirked at him from across the room, obviously having noticed his stumble. "Just hot drinks with a beautiful woman." His use of the word *hot* was intentional. Meant to rub Jason the wrong way.

"I see you're both dressed for running. Strange, I didn't see either one of you on the run."

Remington and Kevin shared a laugh. Fresh, honest, compelling laughter.

Jason realized this was the first time he'd ever heard Remington laugh in such a carefree manner. "Is it a private joke, or can anyone be let in on it?" He wanted to make her laugh like that.

"Kevin stopped to offer me a lift."

"Then Remington talked me into ditching the group for hot chocolate," Kevin finished.

"Kevin, I thought you would have been a better role model for Remington. She's training for her first marathon. You know the importance of long runs. Even in the snow."

Remington made a noise of disbelief. "Don't be

such a stuffed-shirt. We're going to run. Just not at 6:00 in the freaking morning. We're thinking about starting our own running group. One that runs at a more reasonable hour. Say, 10:30."

Jason pinched the bridge of his nose. "According to Ruby Rae, that will be better for Kevin given his rotating door of women and late carnal nights."

Kevin snorted. "Is the old bat keeping tabs on me because she wants to…or did my boss have her keeping tabs on my night activities while he was out of town? Perhaps he's afraid of a little competition."

"Boss? Do you guys work together?" Remington asked.

"Yes," they both said, still eyeing each other like boxers in a ring, daring the other to throw the first punch.

Jason broke the stare. What in the hell was wrong with him? Kevin wasn't his competition. There wasn't a competition. He turned toward Remington. Looking at her was a whole lot better than looking at Kevin's ugly mug.

A red long-sleeve running shirt stopped an inch below her hips. Running tights clung to the curves of her legs, replacing the shorts he remembered from their previous runs. Perfect body. Lots of focal points. A desire to strip her out of her clothes and touch her skin, feel its satiny smoothness, breathe in the fragrance of her perfume, swept through him. "Kevin's a part of my design team. So are Maverick and Tom."

"No kidding? Are you the one with the idea to

make it look like a beachside town?" she asked Kevin.

Kevin beamed at her. "Do you like?"

"Love. Jason, would you like some hot chocolate?"

He nodded and watched as she poured milk into a cup. The material of the tights outlined her ass nicely as she reached on tiptoe to pop the cup in the microwave. With her arms stretched high, the top pulled away, displaying the velvetiness of the small of her back. He didn't notice any panty lines. Was she wearing any?

Remington turned and leaned against the cabinet. "Kevin, I thought you were in real estate. Why the secrecy?"

Kevin walked over and joined her at the cabinet, mimicking her stance and staring at Jason. "I thought it was a secret. I think you have him so rattled he doesn't remember his name, let alone the parameters he's set up for his team and our latest project." He held up his hand and gave Remington a fist bump.

Her cheeks reddened. "I'm sure it has nothing to do with me if he's rattled."

Kevin ran the back of his hand down the side of her face. "I wouldn't be so sure. I've never known him to be so tense around a woman."

Jason wanted to punch Kevin. Tell him to keep his damn hands off Remington. What right did he have to do that?

Remington's eyebrows pulled together, and she looked from one to the other. "Ruby Rae said you were marketing Knotty as a singles town."

Remington brought Jason a cup of hot chocolate and resisted the urge to lay a hand on his arm in familiarity and feel for a pulse. She wanted to make sure he was truly alive and not just pretending.

Jason sipped the hot chocolate. "I didn't start out to make Knotty a singles town, but with Think Tank Innovations placing its first-year employees here, and then the college wanting to house a group of seniors in the orphanage, it's morphing into one. And I decided to market it as such to potential retailers."

"Tell me about the seniors."

Jason laughed. "The local university has a group who are majoring in supernatural stuff. I've agreed to lease the old orphanage to them as a dormitory. They seem to think that Knotty is haunted and hexed."

"You don't believe in that nonsense…do you?" she said.

"Not at all," he replied with zero hesitation.

Crap.

Kevin pushed away from the counter and placed his cup in the sink. "Listen you two, I promised Sara Ann and Ruby Rae I'd stop by this morning and dig their car out. They want to make a grocery run before the next storm."

"Thanks for dropping by." Remington walked him to the door. "I'll see you later." She reached up and hugged him.

When he'd pulled out of her driveway, Remington shut the door and turned to see Jason standing behind her, his lips compressed.

"What's your problem?"

"Have you two had sex?"

CHAPTER NINETEEN

REMINGTON RAN HER TONGUE OVER her front teeth and counted to three. Her insides needed to calm the hell down so she could think. She'd been ready to have sex with Jason two nights ago and now he had the nerve to ask her if she'd had sex with Kevin. Did he think she was the type to sleep around?

Of course, he did. Why else would he ask?

She clenched her hands, her nails digging into her palms. But the self-inflicted pain wasn't enough to drag her mind away from the anger singeing her insides.

How dare he stand in her kitchen and accuse her of being a loose goose? "Who I sleep with is none of your business. You should leave." The hurt in her voice pissed her off. Emotions were not a part of the deal they'd been brokering. Why couldn't she remember that?

He didn't blink or move or smile. "I thought you and I were forming a mutually beneficial arrangement. Have you and Kevin had sex? Because if you have, I'm not interested."

"Could you be any more sanctimonious?" She refused to let any rhyme enter her head. No telling what she'd do to him if she did.

He stared like a hard-ass who had right on his side.

She gave an undignified huff of disgust. "Not that it's any of your business, but no."

He blinked, his features softened, and he ran a hand through his hair. "Good."

"I guess that's all in how you look at it." She refused to believe the message she read in his eyes. No way he was falling for her. There was still a curse on Knotty, so even if her uncurse worked, out of the two of them, only one of them was going to fall in love with the other. And, well...

Without warning, he yanked her against him. "Don't sleep with him." The words had no give in them. Spoken in a no-nonsense, *don't fuck with me* command.

How dare he manhandle her and tell her whom she could or couldn't sleep with? She waited for the outrage to fill her up. The emotion didn't come. Instead, her knees weakened.

Her freaking willpower really needed to be sent to resolve boot camp and get its wimpy ass kicked into shape.

Jason forced one leg between her knees and moved in closer. Like he was laying claim to that part of her body.

"You can't dictate who I can and can't sleep with. All we have is a business agreement." She said the words with as much matter-of-fact as she could muster, which wasn't much.

"I know. But I'm adding some conditions to the

contract. For one, neither of us will pursue relations with another." Jason pressed her against the door, and his head dipped, his lips brushing hers. He moaned.

"You can't just change the rules whenever you want."

"Trust me, I know how contracts work. Take it or leave it."

She turned her head, evading his lips. "*You* were pretending *I* was Beth." She weaved her hands in his hair and yanked. "Where do you get off with the jealous act?"

"Damn it. Why would I ever pretend you're anybody but you? You're pretty fucking spectacular."

She blinked. "Of course, I am, but that didn't stop you from calling me Beth."

He placed a warm palm against her cheek and turned her head until their lips were lined up. "I don't know why I said her name. What I do know is I feel things around you I'm not used to feeling."

She opened her mouth to argue, but he didn't give her a chance. His lips crushed hers, effectively taking her ability to think away. His tongue parted her lips and found her tongue and thrust as if entering her body on a sexual quest.

Hot, raw desire consumed her.

With a muffled curse, he slid his hands under the elastic of her tights and pushed inside them. "I've been wondering ever since I saw you in the kitchen if you were naked under these."

His hands cupped her bare ass, and he gave a low-throttled growl.

"Yep." She gasped at the sensation of his strong fingers spreading wide and gently squeezing. The tights had a built-in panty.

Suddenly, he removed his hands, swept her up in his arms, and strode to her bedroom. He sat her down, tugged her top off and dropped it on the floor. Pushed her back on the bed and slid off her running tights.

And she simply let him.

And then he stared.

And she got all hot and bothered.

And he smiled.

And weirdly enough, she regained her ability to think.

Was he documenting her every flaw? Starting with her overly large breasts? They were larger than Beth's. Much larger than the skinny bitch from the orphanage. What if they were too large for him? She covered them with her hands. What if her hips were too wide? Too fleshy? What if—

"Don't," he growled. "They're beautiful. You're beautiful. Let me look."

She slowly let her hands fall away. This was, after all, just about sex. A contract. If he didn't like full-figured gals, his loss.

His eyes traveled over her body like melted chocolate over Chubby Hubby ice cream.

She nibbled her bottom lip, her body tingling in places she was pretty sure had never tingled before without the help of her vibrator, Mr. Bob.

Was she affecting him? What if she disappointed him? Oh God. She probably would. It wasn't like she'd had any practice since Linny's declaration of her lack of skills in the bedroom. "I should warn you, I'm not very good at making love."

Jason's hooded eyes opened slightly. "What?"

Did he sound angry?

Remington picked at the cotton of the bed-spread, wishing she had more experience. But she didn't, and she might as well be honest with him so he'd know and not be disappointed. "I'm not good at what we're about to do." She scooted to the edge of the bed closest to the wall. "I haven't had much practice. But I'm willing to learn. That's why I'm doing the Tantric thing."

He toed out of his jeans, not taking his eyes from her. "Who told you that you're not any good at making love?"

"Linny. He told me I was a disappointing virgin. That most virgins have more intuitive moves than me." She let her gaze lower to his boxers and saw the impressive ridge of his erection pushing against the material, and she gulped.

Wowza. Jason was twice the man Linny had been. Did that mean she'd cause him twice the dis-appointment?

Jason placed a hand under her chin and lifted. "Haven't any of your lovers since then told you what an idiot he was?"

She briefly glanced into his eyes. They were dark like a cave. Did desire have that effect on them? Remington looked down at her hands clutch-ing the blanket on either side of her. She should probably loosen up, not appear uptight. She let the blanket slip from her fingers.

Jason slid onto the bed. "You didn't answer me."

She licked her lips. "I've only had one lover."

He coughed abruptly. "One?"

"Mmmm mmm." She sneaked a peek at him. How disappointed was he?

He closed his eyes. "You're killing me…Smith."

Her last name on his lips was an aphrodisiac.

The desire in his voice took her breath away and replaced it with sweet bits of confidence. "I am?"

"In a good way babe. In a good way." He opened his eyes.

"Yay me." She worked to catch her breath.

"Yes…*yay you*. Later, I'll teach you about Tantric." He gave her a slow sensuous smile. "But for now, I'm going to simply make love to you." He pushed her down gently and kissed her. "Is that okay?"

"Sex," she said.

"What?"

"We're going to make sex. We have a sex contract."

A tiny frown wrinkled his forehead. "I don't want to have a contract," he whispered. "Did you know your lips taste like syrup?"

He tasted like a dangerous fire licking its way to her stomach. "I had pancakes for breakfast with Kevin."

"I'm going to fire him. Send him back to Seattle."

"You're kidding right? About the contract—right?"

His smile was noncommittal. "We're going to take this sex slow." His voice was low. "Very, very slow."

She ran her hands up and down his back, letting her nails scrape lightly against his skin. Her hips pushed upward against him of their own will. "You have too many clothes on."

He laughed. "Impatient little thing, aren't you?" He spread her legs apart and appraised her body. She thought she felt him tremor. She knew she felt herself tremor.

"Is that a bad thing?" It was scary letting someone look at her so intimately, but it also turned her on. The first few chapters in her Tantric workbook had been about exploring each other's bodies before having sex. She needed to become comfortable with this.

He leaned down and kissed the underside of her breast. "We're going to take the first time slowly." He ran a fingertip lightly against her. "When I'm finished with you, Linny will be a name you can't remember."

Remington moaned. "Who?"

His grin turned wicked. "Exactly." His voice was thick and heavy. "Remington Smith, there's something about you that causes me to wish I had a heart that worked."

She closed her eyes and tried to remember the things she'd learned from Tantric. "I'm not going to fall in love with you, so you don't have to pretend this is about emotions."

The sound of a woman's curse caused Remington to jump. Her eyes flew open.

She glanced at Jason. His gaze was on the window above their head. "Who is that?"

"Jason, are you in there?" the woman said. She pounded on his front door hard enough they could hear the rumble in Remington's bedroom.

Jason climbed to his knees, Remington scrambled to do the same, and together they glanced out her window.

Looking out the curtains, she saw a woman peeking into Jason's living room window. A familiar woman. Long, blonde hair. When she turned, Remington saw her face, and the fog clouding her brain vanished.

"Her again?" Remington whispered. Why? How?

Jason didn't respond. He calmly pulled the curtain further aside.

"You owe me a fucking explanation," the woman called out. "I worked my ass off, and you fucked me."

Remington heard Scotch growl. She found herself hoping Scotch would get loose and bite the woman.

"Are you a couple?" Remington whispered to Jason. Of course, they were. Why else would a woman be making so much noise at a man's house?

Max, who'd been sleeping by the door, scampered under the bed.

"Of course not." Jason flicked the locks on Remington's window and slid it up. "My door's unlocked. Let yourself in. I'll be right there."

Remington collapsed on the bed, not wanting to be seen. "You've got to be fucking kidding me." She stared up at Jason. Was he going to leave her to go to another woman?

He ran a hand through his hair. "What in the hell did you want me to do? Let her keep yelling until all of Knotty comes to see what's going on and finds me in your bed?"

He had a point. "Did you invite her over today?"

"Not exactly. I just left her a message that we needed to talk."

God, they *were* a couple. Had he asked to talk to her so he could break up with her and go with Remington? Did anyone go with anyone these days? What was the new term the young kids used? Shit! Why was she worried about terminology? Remington scrambled to her knees and pulled the sheet with her. "Then I would have expected you to keep your mouth shut and let her go home on the same broom that brought her here. To hell with the gossip."

"I care about your reputation. I don't want the whole town to know we're sleeping together."

"Are you sure about that?" The memory of a high school boy telling her he wanted to meet her after the prom but couldn't take her to the prom because people would talk flooded her. "Are you sure you just don't want anyone to know you have a thing with the nobody orphan?" The boy's family had referred to her as…a nobody orphan. She knew because he'd told her.

Until now, she'd forgotten about that boy who

had wanted to kiss her but not date her. She'd forgotten how dirty he'd made her feel. How worthless he'd made her feel.

"Don't be ridiculous. That isn't what I said."

"But it's what you meant, isn't it?"

"Hell no. Will you just give me a rain check? I'll be right back."

Remington sputtered. "A rain check? You...bastard." She crawled across the bed, yanked open her underwear drawer, dug through her panties. Her fingers came across a package of condoms. Beth's gift to her. She flung them at Jason.

"What? Do you think I'm going to need these with her?" Jason asked.

Remington glanced over her shoulder at him and saw him holding the condoms.

His smile told her he thought her reaction funny. That he thought she was overreacting.

She opened her mouth to tell him what she thought. That he could wipe that damn smile off his face. But all that came out was a growl of frustration. Lucky for him.

She turned back to her panty drawer and found what she'd really been looking for. Hank. She pulled him out, turned and pointed her Smith and Wesson at Jason. "Get out."

He glanced at her gun, and his smile grew bigger.

"I'm warning you, size doesn't matter." Really, of all the nerve.

"Oh honey, I plan on teaching you otherwise." His body shook as if holding back a desire to laugh.

How dare he say sexy things to her at a moment

like this. "I'm a damn good shot with this thing." Too bad she hadn't gotten around to reloading it after her and Kevin's target practice session. If her pistol had bullets, she'd shoot the door behind Jason's back and get his attention. That would wipe the stupid smirk off his face. Then again, it would also wipe out her door.

"Do you have any idea how damn sexy you are waving that thing at me while you're butt naked?" He strode across the room with zero hesitation and kissed her on top of the head. "Do you have a hip holster for it? I'd like to see you in it with nothing else on when I come back."

She lowered the gun. Did he really think she was sexy? Was he coming back? "Jackass." As insults go, it was a pretty good one. Concise. To the point. Accurate. Or it would have been a fine one if she hadn't let the last word come out like a whispery caress instead of a harsh curse.

"Beautiful."

She cleared her throat. "Ass." There. She'd said it right. No doubt she meant it that time.

CHAPTER TWENTY

REMINGTON SWIPED AT THE TEARS on her cheeks and paced a circle around her small bedroom. What in the hell was wrong with her? She'd gone from never crying to crying all the time. Even when she wasn't sad. Like right now. When she was frustrated. "Damn it, damn it, damn it." As long as she was cursing, she couldn't think rhymes.

At least no one was around to see the water-works. Other than Max, who'd been watching her from his perch on a stack of dusty old books and giving her a look that clearly said, "Paw...uke."

Remington scrubbed a hand down her face. Max was right. Her behavior would cause any-one to puke. *Ugh.* Remington yanked her running clothes off the floor and pulled them on. What she needed was exercise. Exercise to exorcise the sex-ual frustration turning her brain to mush.

She'd be damn if she'd still be standing here cry-ing when he returned. *If* he returned.

She grabbed her cell and called Kevin who answered on the first ring. "I know it's not ten-thirty yet, but let's run," she blurted, not bothering with hello. Jason had been with that woman for over a half-hour. Jealousy gnawed at Remington's heart. He obviously wasn't going to come back and woo her into a state of submission.

"Sure. I'm almost finished shoveling the side-walk. Why don't you meet me at Ruby Rae's and Sara Ann's?" Kevin said cheerfully.

Remington rubbed the back of her neck. "I'm on my way." She might as well put all of this unwanted adrenaline to a good use.

She had to run slowly on the snow-packed side-walks. Which left her with plenty of breath to curse Jason. So, why was she cursing herself instead?

If she'd been any good, Jason—logical reason or not—never would have left her to go see that woman in the first place. He would have simply ignored the bimbo hollering his name at the top of her lungs and hung in there with Remington until she'd been hollering out his name in the throes of pleasure.

Bottom line, Linny must have been telling the truth. Part of her, a big part, had been hoping he'd been lying. That he was a toad. That she was a freaking miracle in bed.

The fact was, she was going to fail Tantric sex, and there were two mayhem ghosts released in Knotty, and it was her fault, and she was going to die trying to run a full marathon, and so none of it mattered, anyway.

Her breaths were coming hard and fast by the time she made it to Ruby Rae's and Sara Ann's. Mostly because the cold air wasn't lung friendly. But somewhat because she'd worked herself into a tizzy of despair. Kevin and the ladies were waiting on the sidewalk. No doubt gossiping.

"Good morning," Ruby Rae said. "We missed you this morning."

"Yeah, sorry about that. Kevin and I decided to drink hot chocolate instead." Remington grabbed her side and tried to slow down her heart rate and took care not to look either of the ladies in the eyes. She swore they were psychics, the way they found out things no one else knew.

Sara Ann laughed. "Well, I can't say I blame you. He's a fine specimen of a man."

Kevin took Remington's arm and turned her toward the road. "I think we'll leave on that comment."

"You kids have fun," Ruby Rae hollered.

"Yeah. Save some energy for tonight's board game," Sara Ann added. "Five o'clock sharp. Don't be late."

"We won't."

The first mile, they ran in silence. The second mile, they ran in silence. The third mile, Kevin cleared his throat and said, "Are you going to tell me why you're pissed?"

Remington pulled her brain away from her thoughts. "What do you mean?"

"You're foaming at the mouth, and it's not because you're out of shape. What's going on between you and the boss?"

"What makes you think this is about him?"

"Well, for starters, I thought I was going to get deep-fried from all the electrical sparks you guys were throwing off as you stared at one another in the kitchen."

Remington picked up her pace. "You misread those looks."

"I don't think so."

"Right now, as we run, he's held up at his house with some bimbo from his past."

Kevin didn't reply right away. "There are lots of bimbos in his past," he finally said. "Which one are you speaking of?"

Remington slowed down, because Kevin wasn't trying to keep up with her. "I didn't ask her name. She showed up, and he took off like a rabbit caught in a fox race."

Another mile went by in silence. "I wouldn't worry about someone from his past. I've never known him to be serious about any of them."

"Who he sees isn't any of my business." She took off her gloves and shoved them in her jacket pocket. The sting of the cool air helped distract her from the pain. "But why doesn't he believe in love?"

"That's something you're going to have to ask him. It's not my story to tell."

Remington snorted. "Well then, I'll never know, because the last thing I'm going to ask him is to share his personal life with me." She sprinted until the end of the street. Hell. She'd undone his hex. He could fall in love again.

Kevin caught up with her. "It's hard to build a relationship with a man if you don't ask questions of one another."

They ran in silence for a block while Remington regained her ability to talk. "I don't plan on building a relationship with him. At most, I might have sex with him."

"Is that what you want or what he wants?"

"Both."

Kevin laughed softly. "I find that hard to believe." He glanced sideways at her. "You don't come across to me as the type that just has sex with a man."

Remington stopped running for a moment and glared at Kevin. "Well, you're wrong. I am. In fact, my plans are to move to New York and teach Tantric sex to couples until I can land a gig designing costumes for Broadway stars." Before he could reply, she started running again.

Kevin whistled and caught up with her. "Wow. Did I ever read you wrong."

She took her gloves out and put them back on. "You didn't read me wrong. I'm shy. I'm inexperienced. All of that." They turned down another street that had a hill. Neither spoke while they struggled the steep incline. At the top, Remington said, "But I'm doing what I have to do to achieve my dreams in life."

"I get the feeling there's a whole lot more going on in your life than you're telling me."

"Nothing important."

They turned a corner to a road that flanked the cemetery. Remington's thoughts went to Beth.

"Okay. I'm going to tell you why he doesn't believe in love. There's the obvious—his mom left him and his dad. Has he told you about that?"

"Some."

"And the not so obvious, he fell in love once. With an older woman. Had his heart crushed."

"How do you know this?"

"Because it happened right before he went to college. That's where we met. We got drunk one night, and he told me all about it."

"But you're younger than him. How did you meet in college?" That older woman must have been his Tantric instructor.

"I'm a child prodigy. Started college at the age of sixteen."

"You don't act smart."

"Ouch. Jason never got over the two women in his life that he loved who didn't love him back."

"I can relate to that. Not having someone love me back."

"Sorry. I forgot you were an orphan. Maybe that's why you and Jason seem to have a connection. You both have abandonment issues."

"What are you, a psychiatrist?"

"Minored in psychology. Double major in business and marketing."

"Smarty pants."

"Hey, when you make it to New York, let me know. I have a friend on Broadway. I'll introduce you two."

"That would be cool. Thanks."

They finished their run at the orphanage.

"You kicked my ass today," Kevin said. "Remind me not to run with you again when you're mad… unless I'm in the mood to do speed work."

Remington smiled. It felt good to be in shape. The exercise had taken a bit of the edge off. "How far did we go?"

Kevin glanced at his watch. "Almost eight miles. You've really improved since the girl who met us on the first day and thought seven blocks was a long run."

They both laughed.

"I've got some work to do, I'll see you at game night." Kevin gave her a sexy smile before turning and jogging away.

Remington watched his butt disappear down the road. He had a nice ass. Why couldn't he turn her on the way Jason did? Sighing, she bent her left leg, stretched it behind her and stared at the orphanage.

With all the new snow, the two-story structure appeared enchanted. Almost like a fairytale castle. Other than the fact that there was an eighteen-wheeler backed up to the front, its gate down as if about to load something into its dark yawning mouth. And two ghosts wearing old-time prison uniforms sat on its roof. Hell. Were they the released mayhem ghosts?

A black Lincoln was parked next to the unmarked truck, and Sue's old battered pickup, covered in snow, stood lonely at the other end of the parking lot. Sue did night duty at the orphanage. She'd done so when Remington was there and must be at least eighty.

Curious about the truck, Remington walked inside the orphanage. "Hi Sue."

Sue glanced up from a box stuffed with books.

"Hi Remington. What brings you out on this cold winter morning?"

"Went for a run. What's going on here?" She did calf stretches against the door.

"We're being shut down."

Remington dropped her heels to the floor. "What?"

"You heard me."

"But…what about the orphans?"

Sue pulled a blue embroidered handkerchief out of her bra and blew her nose. "According to the official letter we all received, they're being accommodated elsewhere in the state."

"Official letter?" Sue must have misunderstood.

"State of Missouri. Permission to shut it down officially granted."

"Permission? Who asked for permission?"

"Jason Hart."

"He said he was going to build them a new orphanage, not send them away."

"That's what he told Mr. Drathers when he sold the orphanage to him, but I guess Jason changed his mind. You can't believe anything these young whippersnappers tell you these days."

"Have you talked to him?"

"He's not answering his phone."

"How about the orphans out with trial families? Do they get to stay with them?"

Sue stuck her hanky back in her bra. "You'd think so, but no."

Remington sank to the floor. Johnny B had been out on a trial family run. "Johnny B must be brokenhearted."

Sue nodded stiffly and sniffed. "He hasn't talked to anyone since he got back. Not even me. Just lies on his bed looking at the ceiling." Sue glanced down. But not before Remington picked up on something in her eyes. Something like worry? "I guess Jason is pushing through with his plan to turn the orphanage into dormitories for college students playing around with the afterworld." Her tone dripped disapproval.

Remington was about to comment on the fact she believed in ghosts when a realization hit her. "Doesn't it have to stay open for the marathon?" Her training had been going well. Really well. She actually liked running, not the early morning stuff. But the exercise made her feel better about herself. Like the other runners didn't see her as Remington the orphan, but instead, as Remington, the runner. "Isn't there some type of implied contract between them and those who signed up to run the marathon that the orphanage would be viable and could use the money?"

"I would imagine as long as he refunds everyone's entry fee, there won't be a problem."

Remington paced. "I don't understand why he changed his mind. He promised Johnny B."

"Goes to show you never really know anyone."

"I just don't get it." What wasn't Sue telling her? There had to be more to this.

"No one does," Sue said, walking to the coffee pot and pouring a cup. "I guess his plan to build an up-to-date orphanage with a swimming pool and tennis courts turned out to be too expensive. Want some coffee?"

"No thanks." Remington walked to the file cabinet. "Sue, I need my file." She opened the top file drawer. Empty. "Maybe there's a hint of who my parents are." She opened the bottom file drawer. Empty.

"Sweetie, those files are all on that moving truck out there. Along with all the computers. It happened really fast. We didn't have any warning. But I can tell you, there's never been a file on you. Nothing to put in the file."

"Nothing? No hints? Possibilities on who might have dropped me off and ran away that night?"

"Nothing."

"When are the orphans being moved?"

"Tonight.

"So soon?" When Jason had left her to go to the bimbo, she hadn't thought her day could get any worse. She'd been wrong. Life had flung two lemons at her this morning. When would the third one hit?

"Afraid so."

"Do you care if I go tell Johnny B goodbye?"

CHAPTER TWENTY-ONE

JASON STOOD AT HIS LIVING room window and watched Remington march up his sidewalk. Her posture rigid, her lips moving, her arms swinging wide as if to emphasize the words he couldn't hear. The way the afternoon sun hit her hair, it looked like sparks were shooting off her head.

When she reached his porch, he dropped the curtain and cleared the lump in his throat. Should he pretend not to be home? No, he couldn't do that to her. He had to face her. She had every right to want to skin him with a dull knife that had been left out in the rain to rust.

Although, in his defense, he still didn't see any other way to have handled Bernadette's ill-timed visit. Then again, laughing at the way Remington handled her sexual frustration wasn't exactly white-knight of him.

Hopefully, she would take a calming breath before attacking his front door with her fist.

She didn't.

And the headache building behind his eyes doubled in intensity.

He rubbed his temples and then opened the

wooden door about two inches. "Are you going to shoot me?"

Remington glanced toward her house and stomped her foot. "Son of a bitch, I didn't bring Hank."

"Hank?" Who in the fuck was Hank?

"My gun."

He grimaced, ran a hand through his hair, and opened the door wider. He should hide that toy of hers before she committed a crime of passion on his ass.

Once again, the sunlight struck her hair just right and a spark appeared. Up close, he could almost hear the crackle of electricity. Her hands balled into fists. "I'm—"

"I came back over to apologize about this morning and beg you for forgiveness, but you were gone." He needed to get that information out there in case it helped his situation any. Not that he held much hope. He'd even looked in her windows to make sure she wasn't inside ignoring his knocking. Noticed she'd rearranged her furniture.

Those weren't really sparks coming off her head, were they?

Her eyebrows squished together. "You didn't think I was going to actually *wait* on you…*did you.*" Her tone would have withered a lesser man's jewels. His were not one hundred percent unaffected.

By not waiting, did she mean she'd turned to someone else? To Kevin? Jealousy tied his gut in barbwire. "I'm sorry. My brain doesn't function right when it's being rattled by someone as sexy as you. It was a mistake." He meant every word of what he said. Remington was special.

She harrumphed, sounding like Ruby Rae in a tiff. "Damn straight it was."

He nodded. "I'm a dumbass."

Remington gave him a sharp nod and then pressed her lips together and scowled. "Are you going to let me in or what?"

He opened the screen door and stood back. Between Detective Meek's revelation about the orphanage, and Bernadette's demands, his life had become a cluster fuck in the last forty-eight hours.

Why in the hell had he thought telling Bernadette the truth about the orphans would make her go away quietly? He should have known better. The woman was the mold other bitches were made out of. Instead of saying *thank you* for his honesty, she'd blackmailed him.

It was his dick's fault. He'd been thinking with it and not his brain. He'd been so wrapped up in trying to get back to Remington he hadn't thought his revelation to Bernadette through.

At the moment of the reveal, the truth seemed the quickest way to get rid of her. What a fucking idiot he'd been.

Remington pushed by him in a swirl of fragrance that reminded him of a summer thunderstorm in the city. Her damp curls clung to her cheeks. "Your apology is meaningless. You and I are over."

"Because I tried to save your reputation from being muddied?" He fixated on the eyelash sitting precariously on the tip of her nose. Pretty sure it was a trap. If he touched it, an ambush would be sprung.

"That's ancient history. Why are you dressed up? Hot date with the bimbo?" A smirk caused her freckles to blend into one.

He glanced down at his v-neck sweater, jeans and bare feet. What was she talking about? Of course, compared to her baggy, low on the hips, red sweats and form-fitting T-shirt, he did look dressed up. He read her T-shirt. *Shut up and kiss me* blazed across her chest in bright orange bubble letters. "The question is—did you put that on for me?" He motioned with his head toward her shirt, trying to coax a bit of the free-spirited Remington out to play. The one he'd met that first night, standing by her battered Bug, giving him hell about being too much of a lady's man.

She glanced down at her shirt. "Don't be ridiculous." She crossed her arms in blatant mockery of the way he held his. "You've kissed my lips for the last time. I'll find someone else to help me with my Tantric lessons."

The lady knew how to throw verbal jabs. "A man can hope, can't he?"

She rolled her eyes. "He can. But if his name is Jason Hart, it won't do him a damn bit of good."

He repressed a smile. "Is that so?" He dropped his hands to his sides. The more he got to know her, the more he realized there wasn't anything about her he didn't like. Even her mean streak.

"Stop trying to distract me. I came over here for a different reason." She shifted her stance.

"If not to give me hell about Bernadette, then why?"

"I…" She stopped. Pinched the bridge of her nose. Stared off in the distance. Then she dropped her hand and looked him in the eyes. "Why are the orphans being moved out of Knotty? Why aren't you building them a new orphanage? And don't lie to me because if you do…*you're* going to die." Her voice dropped on the last three words. And she leaned toward him. As if emphasizing the truth of what she'd said.

His smile faltered. "Are you going to shoot me with Hank if I lie to you?"

She ran her tongue along the inside of her cheek then shook her head decisively. "I won't have to. I cast a spell on you. If you lie to me, the things-that-go-bump-in-the-night world will take care of your sorry self."

He raised his eyebrows and took a step back.

"That's right… You heard right… I'm a witch. If you say *one* rude thing to me about it, I swear I'll cast another spell on you. This time concerning your balls."

His bravado faded. She sounded very sane, very sure, and very right. He wasn't going to call her bluff. He'd play along for now. "Orphans and a single town don't exactly go together." This much was true. Not a lie.

She had every right to think he was a lowlife loser.

"So, it's true. You're kicking them out of Knotty? At Christmas time." She sounded like he'd just told her he was sending them to a Third World country.

He held his hands out, palms open. He had nothing. No excuses to make it all sound okay. "Yes," was all he could say. Again, the truth. He wasn't used to being the bad guy.

That was his dad's place in the scheme of things. Jason didn't like how it felt. Didn't understand how anyone could willingly spend their whole life playing the part of the jerk. But for now, it was his shield to wear. The safety of the orphans was more important than his ego, his reputation, or even his relationship with Remington.

He placed a hand on her shoulder and pushed her toward the couch. "Business decisions have to be made on facts, not emotions."

She yanked away from him. "You lied to Johnny B. What kind of person lies to an orphan?"

He'd been trying to come up with a way to make this all okay for Johnny B. There wasn't a way. The boy would hate him. "It's business. Plans have changed and my promise to him is no longer viable."

Her eyes told him he'd just cut her and left a scar.

"*Viable?*" she shouted. "You think a word like *viable* means anything to an orphan who trusted an adult to tell him the truth?" There was so much pain in her voice he was surprised her heart wasn't bleeding through her shirt.

Jason scrubbed a hand down his face, wishing he could scrub the taste of failure out of his mouth. "At the time, I didn't realize the town was going to morph into a singles town." He wanted to tell her the whole truth, but that hadn't worked with Bernadette. He wasn't about to make the same mistake twice. Then again, he wasn't going to lie. His balls were on the line.

Remington flinched. Took a step back. "Then unmorph it. Turn it into a family town."

He leaned a hip against the wall. He forced the next words out. "There's more money in turning it into a singles town." Again true. A singles town was a novelty. His waiting list of businesses wanting to open shop in town had tripled since the ad campaign had launched.

She swung around and poked him in the chest. "You're an even bigger ass than I thought."

He laughed. The disingenuous noise sounded like one of his father's laughs. The ones he would give Jason when they disagreed over something. Was this the first step into becoming his father? "I've been told that once or twice."

Remington dropped her hand to her side. "Why are the orphans, who were with trial families, not being allowed to be adopted?" Gone was the gusto of anger in her voice. Left was nakedness. Rawness.

"I was advised that this was the best way to handle the moving of the orphans. Keep them all together." He used his this-is-just-business voice.

Remington scowled. "The families who had them on trial runs—will they still be able to adopt them from the new orphanage?"

"I hope so." Which was true. He did hope the government would change their mind and allow the adoptions.

Before he could discern her intentions, she walked over to him and slapped him. The sound rang out in his living room like an explosion. "I was wrong. You're not an ass. You're a bastard."

He didn't react. At least not in a way she could see. The pieces of him dying on the inside were invisible to her. For that, he was thankful. "That I am."

"That's it? That's all you have to say? You pretended to care about Johnny B..." Her tirade paused, as if she were waiting for him to deny her words. When he remained silent, she continued, "You didn't care. If you cared about him, you wouldn't have pulled him away from a family that wanted him. You should have seen him when I said goodbye."

She raised her hand to hit him again, but this time he caught it, brought her hand up to his lips and kissed the open palm. The silky-smooth skin was a contrast to the anger that pulsed all around them. Did she know how much her accusations rubbed salt in his bloodied heart? He loved Jonny B.

"Don't you dare put your lips on me." She yanked her hand away, wiped her palm against her shirt.

He'd gone to a lot of trouble to find the perfect family for Johnny B. One that had two other little boys for him to play with. One that had loving parents who would dote on him. Parents who had given Jason permission to see Johnny B anytime he wanted. He'd worked on that adoption while he was in Seattle. It was to be Johnny B's Christmas gift from him.

He looked away. Emotions were a luxury he couldn't afford. He was doing what had to be done.

"Why did I think you were different? That I actually liked you as a person? That I might even see a future with you?"

For a brief second, his heart stopped. Possibilities that weren't possible at all flittered through him. He jammed them. There were so many reasons he couldn't let her fall for him. So many reasons he couldn't say *I see a future with you, too.* The most important one—Knotty wasn't safe for current orphans or former orphans. The second, his heart didn't seem to know how to work. He should place her on the first train out of the town. "It wasn't an easy decision."

CHAPTER TWENTY-TWO

REMINGTON HISSED. "THAT'S IT? THAT'S all you have to say?" She'd just told Jason she was falling for him, and he hadn't even acknowledged the courage it had taken to say the words. The man was a loser. No better than Linny.

"Yes."

The weight of the air in the room was crushing, making it hard for Remington to breathe or remain standing. "You know what? Forget about my feelings. They're not important." As soon as she got back to her house, she'd hex herself to not be able to fall in love. Then her heart wouldn't hurt. "What's important is that Johnny B is leaving today." When would she learn to stop putting her heart on the line?

Jason spun around to look at her. "What in the hell are you talking about?"

"You know exactly what I'm talking about. You evicted them. They're leaving today."

His color drained, and he rubbed the back of his neck. "Do you think that little of me?"

"Is that a trick question?" Maybe his signature hadn't been on the letter. She flung herself at him, pummeled his chest with her fists. "Please don't lie to me." Hate him or not, she didn't want her spell to take his life.

He wrapped his arms around her and pulled her in, holding her tight. "I didn't know they were going to move them so quickly."

"Why can't you stop that part of this?" Her mouth was pressed against his shirt, muffling her words. "Why do you have to buy the orphanage?"

He kissed the top of her head softly. "It's part of the town. I want the whole town for my project."

She pulled back and looked up at him. "Why can't there be an orphanage in your singles town? It just takes up a small corner. You can't get more single than an orphan. Doesn't that qualify them to live in a singles town?"

He looked her in the eyes. Blinked. "No."

She grabbed his cheeks. "Why not? Your adult singles can act like big sisters and big brothers to the orphans. Please reconsider."

He leaned his forehead against hers. "I'm not going to change my mind—so stop asking me to."

She yanked back. "What's happened to you? Where's the nice guy I've gotten to know? The one who likes orphans and animals…and me?"

"I've already signed the contracts." His voice was a brew of calm. "There's nothing I can do about how the state decides to deal with the orphans. It's out of my control."

"You like it that way, don't you? Now you don't have to feel guilty. You don't have to deal with the mess of a child with no mom or dad." She slipped on her coat. "You don't have to have a conversation with a child who tells you you didn't think they were enough."

"That's not true." The words sounded gritty with anger. "Bernadette and I were working on trying to get as many of them adopted out as possible."

She flinched. Her insides felt like they'd spent the last hour being scraped down a cheese grater. "You mean the movie-star want-to-be is a family woman? The one who dragged you from my naked body this morning?"

He had the grace to look uncomfortable. Guilty. "Not exactly. But adoption is the *in thing* in her married circle of friends right now, so I asked her to get involved."

What? When? "She acted like she didn't know you that day in the parking lot."

"That's because she likes to play games."

Remington glanced out the front door. "Did you sleep with her?" She didn't want to ask, but she couldn't stop the words from tumbling out.

"Not today, no."

"Have you ever slept with her?" The words were splinters in her throat.

"A very long time ago. Before I met you." He looked at her, then closed his eyes. "You'll be leaving town soon, why do you care so much?" He stepped away from her touch.

She grabbed his arm and yanked. "Because Johnny B wants me to stay here and be his mom. I've broken his heart." She opened her mouth to say more but tears fell.

He pulled her into his arms. "You can't stay here.

What woman stays in a town where she's in love with a man who doesn't love her back?"

Remington winced. "I'm used to not being loved back. It's who I am." She said the words because they were true. Not because she wanted his sympathy. "I'd be staying for Johnny B's sake. I could even try to adopt him. They allow single parents to adopt in Missouri."

"Johnny B deserves a mom and a dad."

"Then I'll get married. If you can't be bothered with children in Knotty, I can move back to Branson and design costumes for the stars on the strip."

"Johnny B deserves more than what you can offer him."

"Why are you being so cruel?"

"Cruel? I'm not being cruel. What you're doing is cruel. Johnny B deserves a chance at a happy family. Not a make-do family."

The truth of his words stung. Jason was right. She wasn't good enough to be Johnny B's mom. "When will the transformation be complete?"

"By summer, if all goes as planned. We have six more houses we need to obtain. Yours is one of them."

She lifted her chin. "I'm not selling you my house." It was her house. Her first-ever house. She wasn't selling it to him.

He smiled. The smile of someone who knows something you don't. The smile of someone about to get their way. "You don't have to. There's not going to be a marathon. Running the marathon was part of your to-do list. If I remember right,

Beth said everything goes to the Watsons if you don't complete the list. I'll buy the house off them."

"Bastard." She hadn't known he knew that much about her inheritance. "I can run the marathon route. I've paid my entry fee. That will count."

Jason ran his hand through his hair. Telling her she wasn't good enough to be Johnny B's mom qualified him for a direct ticket to hell. But he had to squash her plans. He couldn't let her pursue a dream he knew could never come true. It would just set her up for further heartache. "Remington, I'm in the business of acquisitions. My father taught me how to get what I want. But you're right. You could run the route on your own. Sell me your house, and I'll give you my condo in New York as compensation for your troubles."

Was she really a witch? Of course, she wasn't. But what were the odds both her and Beth would believe in such a thing?

Her eyes widened and her body stilled. "Who in the hell gives away a condo in New York?"

"I inherited it from my father." He shrugged. "The place means nothing to me. I don't need the money. You could live there and wouldn't have to pay rent." He'd do anything to get her out of town before he had to make the announcement Bernadette was blackmailing him into making. Especially since it would require lying, and his balls were on the line.

"You'd do that?"

"In a heartbeat."

She exhaled a shaky breath. "The condo would be all mine? No strings attached?"

"No strings attached."

"And if I say no?"

"Then I will do everything in my power to prove you didn't complete your to-do list, and you'll lose everything." It wasn't a lie. He would. Not for the reason she believed but it was still the truth.

"Why do you hate me so much?"

He didn't hate her. "This isn't about hate. It's about business. I'm giving you your dream on a platter. You should be thanking me."

"When are you going to tell everyone about the orphanage?"

"Tonight, at game night. And then tomorrow, I think it's best if you left town. Headed to New York."

"God, tell a man you love him, and he's suddenly in a fat-ass hurry to get you out of town. Fine. But I'm not going to game night."

"Yes, you are. And you're going to act like everything is okay. And you're going to tell them you're going away for the holidays."

"Why would I do that?"

"Because if you don't, they are going to worry, and you don't want them worrying about you over the holidays."

"I hate you, Jason Hart." The words were a whisper. But he managed to hear them.

CHAPTER TWENTY-THREE

REMINGTON WALKED TO HER HOUSE ready to commit witchery revenge. In the end, the only magical thing she did was place a no-love hex on herself. For self-preservation. And performed an undo on the lie and die spell on Jason. For his self-preservation. She'd discovered it was a simple level one hex. The antidote was in the book hidden between two pages which had been stuck together with bubble gum. She was pretty sure that was the work of the Mayhem ghosts.

Now, seven of them—Jason, Kevin, Tom, Maverick, Remington, Sara Ann and Ruby Rae—sat around the kitchen table nibbling on salty chips and dark chocolate caramels, talking about the weather, laughing about the anatomically correct snowwoman Tom had built in the ladies' yard after he showed up too late to shovel their driveway for them, but mostly settling in for the latest gossip from Ruby Rae and Sara Ann. Oh…and a rowdy game of Spoons. After all, that's what game night was about.

Remington rode with Jason to the ladies' house. He'd insisted, and she didn't have the energy to argue. After the hex she'd placed on herself, her anger and love had dissipated, leaving behind sadness. Sadness for things that would never be. But, like so many other times in her orphan-life, she'd decided to put on a smile and forge ahead. After all, she had a condo in freaking New York City to look forward to. As consolation prizes go, it wasn't a shabby one. And surely, eventually, one of these days, she'd grow to look at it as the grand prize and not the runner-up.

Kevin shuffled the cards and dealt while Sara Ann placed six spoons in the middle of the table.

"Remington, it's your turn to go first tonight," Tom said.

She thought she felt Jason's eyes on her. She glanced at him. They weren't. He was busy placing his cards in order. She glanced around to see if there were ghosts among them. There were. A lot. Including the two jailbirds.

The play went around the table twice before Ruby Rae cleared her throat. "Jason, I hear you've got some news you're dying to tell us." She gave him an arched look before sipping beer straight from the bottle.

Jason leaned back in his chair. "Well, I do have something I think you'll find of interest." He aimed a slow-cooker smile at Ruby Rae and Sara Ann. The one that caused younger ladies to lose their panties and older ones to titter like teenagers.

"We're all ears," they both said in unison, patting their salon-styled hair in place.

One of the mayhem ghosts moved a spoon in the middle of the table. The movement caused all the players to grab for spoons except Remington. She rolled her eyes at the ghost.

"You lose," Kevin said to Remington.

"Did not. No one actually laid all their cards down."

They all glanced at each other, realizing she was right, and then sheepishly laid their spoons back in the middle of the table.

"Jason, dear, did you grab for a spoon to throw us off what we were talking about?" Ruby Rae asked.

Jason raised an eyebrow and examined the faces of the rest of the table's occupants, skipping Remington's. "Why do I get the feeling you already know what I want to talk about?" he asked Ruby Rae.

"Could be one of us has a way of discovering secrets," Sara Ann said, winking at the boys and poking Remington in the ribs with her elbow.

"Gossip usually isn't accurate." Jason took a swig of beer. "I've seen reputations ruined by the stuff."

Sara Ann nibbled at her chip, repressing a smile. "I couldn't agree with you more. I'm always telling Ruby Rae to ignore gossip."

"That's true. I've heard her say that to Ruby Rae," Maverick said, wading into the fray.

"She's just addicted to the stuff. But as it is, our information isn't gossip. It's truth," Sara Ann replied, her face set in pious starch.

Ruby Rae, who'd been busy texting someone on her phone, snapped to attention. "I do not gossip." She put her phone away. "How positively goadish of you to imply—"

"Ladies," Jason intervened smoothly, "I don't mean to be rude and interrupt, but I do happen to have something I'd like to talk with you about."

Sara Ann laid a card in the pile and nonchalantly reached for a spoon. Ruby Rae didn't see her do it, because she was too busy fluttering her lashes at Jason. Kevin, Tom, Maverick, and Remington all saw it at the same time and, equally stealth-like, grabbed for a spoon. Which left only one spoon on the table.

Jason and Ruby Rae noticed it at the same time. They looked at each other, gazes locked, mouths hanging open, and their hands simultaneously shot toward the one remaining spoon.

"Ah ha. I got it," shrilled Ruby Rae, causing the rest of those at the table to laugh.

Jason shook his head. "I think you all teamed up on me and started the rumor conversation so I would be distracted and not see the throw-down."

Remington tsked him with her tongue. "You are such a spoilsport." It was hard to pretend everything was okay between them when it wasn't, but no way would she ruin the holidays for any of her friends. "Now are you going to tell these women what they already know, or am I?"

"Is it my imagination, or is Remington bossing you around like a fishwife?" Kevin drawled, drawing a shut-the-fuck-up look from Jason.

This produced abundant laughter out of everyone, including Remington. It was as if they were one big happy family ribbing each other with their sarcasm. For the first time in her memory, there was a part of Remington's heart that ached with happiness. Not sadness. Happiness at being a part of a family. She would miss them.

"Okay," Jason said, interrupting her thoughts. "I'll tell them." He sat up straighter, lifted his chin to an angle of pride, and his eyes shone with what looked like a desire for approval. "I know you know I'm renovating Knotty, and it's going to become a singles town."

"Indeed, we do."

"What you don't know is that the orphans, unfortunately, are being moved as a result. As much as I would like to build a new orphanage for the orphans, it's not in their best interest."

"You don't say," cooed Sara Ann, like a cat who'd already devoured the cream and was daring anyone to accuse her of the deed. "I knew that too," she added. "I talked to Sue today. Told her not to judge you until you've spoken to her."

Remington blinked. Why weren't they mad? They loved Johnny B as much as she did. Did family always wait to hear both sides before forming an opinion? Or was this adopted family of hers unique in that aspect?

"Thanks for having my back. Remington is annoyed at me, but I truly think it is what's best for the children."

Remington winced. He'd just pointed out to them she wasn't one of them. If she was, she would have reacted as they had. With an open mind.

"The majority of the housing will be leased to individuals, whose average ages will be twenty-two to twenty-five, and who work for TTI. But there will also be some college students who are studying the paranormal."

"Paranormal? In our town?" Ruby Rae inquired with a fluttering of her lashes.

"You've all heard the rumor Knotty's haunted as a result of the tornado. And the rumor that Knotty is cursed."

"You say that as if you don't believe the rumors," Remington provoked.

"Remington, please. Let Jason finish. You were saying?" Sara Ann asked.

A flush warmed Remington's cheeks. She'd just been reprimanded by Sara Ann. Was she mad at Remington for not having Jason's back? Did family always back family? If she did something wrong, would they have her back?

"It will be a small town with a big city feel. We'll have entertainment, upscale shopping, and unique businesses."

Remington's stomach twisted into a knot. She wanted to stay. She didn't want to be the black sheep that had to leave because she didn't belong. She wanted to live in a small town that felt like a big town but had people living in it that felt like family to her. Then again, that wasn't her dream. Jason had offered her a way to achieve her dream. And she'd said yes. So, why wasn't she happy? A dream realized should outweigh everything else.

"Are you going to cart in some old men for these two old ladies?" Ruby Rae asked.

"Speak for yourself, sister. I don't need an old

man. I want some nice middle-aged ones who still know how to take a lady dancing."

Jason glanced at Remington. She lifted the corners of her lips.

"To be honest with you, I think the clientele will be too young for you to enjoy," he admitted.

Sara Ann banged her beer down, causing everyone to jump. "You're not going to have anything here for Ruby Rae and me?"

Jason gave her a thoughtful look. "Truthfully, I thought you would prefer to sell your home to me. In return, I could set you up in a nice condo in Arizona. Someplace it doesn't snow," he said in that warm, deep-chocolate voice Remington found so intoxicating.

"Then you thought wrong. This is our hometown. Our families settled this town. We're not going anywhere." Ruby Rae's pencil-thin eyebrows raised to her hairline.

Sara Ann patted Ruby Rae's arm in a calming fashion. "If you're in charge of this town," she said to Jason, "I don't see why you can't build a section for single senior citizens."

"I agree," chimed in Ruby Rae.

"We have just as hard a time of it as young singles," Sara Ann continued. "We'd like a place to hang out and have a good time without everyone worrying that we're not married or that we're widowed."

Jason crossed his arms and leaned back in his chair. "I've given that a little bit of thought. If I rework some of my plans and include a senior section, are you saying you'd want to stay?"

Ruby Rae and Sara Ann looked at one another. "Can we have our own condo units—I'm tired of living with her?" they both asked in unison.

Everyone laughed.

So, he wanted them to stay, just not Remington. The town wasn't big enough for her and him to coexist.

"Sure. Why not? Sell me your house and I'll build a senior citizen condo. That way you won't have to worry about mowing or maintenance or anything. You can have a community flowerbed and garden. And units completely away from one another."

"Where's he planning to build?" one of the jailbird ghosts asked Remington.

"Where are you going to build?" Remington asked Jason.

"In the spot where I'd planned to build the orphanage."

"Nope, that won't work," said the other jailbird ghost.

"*Why not?*" Remington asked him in her thoughts.

Her congress of other ghosts blew into the room.

"Hush up," the detective said to the jailbirds.

"Why?" they both asked.

"Because she doesn't know, and we like it that away."

"*What are you guys going on about?*"

Instead of answering her, they all disappeared.

"I'd want Ruby Rae to live close enough to have coffee with me in the mornings without too much trouble," Sara Ann inserted, drawing Remington back into the conversation of the living. "Maybe we could have one connecting door or something."

"Only if it locks on my side," Ruby Rae said. "I don't want you interrupting my coitus sessions."

"Like you're going to have coitus with anyone." Sara Ann frowned.

"I'm more likely too than you are. You're in love with—"

"Don't you dare finish that sentence. One more thing." Sara Ann directed this at Jason. "I can't sell you my house."

"Oh, why in tarnation not? What's so special about this drafty place?" Ruby Rae asked.

"None of your business. But I'm not selling it."

Jason steepled his fingers. "Would you be interested in turning it into a bakery of some sort? It's located in the center of town. All the seniors could bake goodies and sell them from here."

Ruby Rae lit up. "What a perfectly marvelous idea. I could sell my cinnamon rolls. They'll become famous."

"I'm sure they will," Jason said.

"You'll have people wanting to move here just so they can have my rolls one day a week," Ruby Rae bragged.

"Why one day a week?" Sara Ann asked, appearing put-out that she had to ask the question.

"Anyone with any marketing sense knows, if you make something too readily available, it'll lose its specialness. I'll create demand by having them available only one day a week. Saturday mornings,"

Ruby Rae answered.

"Mmmm. Then I will make my potato soup available on Friday nights. And, I'll make my momma's famous sourdough bread to go with it. It'll be carry-out only. I don't want to have to wash dishes."

"Very smart thinking," Ruby Rae said to Sara Ann. "Let's see. We'll have seven days, three meals a day. We need twenty-one senior citizens willing to take on the responsibility of a meal to sell during their timeslot."

Sara Ann sat up straight. "Those who want to rent a condo will have to fill out an application and provide a sample of their food item."

Ruby Rae clapped her hands in childlike glee. "Oh…and we can call ourselves the twenty-one club."

"Boss, do you think you should pull them in before they run away with your town and your ideas and make it a seniors-only town?" Maverick asked.

Jason laughed. "I like their enthusiasm. Let them talk. We'll find a happy middle. It feels good to hear someone besides us show some enthusiasm for our idea."

The two ladies stopped talking midsentence. Sara Ann recovered first. "Boss? Do you guys work for him?"

"Of course not," Ruby Rae said, "We would have known that. No one keeps a secret from us. Isn't that right, guys?"

The guys all stood at once and started making excuses to go.

Ruby Rae clutched her heart. "Do you mean to tell me you young bucks have been eating my cinnamon rolls and holding out on me? How can that be?"

Remington got up quietly, ready to leave before they realized she too had known something before them. She had one arm through her coat sleeve when Ruby Rae nailed her. "Hold it right there, missy. You knew too. Didn't you?"

Remington turned toward them, feeling like a traitor. "Really, I only just figured it all out."

Sara Ann went to the liquor cabinet and poured herself a shot of the strong stuff. "Well I...never. Our own kind has been holding out on us, Ruby Rae." She swallowed the amber liquid without making a face or coughing. "I don't know if I'll ever be able to forgive them." She poured another shot and handed it to Ruby Rae.

"Me either, Sara Ann." Ruby Rae swallowed her shot. "It just doesn't feel right to hang out with people who don't trust you enough to tell you their secrets."

"I know. It just breaks my heart. I thought we were friends."

"I'm leaving tomorrow to take care of some business dealing with my job. I won't be here for the holidays." Remington's blurt drew everyone's gaze.

Kevin cleared his throat. "I'm gay, and I'm hoping there will be some gays who move into Knotty's new single's town." His coming-out speech stole the attention from Remington and caused the women to nearly lose their teeth.

"How did I not ever know that?" Jason asked, a pulse ticcing in his cheek. "We've known each other since college."

"I didn't want you to know. I didn't feel like it was anyone's business but mine."

"I prefer chili over potato soup," said Maverick, on the heels of Kevin's confession.

Sara Ann gasped, clutching her chest.

"I'm only six-three, not six-four," Tom said.

Remington and Jason looked at one another. He jerked his head toward the door. They tiptoed that direction.

"I know a guy who is gay. He does my hair. Would you like me to set you two up?" Sara Ann said.

And then Ruby Rae said, "Oh dear. What are you thinking? A hairdresser is all wrong for Kevin. He doesn't have any hair. Haven't you noticed his receding hairline? No…he needs a good body-builder. One who will appreciate those muscles of his."

Sara Ann harrumphed. "I have noticed those. That's why I never got around to noticing his hair situation, I guess."

Ruby Rae said, "If I were fifty years younger, you wouldn't be gay."

Jason shut the door, closing off their conversation.

Remington sighed. That was probably the last time she'd see any of them. It was better this way. She didn't want to do the whole goodbye scene.

Jason chuckled. "Well, that went well…don't you think?"

CHAPTER TWENTY-FOUR

REMINGTON'S LAUGHTER FILLED JASON WITH awe. Any other woman would give him the silent treatment. Instead, she'd graciously accepted his offer of a ride to game night, joked and laughed with everyone, and giggled with him on their way home. Could she be any more perfect? Or confusing?

He parked in their shared drive and turned in his seat. "You're an amazing woman." Energy buzzed through him, pushed him to declare all sorts of dorky things.

Her smile wobbled and her laughter died.

His buzz stalled.

An emotion he couldn't define, or didn't want to define, filled her eyes, turning them a cloudy green. She made a garbled noise, glanced away, and fumbled for the door handle.

Shit. "Did I say something wrong?"

The seatbelt brought her up short. "Damn it."

He reached to release the buckle, and his arm skimmed her breasts.

They both inhaled sharply.

She pushed back into the seat. "I'm going to miss all of them." She clasped her hands in her lap and stared straight ahead. "They make me feel like…" Her voice trailed off.

"Like what?"

She slowly turned and glanced at him. "Like I have a family."

He tucked strands of hair behind her ear. "When I was a boy, I used to wish I had a family that had game night once a week. A family with eccentric members like Ruby Rae and Sara Ann. They make me feel like I have a family, too."

She nodded. Opened the door. "Thanks for the lift."

"Remington?"

She glanced at him. "What?"

He rubbed his palms on his jeans. "Forgive me for not being the man you thought I was."

"No one ever is what they appear to be on the surface."

Even though he knew she hadn't meant the words to be hurtful, they tore through him like acid. They left behind a burnt path that oozed pain like a festered scab oozes puss. In her beautiful eyes, he was a disappointment. "I love your gorgeous surface, but you are even better below the surface."

She sighed. "How is it exactly you think I'm better below the surface than on top of the surface?"

"On the surface, you are a quirky woman who thumbs her nose at relationships and blurts out what's on her mind. Beneath the surface, you are layers of heart and hope and happiness. And you want to be loved."

She nodded. "You forgot the part about my

being a witch, and I cast spells, and while we're baring our souls, I also talk to ghosts. To Beth. With all of that on top of the surface, it's no wonder my undersurface is better."

Ghosts? Beth? He sighed. She didn't mean it. She was pushing him away. "Remington, don't." A thickness in his throat made it impossible to continue.

A harsh noise erupted from her. "Don't what? Don't be that way? Don't hold you accountable for your lies? Don't turn a fun evening into a fight? Don't what—exactly?" Her volume increased with each word.

Don't stop loving me.

He leaned back in his seat. Rubbed a hand down his face. When had his life gotten so complicated? "I deserve that." He stared out his driver's side window. "And I don't deserve what I'm going to ask you next. But I'm going to ask you anyway." He glanced at her.

She tugged at her coat collar. "What's that?"

"Come home with me. Give us one night." He wanted more than one night, but Bernadette's blackmail demands weren't going to be put off past tomorrow. And his gut told him Remington wasn't safe in Knotty. He had to push her out of his town.

She shook her head, sending her curls in a cascade of movement.

"Please." The word he swore once never to say again passed his lips with ease, and everything inside of him stopped. His pulse stopped beating.

His lungs stopped breathing. How had he allowed the word to pass his lips?

As if in tune with his shock, a rumble of thunder shook the truck, and the sky broke open with lightning and heavy snow showers.

He stared unseeingly out the window.

"Why would I do that?" she asked.

This was the part where he should say never mind…it's a stupid idea. This was why he should have never said please. Why he'd sworn he'd never say please again. But that was before he'd met Remington. "You're going to leave tomorrow. I want one night of holding you, one morning of waking up next to you." He didn't deserve her. She deserved to be loved by a whole man. Not one who could only offer a screwed-up type of affection. But he wanted her. And *please* was the price he was willing to pay to get her.

He didn't trust himself to know what love was. The last woman he'd thought he was in love with had been Bernadette and that had been a cluster fuck. And before that, Moon…his Tantric instructor. She'd laughed and told him it was lust, not love.

He'd never seen true love, so how could he know what it looked like?

He tapped his fingers on the steering wheel and waited for Remington's response.

Remington cocked her head to the side. Stared out the window. Then she pushed opened the door, got out, and walked toward her house. Not once looking at him.

His chest tightened. "Wait." He leaned across the passenger seat and yelled, "Is that a yes or a no?"

She flipped him the bird. Her stride never broke.

CHAPTER TWENTY-FIVE

REMINGTON LET HERSELF INTO HER home to the commotion of Max doing the I've-got-to-pee hop, the music of her phone, and her heart shouting at her to not look back.

She answered the phone—no one on the other end. She picked up Max and took him outside to do his business.

The bite of the wind against her cheeks brought a welcome pain. The smell of a wood fire relaxed her a smidge. The sight of Jason standing in his living room next door, looking out his window at her, made her want him. *Damn it.*

The hex had taken away the love but not the lust.

This would be her last night in Knotty. Her last night of being near Jason. The thought deflated her spirit like a boob smashed during a mammogram.

She turned so she couldn't see Jason. Looking at him was like looking at chocolate cake when you're on a potato chip diet. A fresh inch of snow covered her front yard. She hated the sight. And she hated that she hated the sight.

Before she'd met Jason, before she'd moved back to Knotty, snow had filled her with thoughts of fairytale endings and Hallmark movies. Now, it filled her with thoughts of yesterdays without tomorrows.

The wind picked up, and, as if singing a woe-is-me melody, the tree branches screamed and moaned from the weight of ice and snow piled on them.

As she waited on Max to finish his business, she thought of things. Not happy things.

Things like the unfinished to-do list, and the Watsons getting her inheritance.

Things like the curse on Knotty, and the future singles doomed to broken hearts.

Things like ghosts with secrets. Secrets she'd never cracked. Unless their secret was about the location of the crack. In which case, that had been easy peasy to figure out.

The wind picked up another notch, blowing snow up off the ground and smacking Max in the face, causing him to whimper and run toward Remington. She held out her arms and Max jumped into them.

"Do you want to hear a joke?" Beth said, appearing with no warning.

"Sure," Remington answered. "Who couldn't use a good joke in the middle of a thunder snowstorm?"

Her friend looked quite lovely wearing a white parka and jeans. Her feet were bare.

The three of them went inside.

Beth perched on top of the doorframe and pulled a tiny tin box out of her coat pocket. She opened it and withdrew a small, square card that sparkled in the air. "What types of rocks do ghosts collect?"

Remington took a seat near the window where she could see Jason's house. "I don't know." She saw Jason still standing in front of his window, looking right at her. "What?" She pulled her gaze away from his and made eye-contact with Beth.

"Tombstones."

Remington groaned. "That's bad. Where'd you get that joke?"

Max meowed and burrowed behind Remington's back. The dog still wasn't used to Beth.

"I found a box of jokes in an attic. They're great. You should hear them all. Here's another. What do the ghosts of dead gingerbread men wear?"

"What?"

"Cookie sheets. Get it?"

Remington groaned. "Unfortunately, yes."

Beth put the tin can away. "So, I found a ghost witch manual. I can now cast spells on ghosts."

"Cool." What kind of spells would a ghost cast on another ghost?

"Secret-spilling spells," Beth said.

"Stop reading my mind."

Beth came down to sit beside Remington. "Do you want to know what I found out from the ghost I cast the spell upon?"

"I'm leaving tomorrow."

"I know," Beth said.

Remington's congress of ghosts appeared. The detective was pushed to the front. "You received that information by trickery. We request you do not share it with this witch."

Remington sat up straight. "You say *witch* like it's a bad thing. I'll have you know, I'm not your typical bad witch. Not once have I tried to scare a child. Nor have I turned anyone into a pumpkin."

"Be that as it may," the spokesman said, "we wish for you not to be told our secret."

"I don't need her to tell me your secret," Remington said. "I already figured it out."

The ghost took a puff of his pipe and blew out smoke rings. "I find that hard to comprehend."

"Do you really know it?" Beth asked her.

Remington nodded. "I think so."

"How? I just learned of it."

"Speak, human. What is our secret?"

"You wish to keep the location of the crack in Knotty from humans so that none of us will cement it together and keep you from coming and going from the second veil into the living veil."

"Wow. I'm impressed." Beth held up her hand for a high-five. "Not surprised, though. You always were super smart."

Remington tried giving Beth a high-five, and of course her hand went straight through Beth's. The ghosts laughed. Had Beth really always thought she was super smart?

"Yes," Beth said to Remington.

Remington smiled at her, not bothering with the *don't read my mind* admonition.

"Do you know the location of the crack?" the spokesghost asked.

"You want everyone to think it's where the school was. That's why you keep haunting that spot. It's actually where the old tree used to be in the area where the new orphanage was to be built." That's why the sun shone so bright there, and why it had been cold when she'd stepped onto the site.

"Son of a zombie," the ghost said.

"I don't know why you made such a big deal of keeping it a secret from me," Remington said. "It's not like I want you all trapped in the second veil. If you haven't noticed, my best friend is one of you."

"Sam, I told you she wasn't evil," another ghost said. A ghost child.

"You can stop worrying. The orphanage is no longer going to be built there."

"That doesn't mean something won't be built there," spokesghost said. "Like a senior home."

Remington understood their fear. It was a legit one. Humans always ruined things for the other-normal in the movies. "Would you like for me to tell Jason not to build anything where the tree stood?"

"No," spokesghost said.

"Yes," all the other ghosts said.

"Which is it?"

The congress of ghosts gathered in a circle and whispered. Beth even joined them. After a few minutes, spokesghost said, "Yes. Please."

Remington nodded. "Will do. Now, I wish for all of you but Beth to leave. My friend and I need to say our goodbyes."

They all disappeared.

Beth dropped an arm around Remington's shoulders. Remington felt the weight of it. "Before you leave, I have a gift for you," Beth said.

"What kind of gift?" She glanced at Jason's house. She couldn't see him. He'd turned the light off in his living room. Was he still standing at the window watching her?

"The best kind. But first, I have some good news," Beth said.

"What's that?"

"When Jason said *please*, and the thunder and lightning snowstorm occurred…that was the spell being broken on Knotty."

Remington exhaled a sigh of relief. Future single residents were free to fall in love with one another. Knowing that made it easier to leave. "I don't understand."

"You know when Snow White was cursed by the witch, and the only thing that could undo the curse was prince charming kissing her?"

Remington tensed. Her intuition told her to prepare for a sucker punch. "Yes."

"That's the type of curse C-Squared LW cast on Knotty. The curse could be undone by something happening in Knotty that would never happen."

"What's that got to do with Jason saying please?"

"Jason swore when he was a child, and his mom left, even though he said *please don't go*, that he'd never say *please* again."

Bam. "What? No one told me he never used the word *please*. Why didn't you tell me?"

"I forgot until I remembered."

She should go apologize to Jason. "I'm glad the spell is broken." One less to-do on her list. But one more added on her should-do list. She should apologize for causing him to use the word *please*.

"You don't owe him an apology," Beth said. "He's a big boy."

"Stop reading my mind."

"Then stop thinking stupid thoughts."

Remington huffed. "You can't give me a gift because then I'd have to get you a gift, and I don't know what you're supposed to get a dead person." She pushed thoughts of Jason to the back of her brain. "Anyway, I could never surprise you with a gift, because you'd just read my mind to find out what it was before you opened it."

"Very funny. Anyway, I don't need a gift."

"I'm not going to be able to run the marathon, because there's not going to be one," Remington told her.

Beth considered her for a second. "I have a confession."

"What?"

"I didn't place all of those conditions in the will. You get everything no matter what. You could have never shown up in Knotty, and you would have still inherited my house, my life insurance, and all my things."

"You didn't? I do?" Should she feel relieved or abused?

"Nope and yes. I just wanted you to come back to Knotty. I thought this would be a place you could find family and happiness."

Remington decided to feel relieved. "I can't keep an eye on Johnny B, because he's been shipped off to a new orphanage." She should have stayed this morning. Followed the black sedan that took the orphans away and found out where they were going. Why hadn't she thought to do that?

"I really thought you or Jason would be able to help him find parents."

"Jason wants to buy my house and he'll give me a condo in New York for my trouble."

"It's not the worst idea in the world." Beth stared at her fingernails. "You have always wanted to live in New York."

Remington pulled her knees up under her chin and wrapped her arms around her legs. "I failed my second Tantric test. I've been kicked out of the class."

Beth laughed. "I only put that in my will because I wanted to study it and didn't have time. So, I pawned it off on you. Anyway, I was perusing your closet earlier. The T-shirts you've designed are hilarious. Have you ever thought about selling them? You could do that in New York while you were trying to get hired as a seamstress for Broadway. If that's what you still want."

"Do you think it's what I should want?"

"If living in New York will make you happy, then yes." Beth grabbed both of Remington's hands and squeezed. "I'm sorry I made you take a detour in Knotty."

Remington pulled her hands away. "Don't be sorry. I'm glad you tricked me into coming back, because you're here. I get to talk to you."

Beth leaned forward and kissed her on the cheek.

"You don't know how much I like having a living person to talk to." She sat back. "Dead people aren't that fun. They're all stiff."

Remington laughed. "Why don't you follow me to New York? I'd be okay with you always being underfoot."

Beth flipped her the bird. "Underfoot my ass."

"Whatever."

Beth's smile died. "My unfinished business is here in Knotty. I have to stay within fifty miles of the city limits."

Remington closed her eyes. She didn't like the idea of losing Beth. Ever. "Will I get to talk to you when you're in the third veil?"

A gust of wind blew through the living room walls, and the mayhem ghosts appeared.

"Leave," Beth ordered them. "Or, I'll curse you."

They left.

"Can you cast a spell on them to thwart any mayhem they plan to bring to Knotty?"

"Already did. Only time will tell if it worked."

Remington hoped it worked. "Beth, can I ask you a personal question?"

"Sure."

"Did you and Jason have an affair?"

Beth sat up straight. "I don't think so."

"Would you have cared if we'd had an affair?"

Beth stood up. "Why would I care about that?" she said, with a display of open palms. "In case you haven't noticed, I'm dead. I just wished you hadn't fallen in love with him."

Remington stood up as well. "Don't be. I'm not

in love with him anymore. I conducted a spell on myself."

Beth grabbed Remington's hands and twirled her in circles. "Brilliant."

Remington had to wait until the twirling stopped to speak. "Do you have feelings when you're dead?"

"Not the kind you have when you're alive." Beth cupped Remington's cheeks with both of her hands. "Have a one-night stand with Jason before you leave tomorrow."

Remington's stomach dropped to her toes. "Why would I want to do that?"

Beth gave her a sad look. "You'll have a great memory to take with you."

The tinkling of a bell caught their attention.

Beth sighed. "That's the big man. I've got to go. I'll be back."

"Tonight?"

"Not sure, but remember you owe me a séance before you leave town."

Remington shivered. "I'd forgotten about that."

Beth shook her head. "By the way, I've heard, and I can't prove it, but I've heard you get to have sex when you're in the third veil. So, don't feel bad for me when that happens."

With those words, Beth disappeared. Feet first.

Still no *smile if you love me*.

Max hissed until she was gone and then whimpered...like a wimp.

What if Beth wasn't Beth, and that's why her memory sucked rubber duckies? Because she never had the moments to remember?

Remington went to the kitchen and fixed herself a cup of hot tea. "Have a one-night stand," she muttered to herself. "What a ridiculous idea." She carried her cup to the bathtub, set it on the edge, ran a hot bath, and poured in a half-bottle of rose petals bubbles. She needed clarity.

She stripped out of her clothes, grabbed the spell book off her bedside table, and then gingerly stepped into her hot bath. The burn took her breath away, and she dropped the book in the water. "Damn it." She hastily fished it out of the water and dabbed it dry with a towel. Then she sank into the fragrant bath.

"I need clarity." She closed her eyes and heard pages rustling. She opened her eyes, and what she saw almost caused her to knock the book back in the water.

The spell of lucidity:

You will need oil of myrrh.

What in the hell was myrrh? The only oil she had was KY Jel. It would have to do. She retrieved the pink bottle from under the sink and read the spell.

Step 1: Rub your third eye chakra, (between your eyes), with oil of Myrrh and say:

Remington poured a drop of KY Jel on her middle finger and rubbed it between her eyes and chanted: *"By the supremacy of water, earth, air and fire, it is lucidity I seek to acquire."*

Step 2: Dab some oil on your heart chakra (between the breast bone).

Remington did and then chanted: *"By the com-*

mand of The and Thine, my thoughts and needs will be realigned."

Step 3: Anoint your midsection (your belly button) with the oil.

Remington did and chanted: *"By the control of all that is light as air, I appreciate what it takes to get me there. So it shall be. So it shall be."*

The bubbles in her bath multiplied, and the heady fragrance enveloped her causing every little detail in her bathroom to become very clear. Like the cobwebs in the corners. The jailbird ghosts sitting on the top of the showerhead. Remington closed her eyes and slipped deep into the bubbles. She took several cleansing breaths.

She was going to swallow her pride. Take Jason up on his offer. One night of sex.

CHAPTER TWENTY-SIX

R EMINGTON WAS ON A MISSION, so she didn't knock. Instead, she threw open the door, channeled her inner Hollywood actress, and in a dramatic fashion, announced, "I'm here to take you up on your offer."

Jason wasn't startled. Why the hell not? Had he been that sure she'd cave? Damn it.

He stared at her from his lazy chair by the fire, a book in one hand and a look of amusement on his face. "Which offer was that?" He spoke as nonchalantly as if they were talking about the weather.

She shook her head making her hair swing. "A night of sex." Then she tossed her Tantric workbook on his coffee table and struck a pose. "I want to see if you're any good."

His book slipped from his fingers. "You do?"

She let her hands fall to her sides. "Yes." God, she hoped her hex on her heart didn't fizzle.

"What changed your mind?"

"Really? That's your response?" She plopped her hands on her hips and leaned toward him. "Are you freaking kidding me?" She took a deep breath. Tried to calm down. It didn't work. "I'm offering you sex, and you want to talk about"—

she zig-zagged her hand through the air and did an impressively loud snap right as she uttered— "why?"

Jason's eyes widened. "I've never met bad-ass Remington."

"Not the point." She slipped her coat off and tossed it on the couch and noticed the mayhem ghosts sitting there, whispering to one another. What in the hell were they up to?

"You're right." Jason glanced at the workbook she'd dropped on his coffee table. "Is that why you came over?"

Remington closed her eyes and channeled her clarity hex.

"For help with Tantric?" Jason continued. "Not simply because I asked you to?"

She opened her eyes. The ghosts were gone. "Yes." She'd only brought the book with her as a prop. Something to hold, to use as an excuse for caving to his whim if he said he'd changed his mind about wanting one night with her.

He sat up in his chair, pushing the footrest down. "Which parts?"

She licked her dry lips. "I'm on chapter five— the chakras. Do you know about those?" He didn't know she'd already flunked out of the class. She could live with that deceit.

He chuckled, a deep, sexy noise that stirred her senses and made her forget her uncertainties.

He stood.

Remington gulped over the sudden knot in her throat, not sure how this would play out.

Jason wore a pair of pajama bottoms and nothing else.

She keenly appreciated the bare skin on display. "Aren't you cold?" All of his naked manliness produced tingles by the gazillion in her body. His broad shoulders tapered down to a flat stomach and narrow hips. His chest had a slight layer of hair. She was dying to find out if it continued past the waistband of his pajamas, which sat very low on his hips. They were held up with a drawstring—just begging to be tugged.

"No."

Remington resisted the urge to reach out and yank the string and watch them drop. See how far the hair traveled down Long and Lanky's body. Instead, she tried to force her eyes to look up. They did, about twelve inches, stopping at his pecs. They were large, perfectly hard, and beautiful to visually inhale. She strolled to his liquor cabinet and poured herself a shot of whiskey. She downed it like Ruby Rae and Sara Ann...only she coughed and sputtered when it hit the back of her throat.

Jason strolled over to her. "Do you often visit your neighbors for a booty call?" He ran his fingers through her hair. Sensually rubbing the strands between his thumb and index finger.

Remington raised her chin a fraction. "Just when I have sexy neighbors." He was so much taller than her that she had to raise her chin much more than a fraction to meet his gaze. And the scenery along the way didn't entice her to hurry the journey.

"I see." He sat on the arm of the couch and then

leaned down and lifted her leg until her foot sat on his bent thigh. She placed her hands on his shoulders for balance. "You're that kind of girl?"

Her palms burned from the contact. "Definitely."

Slowly, rubbing her calf muscle, he removed one snow boot and then the other.

"Perhaps we should start with sex. Work our way up to Tantric methods." His fingers slid up the inside of her leg as she let her foot drop to the floor. Right when his hand would have grazed her girly parts, he let it fall away.

Her breathing sped up. "I can multitask. Can you?"

He lifted both eyebrows, and she dug her nails into his shoulders, glad she hadn't yet let go of them.

"The chakras ceremony is a very intimate encounter." He stood, and her fingertips scraped slowly down, through the hair that covered his chest, before doing their own last-minute falling away.

"I know." Her voice had a husky quality.

He pushed her softly back, one step at a time until her back came up against the door. Then his head dipped, and he captured her lips.

She groaned.

His tongue tangled with hers while his hands roamed freely over her backside. "Once we start, you can't change your mind." He pressed himself hard against her, leaving her in no doubt as to his own desires.

"Who's changing their mind?"

He lowered his mouth to a spot right beneath her chin and nipped. "Are you sure?"

She shivered. "Yes." The sensation of his tongue licking the spot he'd bitten and then traveling lower took her breath.

He picked her up and walked into his bedroom where he sat her feet-first onto the floor. "While I set up the room for the ceremony, why don't you make yourself comfortable?"

Jason watched Remington walk into his bathroom and waited for the door to shut before he moved. His breaths were more ragged than they were after running a marathon. He would have tonight with Remington. Tomorrow, he would send her away, and Bernadette would come. Tonight had to be special.

His mind replayed the steps to a chakra session. Moon had been a free spirit, in love with the world. For her, teaching sex had been a calling. She'd embraced her physique. Loved both the female and male bodies. Loved teaching others to love.

Remington wasn't anything like Moon. Remington was shy. Unsure of herself. An innocent. If that was going to change about her, he wanted to be the one to teach her. To introduce her to the beauty of sex…to the beauty of her body.

He went around the room and lit the candles. Then he piled the pillows on his bed up against the headboard. Lastly, he slipped out of his pajama bottoms. Part of Tantric was being at ease with your body. Nudity was embraced.

"Do you have a tattoo on your ass?" Remington said, causing him to jump in surprise. An extremely unmanly response when your role for the evening is to be master.

He glanced over his shoulder and chuckled. "What are you doing looking at my ass?" He'd forgotten about the tattoo.

She stepped across the room wearing one of his T-shirts and leaned down to get a better look. "That's what I thought. You have a pink ribbon on your ass?" She reached out and traced the breast cancer survival symbol.

He turned to face her, and she quickly popped up, pink tingeing her cheeks.

"Beth wanted to get one and the doctors wouldn't let her. So I got inked instead."

She nibbled on her lip, and her eyes clouded. "Were you in love with her?"

The question caught him off guard. "The day I met her she was in tears." He visualized the bright, summer day he'd first met Beth. "She'd made an appointment to get a tattoo and the artist told her he couldn't do it without her doctor's permission. The doctor wouldn't give his permission." She'd been sitting on her back porch crying. He'd gone over to introduce himself and to check on her. "I offered to sacrifice my ass for the cause thinking it would make her laugh." It had worked. "And she took me up on my offer." Which had made him laugh. They'd bonded over that moment.

Remington grabbed his shoulder, turned him

sideways and eyeballed his tattoo. "Why on your ass?"

He grabbed her hand and inched her toward the bed. "I don't know. That's just where she was going to get hers, so that's where I got mine."

His platform bed sat under the window with a view of the snow-covered landscape as its back-drop. He gently lifted her up and set her on the king-size mattress.

Her smile evaporated.

"Are you okay?" He wanted to smooth away the worry lines between her eyes.

She shrugged. "It's like you took my place in her life. I'm the one who should have a tattoo on her ass. Not you."

"You can still get one." There was something about Remington that mystified him. Made him want to be a better person.

She looked down at her hands clasped tightly in her lap. "It wouldn't be the same."

"She talked about you nonstop."

Remington's chin shot up, and her eyes met his. Emotions fought over the right to arrange her eyebrows. Surprise won. "Really?" The one word barely a whisper.

He nodded. "I know more about you than you probably know about yourself."

"Like what?"

He shook his head. "Tonight is about Tantric sex."

Jason pushed thoughts of business dilemmas to the back of his brain and thoughts of the way his heart hitched around Remington to the delete file in his mind.

He just wished he knew what in the hell Beth had been mad about, or if it had even been Beth he'd seen the other night at Remington's.

Sitting on the edge of his bed, Remington looked like a frightened hooker on her first call. Her eyes were wide, her breathing rapid.

"Relax. I'm not the big bad wolf—unless you want me to be the big bad wolf." He walked away to relight the candles in his room. For some reason, they'd all gone out. When he was done, he put on soft instrumental music and turned the thermostat up.

He couldn't believe he was going to teach Remington about Tantric sex. It pleased him he was the first she would experience this with. He went to the bed and ran his hands down her arms. "To do this, you'll have to trust me. Do you trust me?"

"Not even for a second."

His chest tightened. "Can you try?"

"Yes."

"Good," he said. "Stand up."

Slowly, she slid off his bed and stood. Her movements were graceful, reminding him of a pampered cat.

He reached to the hem of her T-shirt, *his* T-shirt, and inched it up her thighs, over her hips. His breath stalled in his throat when he saw she wore no panties. "You're killing me, Smith."

"You seem to have a thing about women and their potential pantilessness, so I thought I'd indulge your fantasy."

He pulled a deep breath into his lungs and continued tugging the shirt up over her bare breasts, over her head. He leaned forward and teased a nipple with his tongue until she groaned. He stepped back, tossed her shirt to the floor, and stared. "Beautiful." Too beautiful for words.

Remington stood naked in front of him with a snowstorm in the background. Never had he seen a more stunning sight in his life. If he was smart, he'd run like hell.

"You're staring." She raised her hands and covered herself.

"I can't help it." He removed her hands. "Don't cover your body. Let me soak in the sight of you in moonlight, in my bedroom, naked." He didn't believe in forever, but the sight of her standing there made him want to. That was something he'd never felt before, and he didn't know how to react.

Her hand came out and brushed the hot length of his erection, turning his brain to mush. He groaned. "Careful baby, or we won't get anywhere in my teachings."

She didn't break contact immediately. She ran her soft palm up and down his shaft. "You're huge. I don't know how any woman could ever give you a blowjob," she said, her eyes wide, and then she blushed.

He resisted the urge to throw back his shoulders and crow. Instead, he removed her hand. Tantric was about self-discipline. Right now, it was to be about her pleasure. Not his. "Sit on the bed."

She did and crisscrossed her legs.

He shook his head at her. "Darling, you make it hard for a man to have good intentions."

She gave him a shy smile. "Sorry."

"Don't be." He gathered massage oil and pillows before settling himself behind her on the bed. His legs spread on either side of her hips. "I'm going to teach you about the Chakra Wave."

"Okay." Her voice was husky with need.

He placed a pillow between his legs. "Lean back against me until you're comfortable." He gritted his teeth and counted to ten while she did so.

"Now what?"

"Now, breathe with me." He poured massage oil on his hands.

They inhaled and exhaled in unison until he felt the tension leaving her body and his. "Now, when you're ready, take my left hand and place it on your mound of Venus, which is referred to as your Yoni in the teachings of Tantric."

"Your left hand on my Yoni?" she murmured.

"Place it where you'll feel a tingle. Don't be shy."

She lifted his left hand and guided it to her Yoni. He bit back a groan as fire exploded in his veins. "Is this your sweet spot?"

She repositioned it so that his fingers were lightly touching her clitoris.

They both gasped. He wanted nothing more than to push her down on her back, spread her legs and use his tongue on her Yoni. He gritted his teeth, reminding himself of the teachings of Tantric.

"Now, take my right hand and position it right

below your navel."

She gripped his right hand, and after a moment of hesitation, she placed it on her stomach.

"Close your eyes."

"They haven't been open."

"Good. Relax. Breathe slowly, deeply through your mouth." He paused and let her follow his instructions. "Now, inhale so that the breath flows down to your sex before you exhale it out."

Jason closed his eyes and tuned into Remington's breathing. After several breaths, she relaxed her body fully into him, and he began to gently stimulate her with his left hand.

She stiffened for a moment.

He alternated his caresses with tiny pulses. The oil on his hand blended in with her juices. "We're awakening a fire in your first chakra."

"Is that where that is?" she said in a soft, lilting voice.

Her head rested on his chest, and he could smell the sweetness of her sex fill the air. "Squeeze your PC muscle and rock your pelvis slightly."

She did.

He heard the soft sound of her breathing. "Keep doing this until you feel alive with need. Tell me when you're there."

"Now. Oh God, now."

Jason smiled into her hair. "Good. You're doing a great job. Now, feel the color red filling your pelvis with lust, warmth, fire."

Remington's breathing quickened, and her hips rocked.

His hand rode the motion.

She moaned softly.

"Good. Now, we'll move to your second chakra."

"But I like the first chakra," she whispered.

He chuckled. "Trust me. It gets better."

She stiffened. "Trust?"

He leaned down and kissed her temple. "Yes. Trust."

"Okay." Her body relaxed.

"I want you to inhale and draw the energy up to your belly where my right hand is resting. As you do this, visualize the color changing from red to orange." He gave her time to make the transition.

"Inhale and feel the orange burn and spread fire through your belly. Feel it stir up your emotions." Her stomach muscles contracted under his hand. "When you exhale, let the energy return to your sex center. Continue with the PC pumps as you do this."

She became very quiet.

"Do you feel a fire burning in your belly?"

"Yes. But I feel so weird, so wild. Wanton." Desire thickened her voice.

"That's how you're supposed to feel. Let's move to the third chakra." He continued to gently stimulate her clitoris.

"If you'd just keep the pressure right there for a moment, I'd come."

"Not yet. Take my right hand and place it on your solar plexus."

"My what?"

"It's about two inches above your navel."

Her hand shook as she lifted his and moved it to the right spot.

"You're beautiful," he murmured.

She breathed in and out as his right hand rested there.

His left hand continued its playful touching. "Inhale and imagine your energy rising from your first to your third chakra."

Remington shuddered and spread her arms out, palms flat on the bed on either side of his legs. Her hips were becoming wilder in their movements under his hand. His finger accidentally slipped inside of her.

"Oh my God," she panted.

He bit back his own response, quickly moved his finger back to the spot it belonged. "Now, imagine your energy is glowing like the sun. Bright, yellow, hot. Inhale from your first chakra." He cupped her first chakra as he spoke. "Move it up your spine and, as you release, let the energy flow down the front of your body."

"What if I come?"

"It's okay. But concentrate on your chakras. Your third chakra is your power center. It's where you accept who you are and you're proud to be *I am*. It's where orphan Remington is accepted."

"Even unloved Remington?"

The question squeezed his heart. "Especially her."

He placed his right hand over her heart. "Now, we're going to move on to the fourth chakra. Visualize the heat rising from your clitoris to your heart, and as it does this, it turns a beautiful shade of green."

"Like the color of summer?"

"Yes. This color is meant to heal, to love, to give hope and to renew. It's a color that awakens you." Warmth and safety flooded him when he said the word *love*. "Do you feel it?" He wasn't sure if he was asking her if she felt the love or if she felt the color.

"I do."

They breathed, and her tears landed on the back of his hands. "It's okay to cry," he said, past the lump in his throat. "This is your way of releasing tension as you heal old wounds." What old wound was she healing?

He placed his right hand on her throat. "This is your fifth chakra. Circle your energy from your pelvis to your throat and back down."

"What color is it?"

"It's blue." Like the sky. He envisioned himself waking up for the rest of his life next to her.

"Your sixth chakra is here." He placed his index finger lightly between her eyes. "Visualize the color purple."

"Oh my God, I'm ready to explode." Her voice was so husky he barely recognized it as hers.

"Then go for it, babe. It's okay."

"No, I want to finish. Teach…more."

He placed the fingers of his right hand on her crown and gently massaged. "Inhale and draw your energy from your center up to your head, and when it touches the top, see the white light."

"It's breathtaking."

"Yes. You are. Do large circles, move your hips, enjoy the pulsing, hot heat as it paints your body in colors of desire. When you can stand it no more, release it into the universe." He slipped his finger inside of her and stroked the inside of her first chakra. Unable to stop himself, he pushed his rigid dick into the pillow blocking him from her skin.

Remington moaned and arched her back. Her breaths razored in and out. A primal scream filled the room, and she collapsed against him with a shudder. "I can't believe…that was so…thanks."

He wanted to finish off his own needs with his oiled hands but didn't. Instead, he scooted out from behind her. All of him contracted tight. His jaws, his chest, his loins. He placed a clean pillow under her head and tugged an afghan over her. "Rest," he murmured, curling into her backside.

She twisted toward him. "What about you?"

He hadn't expected to feel this way about her. He wasn't sure he wanted to feel this way. He needed time to think. "We have all night." Was he capable of real love after all? No. This wasn't the right time. Plus, there was the whole blackmail issue with Bernadette. And the danger to all the orphans.

"I feel so good but really tired." She closed her eyes. A soft sigh escaped her lips.

"Then rest." Analyzing his ability to love was a waste of time.

CHAPTER TWENTY-SEVEN

WHEN REMINGTON OPENED HER EYES, she knew exactly where she was. And what she'd done. She was in Jason's king-size bed. And she'd had one hell of an orgasm.

People would give up their soul for the kind of orgasm she'd experienced.

And then she'd fallen asleep before her one-night stand had been completed. She yanked the covers over her head. The very least she could have done was give Jason a fabulous handjob. She'd been a big fat zero in last night's sexual equation. And today she was leaving for New York. Unless, of course, Jason begged her to stay. Which he wouldn't.

Linny was right. She was lousy in bed. No wonder Jason wasn't in bed with her this morning.

She heard a noise and glanced around.

The two mayhem ghosts stood in the bedroom.

"Good morning," one of them said. He was chunky and bald.

"Tell Beth her spell didn't work," the other said. He had a black eye and a missing tooth.

Before Remington could respond, they disappeared and loud pounding noise caused her to jump. *Voices.*

Were the mayhem ghosts in the living room talking to Jason?

She strained to hear. Not them. Muted female laughter drifted under the door and into Remington's ears like a snake's hiss.

Remington covered her mouth with her hand to keep from making a noise.

Who in the hell is here?

She glanced at the clock. Seven. Too early for a casual visitor. Then again, this was Knotty, Missouri, where social visitation conventions didn't appear to apply. Maybe Ruby Rae had brought cinnamon rolls. Had she stopped by Remington's house first? Discovered her not home? Damn it.

Were the mayhem ghosts behind this visitor's arrival at the inopportune time?

If Ruby Rae discovered Remington in Jason's bedroom, the darling blatherer would have fodder for a year.

Remington crawled off the platform bed, tugging the blanket with her. She fashioned it into a sarong and secured the loose ends above her breasts.

She eyeballed the window. Not big. Standard size. But she could probably shimmy through it if necessary.

She'd turned one bare foot toward the window for a closer look at her escape route when she heard a female say, "Jason, you didn't answer my call."

Remington froze. It wasn't Ruby Rae.

Jason laughed. The sexy rumble sent tingles to Remington's toes and weakened her knees despite the confused state of her mind and the shell-shocked state of her body. "I was otherwise occupied."

Oh yes you were. Remington smiled remembering his hands on her Chakras. Those little suckers would never be the same.

"Too busy for me?" The woman's voice vibrated sex louder than a vibrator with new batteries.

Jason coughed. "Now's not a good time." His voice was low. Hard to hear.

The woman laughed. A tinkling clamor that grated Remington's hyper-alert nerves. "Darling, we have so much we need to talk about, and with the holidays coming up so quickly, I just couldn't wait another second to see you."

The steady tick of the grandfather clock in the hallway punctuated the lengthy silence between the room's occupants.

Then there was the sound of a gasp so loud it made Remington jump and drop her blanket.

"I haven't caught you with another woman have I?" the woman asked in a voice that wasn't pissed, but it wasn't happy either. As if not really believing what she was accusing him of, but yet…

Fuck. Remington tried to jump-start her brain which seemed fried from last night's pleasure. Who was out there, and what was this all about? Thank God she hadn't, at the tip of the orgasm Jason had given her, declared her desire to undo her love hex. She found the T-shirt from last night, yanked it over her head, and stabbed her arms through the sleeves. She wasn't about to get caught with her panties down.

"Please tell me it's not that little mouse I saw you with back in October? The one you said you were being nice to because you needed her to sell her house to you?"

Remington tried to inhale volumes of oxygen at the same time pain spewed out of her heart which brought on a panic attack, and she fell against the bed for support. She leaned over and grabbed her knees and took tiny little breaths.

She knew who it was. Gnat-Brain.

Remington's desire to stomp into the living room and demand answers and an apology warred with the panic attack holding her captive in his bedroom. *Wheeze in. Wheeze out.*

"That's enough." Grisly intensity turned Jason's voice into a weapon.

Was he angry or did he just not want Remington to wake up and hear the truth?

"Darling, I'm only calling her what I heard you call her."

Remington cringed mid-wheeze. Was that how he viewed her?

"Don't be vulgar."

Remington walked to the door and eased it open. Just a tad. No one noticed.

Probably because Gnat-Brain had just stepped up to Jason and was pushing her boobs onto his shirtless chest. "Darling, I don't want to fight. Did you use sex to get her to sell her house to you?"

Remington's insides twisted like an arm in the hands of a bully.

Her Tantric textbook sat on the coffee table.

Gnat-Brain reached out and picked it up.

"Put that down," Jason said.

Gnat-Brain laughed. "You used your Tantric skills on her."

"It wasn't like that."

Gnat-Brain smiled and took a seat on the couch. "There are shoddier things than using your sexual knowledge to get a woman to sell her house to you." She took a sip of her drink. "I think I'll buy her bungalow when you get your little community built. Should be a hoot having a home in a singles town while we make our plans."

Remington didn't understand what was going on. Without warning, hands shoved her forward. Unable to stop her momentum, she stumbled into the living room.

"Well, well, what do we have here?" Gnat-Brain said.

Remington glanced toward the bedroom door and saw the mayhem ghosts waving at her. Assholes. She turned her attention to Gnat-Brain. "It's not for sale." She glanced at Jason. His normally tanned complexion was an unhealthy shade of white.

Gnat-Brain's eyes narrowed, glowed with evil, completely at odds with the pout on her lips. "I wasn't going to buy it from you. I was going to buy it from Jason. My lover."

Remington squared her shoulders. "Don't you mean ex-lover?" She willed Jason to walk over to her. Say he was on her side.

Gnat-Brain laughed. An evil, obnoxious noise

that caused Scotch to whimper. "Oh, you darling girl, is that what he told you?" She turned to Jason. "Did you give her the chakra treatment?"

"That is none of your fucking business." His gaze met Remington's. "You need to leave."

"Me?" Remington didn't understand. He appeared to be upset with Gnat-Brain, but it was her he wanted to leave. Why?

Gnat-Brain took a seat on the couch. "How did that poor ordinary thing handle all that heat?"

Remington's pride snapped like a towel in a locker room after a monumental win. "Ordinary? You're calling me ordinary? You're nothing but a two-bit bug that no one mourns when it gets squashed. It doesn't get any more ordinary than that." She looked at Jason. Waited for him to back her up.

"Why don't we ask Jason which one of us he thinks is ordinary?"

He didn't reply.

He stood there as if someone had cast a spell on him, and he was trapped in a glass bubble.

Remington's bravado shattered.

Of course, he thought of her as ordinary. She was ordinary.

Not a blinding beauty.

Not a rocket researcher.

Not a wheeler of whit.

Not sexually spectacular.

Just ordinary. Less than ordinary. Ordinary had parents.

She grabbed her book from the bitch, cocked

her head at an impossibly high angle and walked to his front door, grabbing her purse off the hook.

Jason reached out a hand on her shoulder. "Remington, I'm sorry."

Remington didn't turn to look at him. "Save it."

Gnat-Brain said, "Jason, darling, let's make her the first we tell about our engagement."

Remington swirled around. Had she heard right? Engaged?

"Christ sake, shut up," Jason snapped. "Can't you see you're hurting her?"

Jason Hart was a man of many secrets and many talents. He hadn't stolen money from her like Linny, but he'd stolen something far more precious. He'd stolen that tiny part of her brain that was open to the idea of someone, someday, loving her.

"Is that true?" Her voice a whisper of despair.

"It's complicated."

She slapped him across the face, causing pain to explode up her arm, before wrenching open the door and walking out. Right into the mayhem ghost. One of them stuck a foot out and tripped her. She missed the first step and took a nose dive into the snow.

With as much grace as a newborn colt, she struggled to her feet, spitting snow and fury.

"Why didn't you use the steps?" Gnat-Brain asked.

Remington counted to three and forced herself to glance over her shoulder. "Go to hell…both of you."

Gnat-Brain ran a finger down Jason's bearded

cheek. "I want to hear about the sex you had with my fiancé." Her voice pulsed like a purring kitten. "Was it good? Would you be willing to join us in a threesome soon?"

"Remington, I'm…" Jason said something, but the ringing in her ear kept her from hearing his words.

Gnat-Brain checked her nails, pointy red tips. They had probably been poison darts on the set of *OZ* in a previous life. "It won't be the first threesome I've had with him," she said in a conversational tone. "That used to be one of his favorite things to do with the women he dated."

"I'm sure it would be any man's favorite thing to do if he can find two gnat-brains to—"

"That's enough, Bernie," Jason ordered.

Gnat-Brain sneered and ruined her appearance of glam sophistication. She leaned toward Remington. "Tell me darling, how far did you make it in the Chakra wave? I personally didn't get past the first chakra before I ravaged the man the first time we did it."

Remington didn't bother to answer. Instead, she dug her purse out of the snow.

"He hates when a woman makes it through the whole chakra. He doesn't get anything out of it."

Remington stood and trudged toward her house.

"You didn't disappoint him by making it all the way through, did you?"

Remington could feel the heat rise in her cheeks, and her mouth had that funky taste one gets after eating sharp cheddar cheese, but she kept walking.

"Jason, you poor frustrated man. I can tell by the red blotches covering the back of her neck, she did make it all the way through. I forgive you for cheating on me. I can see it was nothing more than a business decision."

Remington fumbled for the key in her purse. *I hate you Jason Hart. I hate you Jason Hart. I hate you—*

"Stop being a bitch," Jason said. "Remington, look at me."

Remington wanted to look at Jason's face. See his eyes. Read the truth. But she couldn't. She was afraid the truth wasn't on her side. When she thought things could get no worse, she heard the crunch of tires in front of her house.

Great. A witness to her humiliating walk of shame. She turned to see who it was.

"Linny?" Were her eyes deceiving her?

Oh, holy snot. They weren't. If it wasn't so tragic, Remington might have laughed.

He parked his beat-up, twenty-year-old Ford next to Gnat-Brain's four-wheel-drive Lexus and jumped out. "Hi, Remington. I'm so glad you were outside." He spoke loudly, exuberantly. Like they were going to have a grand reunion.

"That makes one of us," she mumbled for her ears only. How in the hell had he found her? Had her old landlord given him her address?

"I didn't know which house was yours. I was just going to go door-to-door." Obviously, he hadn't correctly read the underwhelmed posture of her body. In horror, she watched him run in slow motion through the deep snow toward her. Arms outstretched.

Linny swooped her up in his arms, causing Remington's book to fall out of her limp fingers. She didn't make a sound—couldn't make a sound—she had no idea what the appropriate noise would be. Her hands automatically went around his neck for balance.

"Darling, where are your shoes and your pants?" he asked, a look of concern on his face.

Remington glanced at her toes. She hadn't even noticed she was barefoot.

Linny didn't wait for her reply. "Let's get you inside before your beautiful feet get frostbite."

"Remington, who in the hell is this?" Jason asked.

Remington glanced at Jason. And at Gnat-Brain. *His fiancée.* "He's my ex-boyfriend."

"That's what I thought. Put her down," Jason ordered in a tone that said, "I'm-capable-of-murder."

"But she's barefoot," Linny said, sounding anything but brave.

"Down," said Jason.

Linny did as ordered.

"Remington, get inside your house. Bernie go inside. Linny and I have some talking to do," Jason said, in a full-blown macho voice.

Remington's hinges sprung. She'd had enough. She was her own person, and no one was going to tell her what to do. Especially a guy who'd spat on her pride. "No, you don't," she yelled at Jason. "Linny isn't any of your business."

Jason momentarily looked confused. "He's the

one who stole from you, isn't he?"

How dare he look at her like she was betraying him? "Yes—"

"Then get inside." Jason brought his fists up in front of him and squared off with Linny.

Remington laughed. Not a natural laugh. A forced one. "For God's sake, Jason. Leave him alone...I love him." It was the only thing she could think to say to hurt him the way he hurt her.

"What?"

"You heard me. Now go back to your bug and leave us alone. We have our own plans to make." Remington grabbed Linny's hand and pulled him behind her toward her house.

"I'm so glad you're talking to me. I was afraid you would shoot me with that toy gun I gave you." Linny tripped, or the mayhem ghost pushed him, and caused them both to fall.

Remington struggled to stand. "It's not a toy. And if I had it on me, I would shoot you. What in the hell are you doing here?"

"Darling, I'm sorry I stole from you. I woke up in the middle of the night and realized I'd really fallen in love with you, and I panicked. Do you really love me?"

"Hell no." After a couple of failed efforts to get up, she extended a hand to him and helped him.

"Thank you."

Dropping his hand, she glared at him.

Unbelievably, he went down on one knee in the snow. "Remington, I've changed. I've realized that love can't be ignored. I love you, and I don't want to spend the rest of my life without you. Can you ever forgive me and give me another chance?" He spoke the words loud enough for all of Knotty to hear.

Remington wanted to die. This had to be the most humiliating day of her life. "Get up. You're making a scene." She didn't bother to keep her own voice low.

"Now do you want me to kick his ass?" asked Jason. "I will. Just say the word."

She glanced at Jason, and might have taken him up on his offer were it not for the arm candy hanging on him.

Gnat-Brain had her hand tucked into the crook of Jason's elbow. The bitch opened her mouth and said, "Don't be silly, darling. Can't you see the love in her eyes? This is the most romantic thing I've ever witnessed. He's proposing to her in the snow."

Jason's gaze scrutinized Remington's face. "Is that true? Are you in love?"

Remington could feel tears burning the back of her eyes. "Yes." She grabbed Linny's hand, yanked him up, and marched them to her front door.

CHAPTER TWENTY-EIGHT

REMINGTON STOOD IN THE MIDDLE of her living room, gulping for air.

"Do you really love me?" A smile the size of the Mississippi River stretched across Linny's face.

Remington sputtered. "Are you freaking kidding me? Really? You think I love you?" she paused, not for dramatic effect, but simply to give her brain enough time to process the mere idea that Linny could think she still loved him. "You stole my New York money. You stole my rent money. You caused me to get fired from my job." She spoke each sentence a tad louder than the previous. Even if she weren't under a self-imposed hex to love no one, she wouldn't still love him.

The mayhem ghosts sat on her couch, feet propped on her coffee table, eating popcorn and watching.

Linny's river smile dried up. "But you said—"

Remington jerked her arm toward her couch and pointed. "You...sit right there. Don't move until I tell you to move."

"Are we going to talk?"

"No. But Jason's going to think we're talking. And then when you leave, you're going to smile and whistle all the way to your truck. And then you're going to drive away, and I don't want to ever hear from you again."

"But—"

"No. No but. You don't get a say in any of this. Got it?"

He stood up straight. Cleared his throat and declared, "I love you, Remington Smith."

"Go to hell…and keep digging until you're at the slimy bottom of hell. And even Hades is too good for you."

"Why are you being such a bitch?"

"Because the one person in this world who finds me lovable is you. A loser. Call me crazy, but I'd just as soon not be loved at all. Thank you very much."

His expression hardened. "Okay, but, if I do what you ask, would you loan me some money?"

Remington's fingers itched for something heavy to throw at him. "What?"

"There are people I owe money to." Gone was whiny Linny. In his place, a very calculating Linny.

Remington shivered as if a coat of evil had just wrapped itself around her shoulders. "Are you saying I'm not the only one you've stolen from?"

He cracked his knuckles, reminding her of a thug. "I didn't steal money from them. I took a prepayment on a job, but then didn't finish the job."

"What job?"

"You?"

"Me?"

"I was hired to get information out of you."

"What kind of information?"

"It doesn't matter. I found out pretty quick you didn't have it to give."

"You're talking in riddles."

"What matters is they threatened to hurt you because they knew I'd sort of developed a soft spot for you by the time I figured out you were a waste of time. That's why I stole you the gun."

"People thought I had information?" Remington's brain cells were whiplashed. "Hank's hot?"

He pulled a toothpick out of his shirt pocket and stuck it in his mouth. "When I realized I was going to have to get out of town, I was cash poor. So, I stole your money. But I left you the gun for protection from these people."

"What sort of people? I don't understand any of this."

"I mean the sort of people that hire people like me to take care of minor problems, and or gather information for them."

Remington blanched. Was Linny a hitman? She picked up her purse and pulled out the money she had and threw it toward him. "This is all I have. Now, get out."

He counted the money and looked at her speculatively. "Just a word of warning. Keep that gun handy. There are lots of bad guys in the world. Some who might want you dead."

"Like who?"

"Doesn't matter. And one more thing…don't believe every man who tells you they love you. They mostly just want in your pants."

"Did you ever love me?"

"Actually, not even a little until I drove into the city limits of Knotty. Then it hit me with a two-by-four. Not to worry. I'm sure it'll soon pass just like the fart I'm about to release." He let himself out.

She shuddered. The asshole was a victim of the town's curse. That's why he tried to propose. Why he was acting like a guy with a split personality. The hex must not be completely broken. There must be a kink in the undo spell. Remington watched him, and the mayhem ghosts, saunter to his truck. The bile in her stomach rose up in her throat.

Had she given a hitman her virginity? Why would anyone hire a hitman to ask her questions?

CHAPTER TWENTY-NINE

"SON OF A BITCH AND shit!" Remington hollered, letting all of her anger at herself, at Jason, at life, spew in the form of words. She shouldn't have let Linny leave without an explanation. He owed her that much. To stand there and tell her everything.

A rhyme came to mind. She blocked it, afraid it was a spell waiting to be released.

"Beth," she summoned, in a tight, sharp syllable.

"Here I am." Beth appeared in front of her wearing a bad maid costume, her fingers in her ears. "Now, stop yelling."

"I can't help it. I'm mad."

"I get that, but buck-up sissy girl. You're falling apart."

Remington exhaled hard. "We need to talk."

"Fine. But first, a joke." Beth pulled out her joke box. Withdrew a card. "How do girl ghosts keep their hair in place?"

Remington muttered bad words under her breath. "I don't know. How?"

"With scarespray. Get it? Scare spray. Not hair…" Beth trailed off, and she stuck her joke box in the pocket of her raunchy ensemble.

Remington sighed. "I get it. I'm just not in the mood to laugh."

"Okay. Sorry. I didn't know. You were out a little late last night. I thought maybe you'd be in a terrific mood today."

"I'm not." Remington sighed. She was angry, but she was finding it hard to concentrate on the anger with Beth's outfit proving a distraction. "What in the hell are you wearing?"

Beth twirled around. "Isn't it great? I found it in that trunk in the attic of the lime-green house on Elm. The one I told you about. The old owners must have really loved Halloween. It's where I get most of what I wear."

Remington didn't want to talk fashion. "Did you find out who your client is?" Her voice was flatter than a crisp sheet of computer paper before going through a printer and just as lifeless. Just like she felt on the inside. Ripped of words.

"As a matter of fact, I did."

"Who's the mystery man? Let's get this séance show on the road."

Beth nibbled on a nail and glanced at Remington through lowered lashes. "Maybe we should talk about this later. First, you can tell me what happened last night."

"There's nothing to talk about. Are you going to tell me who the mystery man is? If I'm hosting a séance for you, we need to get it done."

Beth carefully chose several strands of hair and begun twirling them. "Jason's dad," she finally said. "He asked for me specifically."

Remington laughed. She'd thought Beth had said Jason's dad. Of course, she must have misheard. "Who did you say?"

"Jason's dad."

Remington gasped. "I'm supposed to help you talk to Jason's dad?" Would she tell him Remington was his murderer?

Beth waved the concern off with a flick of her hand. "Don't be such a goose. Accidental murder can't be helped. That's why they call it accidental. You'll summon him. I'll tell him what happened. He'll understand. The séance won't take more than five minutes."

Remington couldn't say no to Beth. It might be the last time she saw her friend. "Fine."

"Here are the instructions. Now this part is crucial. Set your ghost party up right or things can go astray."

Remington took the crumpled sheets of papers from Beth. "What do you mean...astray?"

"I mean you may end up with more than just me at your séance."

"Like the mayhem ghosts?" Remington straightened the sheets of paper in her hands.

"We definitely don't want them at the séance," Beth said. "They could cause things to go all kinds of sideways."

"How do I keep them out?"

"You simply don't invite them in."

"I haven't invited them to anything I've done and they still show." *Assholes.*

"A séance is different. Even their kind have to

follow the rules of a séance. Now back to the instructions."

Remington glanced at the instructions. They were written in English and in Spanish. "Are their kind dangerous or just ornery?"

"Who?"

"The mayhem ghosts."

"Both."

Remington shivered. She'd never done well with being scared. As much as she loved watching old movies, she made it a point not to do scary.

Even *Ghostbusters* gave her nightmares.

Exhaling her anxiety, she read the WHAT YOU'LL NEED column part of the instruction sheet. "I don't have all this stuff."

Beth picked up a paper sack. "Not a problem. I've gathered everything you need."

Remington didn't reach for the bag. "Did you use a spell to get that here?"

"A tiny one." Beth thrust the bag into her hands. "Now, I can't enter the circle you set up without your permission. Be sure and invite me to the séance. While you're setting up your séance, I have another assignment. I think it's someone who used to live in Knotty. Ta ta."

"Wait. I'm not done talking."

"Honey, I'd love to stay and chat, but I have a job. A murder mystery."

"Where?"

"In the second veil," Beth said. "See ya."

Remington's mouth fell open and a shadow of alarm slipped down her throat and swept through her, leaving a coat of fear everywhere it touched. People were murdered in the second veil? Ghosts murdering ghosts. Sweet Jesus, what veil did you have to make it to before a dead person could just enjoy being dead?

Shutting her mouth to keep any more shadows from journeying through her, she walked into the spare bedroom. When she died, would she get stuck in the second veil? She would if she had unfinished business. God, she needed to get things done. No unfinished business for her.

She dumped the items on the bed. Twenty or more candles appeared to be the main component of setting up a séance, along with fragrant pouches of potpourri. She picked up the instructions and read.

Step number one: Set the intention for the room. This is necessary to keep the crazy out of your séance.

"Wouldn't want crazy in a séance."

Step number two: Do not allow unbelievers in the room when you set the intention. It can weaken the protective circle.

Remington glanced at Max, who lay on the other side of the door, his paws inches away from the threshold. "Don't come in here unless you believe in ghosts."

Max placed a paw over his face and meowed.

Step number three: Remove your shoes and set the candles in the middle of the room.

Remington glanced at her feet. She still didn't have any shoes on.

Step number four: Lower all blinds so that the room

will be completely dark except for the candles.

"Oh great. The woman who's afraid of the dark is going to sit in the dark and invite in ghosts. What in the hell is wrong with this picture?"

She glanced around and surveyed the window situation. The room had one window. No blinds. She took the quilt off the bed and draped it over the curtain rod. That would have to do.

Step number five: Place a bowl in the center of your circle and fill it with sage, cedar, sweet grass and lavender.

"So that's what all the smelly stuff is."

Step number six: Light the mixture in the bowl and let it burn for several minutes.

Step number seven: Blow the fire out. The mix will smolder in the bowl.

Step number eight: Starting in the east corner of the room, pace counter clockwise and chant: 'I banish the way I have been taught by my teacher and his teachers before him. I banish the evil spirits who are lurking and looking for a way into my circle.'

Remington read the verse again, memorizing it, and then crossed her arms and high-stepped around the room, reciting her lines, bobbing her head as she went. Max joined in on the fun and paced behind her, yapping.

Step number nine: Pace clockwise and chant: 'I invite ancestors, guides and angels into this circle.'

She executed a ninety-degree turn that would make a military big-wig proud.

Max fell out of formation and jumped on the hope chest at the foot of the bed.

Why did Remington have to invite in all these

spirits? All she really wanted was Beth and Jason's dad. Should she uninvite the ancestors, guides and angels? Then again, she'd never met an angel. That might be cool.

Step number ten: Light the candles and place pillows around to invite relaxation by those in attendance.

Remington shooed Max off the pillows on top of the hope chest, set them on the floor, and lit the candles, creating a charming, romantic scene.

CHAPTER THIRTY

WHEN HIS KNOCK WENT UNANSWERED, Jason let himself into Remington's house. In his hand, her pink lace bra. He'd discovered the frilly garment abandoned on the bathroom floor. His mission—force her to hear him out.

His mission came to a halt when he found Remington in Beth's old bedroom.

Her head bobbed to music he couldn't hear as she walked in a circle, her knees practically touching her chest with each step.

"What's all this?"

Remington yelped and swirled. She placed a hand over her heart. "Holy snot, you scared me."

"Sorry about that." He resisted an urge to storm her personal space and yank her into his arms. His body ached for contact with her curves.

"I'm setting up a séance." She took a deep breath and exhaled slowly. "I thought you were an early guest."

He laughed.

She didn't.

He gulped. "Are you having Ruby Rae and Sara Ann over for an afternoon of ghost stories and wine before you leave town?"

"Why aren't you at your house with Gnat-Brain?"

"She's gone." He ran his hand through his hair. "Why did Linny leave?" He didn't really want to ask the question. He didn't want to care. But God help him, he had to know.

"None of your business."

Fair enough. "Are you really setting up a séance?"

She rolled her eyes, motioned to the séance circle. "Can you think of another reason for all of this stuff?" Her tone added the, *well duh*—her tongue didn't.

He pinched the bridge of his nose. This wasn't going the way he'd planned. "Do you believe in this stuff?"

"What do you think?" She picked up a sheet of paper off the bed and read. "In fact, we should leave while the room marinates." She folded the sheet and placed it on the dresser before walking to him. She put her hands on his chest and pushed. "Let's get out of here."

He didn't budge. "We need to talk."

"I can't think of one thing we need to say that hasn't been said." Their bodies were close, and he could feel her tenseness. See the storm clouds in her eyes.

"I can."

Seconds stretched into almost minutes.

She pursed her lips and pointed to a pillow on the floor. "You have five minutes. And take your shoes off before you come in. This is a sanctioned séance room." The stiffness in her voice told him she was holding back. Not blurting thoughts.

He toed his shoes off and stepped through the doorway. "What's all that stuff you burned in the bowl?"

Remington picked up the paper, cleared her throat and read. "They are the ingredients used to ethereally cleanse a space. The cedar cleans the room, the sage brings clarity to the room, the lavender and sweet grass bring beauty to the room."

He stepped up to her and took the paper. He read the first line. "How to Host a Séance." He raised a brow. "Did you get this off the internet?" It was a joke meant to make her laugh.

Her gaze narrowed. "Beth gave it to me." Her face showed no signs of the whole thing being a practical joke. None.

He didn't believe her. Couldn't believe her. He tossed the paper onto the bed. "This wouldn't be a prank would it?" He reached out and cupped the curve of her face and was pleasantly startled when she didn't immediately yank away. The softness of her skin filled his thoughts with things other than séances and ghosts.

"Whatever."

"The guys put you up to this?" The pad of his thumb rhythmically rubbed her jaw.

She stepped back and took a seat on a pillow. "Why are you here?"

He dropped to a pillow, grabbed both of her hands and gently squeezed. Their eyes met. What he saw caused him pain. "I'm sorry about this morning."

"Is she really your fiancée?"

He leaned back, using the bed as his backrest. He stretched his legs out in front of him. Crossing his feet at the ankles. Stalling while his mind floundered. "It's not a simple yes/no answer." What could he tell her that wouldn't be a lie?

She made a strangled noise. "I'll take that as a yes."

"What if I told you I agreed to something for reasons I can't explain?"

She shook her head. "I don't know the answer to that. Because I don't know what game you're playing."

Neither did he. "Have you ever spoken to a spirit?"

"It's important to create a room where ugly spirits won't like the space," she said.

"You didn't answer my question."

She gave him a look of exasperation. "As a matter of fact, I have. Would you like for me to channel your dad?"

He jerked. "Hell no. Why would you even ask me that?"

She looked away. "Didn't you say he died without telling you how to find your mom?"

"So?"

"If we talked to him, he could tell you where to find her." Her voice was different. Like she'd flipped on her autopilot switch and emotions weren't allowed.

"I don't believe in that shit."

Other than a pulse beating by Remington's right

eye, she showed no signs of aggravation. "You should believe in that shit. In fact, before you came, I invited in some guides, ancestors and angels."

He considered her words and their ring of truth. His gaze swept the room, the candles, the pillows, the darkened window. The pungent smell of burnt incense tickled his nose as he inhaled. Finally, he turned his attention to her. She reminded him of a proud winter rose. One that had been hailed on. Lost most of its petals. But still stood tall. Regally daring anyone to comment. He humored her. "Are they here yet?"

"Not yet."

The hairs on the back of his neck twitched, and he thought he heard a noise. He refused to look around. The imagination was a powerful thing. "While we wait, why don't we finish what we started last night?" The question was out before he could censor the words or class them up.

"I don't have sex with another woman's man."

"I'm not her man yet." He stood and stripped out of his shirt as his eyes raked boldly over her. The long length of her bare legs. The soft slope of her neck. "We've been talking about marriage, but I haven't actually asked her." Damn Bernie and her blackmail.

"Stop getting undressed. We're not having sex."

He unbuttoned his jeans. He was tired of holding back what he wanted to say. "I think I might be falling for you."

"You think?" The color drained from her face. She took a step back. "When you fall for someone,

you won't have to think about it." She held up a
hand to keep him at a distance. "Let me help you
out. You're not falling for me. I'm simply the girl
you want to scratch an itch with before you get
married."

And that's what you call having your heart handed
back to you. Served him right. He was supposed to
be getting her out of town. Not declaring feelings.
"Let's say you're right. Are you saying you don't
want to finish what we started last night? You don't
want that memory?"

She gazed at him through lowered lashes. Her
nostrils flared, and she bit her bottom lip. Blinked
several times. Then she closed her eyes and sighed.
"Of course, I want to finish what we started last
night."

"Me too." He pulled her into his arms. "Me too."
His hand went to her neck, traced the jumpy muscles, felt the rapid beat of her pulse. He inhaled her
lemony fragrance.

"You're a conundrum," she whispered against his
chest.

He kissed the top of her head. "How's that?"

"You confuse me."

He cupped her head in his hands and tilted it for
better access. "Then it's time we stopped talking."
His tongue caressed the seam of her lips, while one
hand slid down her back to her ass and pulled her
tightly against him. Against his erection.

She gasped, allowing his tongue the opportunity
to enter her mouth.

He laid her back on the quilt and deepened the

kiss. Alternating between sucking on her bottom lip and tangling with her tongue.

They both moaned as their bodies pushed for more intimacy.

Jason couldn't remember the last time he'd felt such desire for a woman. Such a need to make sure it was perfect. He didn't want her to ever want another man in her life. Which made him an ass because as much as he might want to, he couldn't keep her.

He had to push her away. Push her out of Knotty.

Remington was lost in the sensation of Jason sucking on her lip. It felt like a direct connection to her girly parts. Like each suck was in fact his mouth on that most sensitive part of a woman's body. She arched up, wanting more. Her hands roamed down his back, intent on pulling him closer.

He laughed and pulled back. Ending the kiss.

Her eyes widened. "Did you change your mind?" One of them should change their mind. Do the right thing. It wasn't going to be her.

"Hell no," he said with such conviction she grinned. "But I think we need to get a little more comfortable."

"That's not a bad idea." She pushed the guilt to the back of her mind. For once, she was going to be bad.

He stood, moved Max from the foot of the bed, set him on the floor. He arranged the candles to the side, giving a soft glow to the room. He stretched out beside her. His lips found hers in another gentle but thorough kiss that left them both breathless.

When he lifted his lips, she murmured. "We shouldn't be in here. It'll cause bad Karma. Maybe we should go into my bedroom."

"We're fine right where we are."

She lifted a hand and skimmed her fingers through his hair, enjoying the sexy texture. "I've never run my fingers through your hair."

"I'm glad you've remedied that oversight." He slid his palm over her face, behind her head, and tugged her into his embrace.

She heard herself whimper. The emotions were so powerful, practical thoughts weren't able to invade her brain.

Jason's tongue became rough and invasive, demanding she allow it to explore her own tongue in an intimate dance. A dance that felt like sex.

She didn't believe in what they were doing. Sure, he wasn't married yet, which some would say meant he was still fair game. But she'd never adhered to that line of thought. Then again, was there a rule that said she had to believe in everything she did? Couldn't she do something regardless of her beliefs? If her dog could act like a cat, couldn't she act like a hussy just once in her life?

Jason's breaths were ragged, and when his gaze met hers, a glaze of hunger—or it might have been panic—dyed his eyes a muddy brown.

She trembled, understanding panic. Panic stole your breath. Caused fear to block your airways.

"I need more than a kiss," he warned.

She nodded.

He raised her into a sitting position and yanked her T-shirt over her head. The cool air caressed her skin, and she trembled. He leaned forward and kissed the valley between her breasts, his unshaven face rough on her soft skin. She moaned.

This was sex. Pure sex.

Her one-night stand was going to happen in the middle of the afternoon with a dozen inches of snow on the ground.

When he moved back, he glanced drunkenly at her breasts. "Beautiful." With one hand, he reached out and gently circled the dark peak of one nipple. He rubbed it between his thumb and forefinger, pinching it gently as he did.

Remington groaned and leaned deeper into his palm. She wanted more than the gentle touch. She wanted him to cup her breast, squeeze and massage it. The heat between her legs at a feverish pitch. "More."

He bowed his head and licked the rock-hard nipple.

She placed her hands on the back of his head and pushed his face into her breast.

He opened his mouth and suckled the nipple, drawing a gasp from her. When he stopped and blew on it, the sensation of cool air against the hot pebble drove her crazy.

Her legs clamped together on the desire riding there. Remington played with her other nipple, tugging and massaging.

He took her hand and moved it above her head.

"That's my job." He leaned forward and captured the nipple between his lips.

Remington raised her hips and pressed them into his. He wore too many clothes. She wanted him naked. She wanted her one-night stand like a junkie wants a hit.

As if he could read her mind, he let go of her hands. He stood and slipped out of his jeans. His erection called out to her, the magnitude of its size causing her breath to catch in the back of her throat. Just as it had last night. She wanted to touch it, to stroke it, to taste it, to feel it.

"I was jealous as hell watching you walk away with Linny wearing nothing but my T-shirt." He went down on his knees and spread her legs. "Wondering if he was going to discover you were pantiless."

"He didn't."

"Thank you." His voice hitched.

Jason lay stretched out with his hands above his head and watched Remington. She straddled him, and her body writhed in a dance of pleasure. He was a lost man. This wasn't just a good fuck. This wasn't just any woman.

There was something about her, about the way he breathed around her, that was different. He wanted to pleasure her like no man had ever pleasured her before or ever would again. He grabbed her hand and pulled her down to him. God, he wanted to love her.

Remington laughed. "You're thinking. Don't think. Just do."

Just do. He wanted to romance her and show her this wasn't just sex to him.

He would take what they had at this moment and walk away with the memory.

With the decision made, he grabbed his pants and yanked a condom out of his pocket. After slipping it on, he then lowered himself over her and entered her with a force he didn't try to control.

"Oh, God yes," she whimpered and wrapped her legs around him. Her body met his with the enthusiasm of a woman living only for the moment.

"Easy, or I'm going to lose it." Never had it felt so right to be inside a woman.

"Just fuck me," she whispered in his ear. "No strings attached. No broken promises. No stolen money."

His mouth found hers, and their tongues warred with one another as he fucked her to a tempo better suited to a race track or a rock concert. Their bodies grew sweaty and slid enticingly against one another. Their breathing labored and noises filled the room with their desire.

Her moans, mixed with his, were all the words they spoke. When she exploded, he heard her scream echo around the room. Only, it wasn't an echo. It was his groan of release.

He collapsed next to her, unable to move or talk. His whole body boneless; and he knew for certain, he wanted to do this again—just as soon as his body would let him. Later, he wasn't sure how much later—it might have been moments, it might have been hours—he took her hand and kissed the silver ring she wore on her third finger and then kissed her fingertips.

"Jason, there's something I have to tell you," she whispered.

"What?"

"I—" Her voice died away.

"Yes?" His voice was still thick with desire.

Remington let out an audible sigh. "I'm hosting this séance for your dad."

Jason tried to think of a response, but *what the fuck* seemed ungentlemanly, but oh, so appropriate. He rolled onto his side. With her swollen lips and tangled hair, she looked like a love angel—perfectly sane—not a woman who thought she could talk to ghosts.

She leaned up on one elbow and twirled strands of hair with her other hand. "I know. It sounds crazy. It probably is. But here's the thing. Beth is a ghost. I see her and talk to her." Her eyes searched his face, as if trying to read his thoughts.

He hoped like hell she couldn't. "Is she here now?"

"No."

"I see." Even to his own ears, he sounded patronizing, so he wasn't surprised when she flushed.

"But I can call for her, and she'll come."

His lips twitched. He'd completely, one hundred percent, fallen for a crazy chick. "How long have you been seeing her?"

"I saw her for the first time the night I moved

in." The expression in her eyes seemed to plead with him to believe, to trust her words.

"I see." The politically correct answer of the moment.

"If only you did see—her, that is—this would all be so much easier." Her curt tone reminded him of a school librarian. A sexy school librarian reprimanding him for bad manners.

He decided to suspend disbelief for a moment. "What does my father have to do with Beth?"

"She's stuck in the second veil until she finishes some unfinished business. In the meantime, she's a fixer of sorts for the second veil. Her first job is to help a guy who was murdered discover who murdered him."

"What a crock. He died of a heart attack. You know that. I told you that." His mind burned with the memory of his dad ordering his mom out of their house and never to return. On that day, his hate for his father had been born, and it hadn't died when his father died.

She reached out and laid her hand on his arm. "I cast a spell on you that caused his heart attack."

He grabbed her hand, rolled onto his back and pulled her down so she was lying in the crook of his arm. "If this is all a big joke created by Kevin and Maverick, I'm going to kick their asses."

A biting wind entered the room, causing them to both gasp. It whipped around the bed, around them, and flew over the candles until their flames were nothing but smoke.

CHAPTER THIRTY-ONE

REMINGTON PUSHED OUT OF JASON'S arms. Sat up and scooted back until she had the safety of the headboard to lean against. Jason sat up with her, and she pulled the covers up around them.

The wind died, and an image began to materialize from the black bluster.

Remington breathed in sharply and tightened her grip on the top quilt. She moved her leg so that it touched Jason's, making him her security-blanket. *Damn it.* She saw something forming in front of her but couldn't make it out.

"You must be Remington."

As the image became clearer to her, she saw a man with Jason's brown eyes. But his voice wasn't deep and sexy like Jason's. It was old, ragged, yet full of charisma. Like a televangelist preacher on the verge of retiring.

Remington nodded, grabbed her T-shirt, held the quilt over herself and tugged it on. Oh shit, oh shit, oh shit, she mouthed to herself. "Jason, I think your dad's here."

She heard Jason curse. Not like a sailor curse. Far worse than a sailor. Like a mother whose child was being threatened.

Remington poked her head out from under the quilt. She wasn't even sure she knew all the words. Some of them sounded foreign.

Jason threw back the covers, stood, reached for his jeans, and pulled them on. "I'm out of here." His features were frozen granite.

Remington squeaked and pulled the covers back up around herself. "Would you hand me those sweats hanging on the back of the door before you run away?" She didn't need a spirit seeing her naked. Especially, Jason's dad.

He tossed them to her. "I'm not running from anything."

"Prove it. Don't go." She went under the covers and wiggled into her sweats. Fully dressed, she popped her head out. "Listen to what he has to say." She didn't want Jason to storm out of here thinking she was a flake.

Jason slammed his hand against the wall. "Why should I? Give me one good reason." His voice held a silken thread of warning.

"Because I asked."

He fisted his hands. "I'll give you five minutes."

Remington turned to the man in the room. "What's your name?"

"Robert Hart." He took a seat at the edge of the bed.

Max growled from the living room. His meow gone.

"Okay, Robert Hart, what would you like for me to tell your son?"

"Tell him I love him."

"He said to tell you he loves you."

Jason stood rigid in the doorway of the room. "Okay. Got it. Are we done here?"

"Tell him to sit down," Robert Hart said.

Remington raised her eyebrows at Jason's dad. "Are you sure you want me to tell him that?"

"Tell me what?"

"Tell him we need to talk about his Knotty project."

"He wants you to sit down, and he wants to talk to you about Knotty."

Jason's eyes widened and a pulse in his neck became visible. "What about it?"

Remington tore her gaze from Jason's and glanced at his dad.

Robert's face wore a mask of bitterness. "I tried to sabotage your project so you would have to come to work with me."

Remington told Jason what his father said.

Jason paled. "Bernadette called and told you that, didn't she? You're just playing me," he accused Remington.

"No." Why in the hell would Gnat-Brain call and tell her that? "I—"

"Stop it," Robert Hart boomed.

Damn it. She wished Jason would sit beside her and protect her.

Jason gave her a funny look. "What happened?"

"Your dad yelled, and it startled me."

"Ask him where Mom is."

"The detective I hired to find her couldn't,"

Robert Hart told Remington.

Remington told Jason.

"Where did he look?" Jason raked his hand down the side of his face and loudly exhaled.

Remington turned to Robert for the answer. Being a medium, relaying bad news to people she cared about, sucked. "He said everywhere. He's had detectives looking for her for twenty years."

Remington didn't care for Robert Hart.

Jason strolled across the room and sat on the edge of the dresser. "Let's say for a moment I believe this nonsense. What does he expect me to do—forgive him?"

Robert Hart smiled like he'd won a hard-fought battle. "Ask him to keep looking for his mother."

"He wants you to find your mother."

"So, this is all about what he wants. What he needs." Jason spoke passionately.

Robert sighed. "That's part of my unfinished business. I have to make amends by bringing him and his mother back together. At least that's what I think my unfinished business is."

Beth wasn't the only one with unfinished business. Remington relayed the message.

"Are you sure you didn't have her killed, and you just don't want to admit it?"

"I didn't have the mother of my child killed," Robert Hart yelled. He began fading in and out. Like he was short-circuiting.

Remington repeated the words to Jason.

Jason pinched the bridge of his nose. "Ask him if he knows where I should start looking?"

Robert shook his head. "I don't know."

"He doesn't remember. But to be fair, Beth has holes in her memory as well."

Jason sighed in exasperation. "Remington, I'm done with the charades."

She turned to Robert Hart. "You heard him." Much to her amazement, Jason's dad disappeared the moment she said the words, and the pressure in her chest vanished.

But then three new ghosts appeared, and the pressure was back. "Who are you?"

"Mother," one of them whispered, before all three disappeared again.

Remington took a deep breath and blew it out hard. Had she heard right? "Jason, I'm not sure, but I think…your mother just appeared. A tall woman with long flowing black hair and a beautiful smile. All she said was *mother*."

Jason rolled his eyes. "First you try to tell me you can talk to Dad. Now, you're trying to tell me Mom is dead?"

Remington bit her bottom lip. "I'm not sure. There were three. The other two didn't speak."

He gave a nasty laugh. "Isn't that convenient? You haven't told me a damn thing that was straight up. All riddles. Get them all back. Let me ask them the hard questions."

"Ghosts, come back," Remington said. None appeared. "Ghosts come back," she said again. Nothing. Damn it. "I don't know how to get them—"

A cold blast entered the room, settling on Remington, blocking her vision. She shoved at the heaviness. Oh, holy snot. This was bad. It didn't move. It didn't budge. Something wasn't right. The weight wasn't the same as it had been with the other spirits. Wasn't the same temperature. The spirit sitting on her felt agitated. Panicked. She heard a clacking noise like the sound of keys bouncing off of one another. Were they lost keys symbolizing lost souls? Were lost souls sitting on her chest? "What is it?" she asked Jason. "Can you see it? Get it off of me."

Evil spirits must have crashed her séance. Damn it, she knew having sex in here had been a bad idea.

Jason didn't speak. He looked at her as if she'd grown two extra heads.

The music from Frank Sinatra's hit "New York, New York" rang out in the room. Then the force left.

Remington fell against the wall and slid to the floor. She curled into a fetal position. "Did you hear that?" Goosebumps covered her body, and she shivered, her teeth chattering.

"Hear what?" Jason came to her, laid beside her, and pulled her into his arms. "Are you okay?" He rubbed his hands up and down her arms helping warmth to spread through her.

"You didn't hear 'New York, New York' playing?"

"No."

Remington rubbed her temples. "I think a spirit was telling me not to go to New York."

He looked skeptically at her. "Did the spirit happen to say why?"

She closed her eyes. Replaying the moment. "I just heard the music, and that is the thought that popped into my mind."

"Sweetheart, I know you think you can speak to ghosts, but this is ridiculous. Mom isn't dead. Dad didn't come and speak to me through you. You weren't told to stay away from New York."

"How do you know?" She opened her eyes.

"Beth wasn't here in this room when all this rubbish happened. You just imagined all of this, because you're tired and you're traumatized by what Bernadette said to you."

"I'm not bothered by her." Which wasn't true, but not the point at all. "You have to believe me. I spoke to the spirits. They told me what I told you."

"You've had a rough childhood. You're getting things confused. You're not able to separate your life from make-believe."

She wrapped her arms around her stomach. "Are you calling me a crazy orphan?"

He took a moment to reply. "I'm just saying you might need help."

"Fuck you." She yanked out of his arms and put space between them. "I don't need you or your opinion. And don't worry. I'm leaving for New York. That should make you happy. Now, you can stay here in the little town you're going to build, and you can fuck yourself into an early grave with no worries of the crazy orphan getting in your way."

"Don't be so—"

"Beth. I did it," she yelled, interrupting him.

"They talked. I'm leaving now."

Beth didn't respond. Remington glanced at Jason. Knew he was going to ridicule her because Beth didn't answer.

Jason's eyes were closed. "Is she here?" he asked wearily. "Can you see her? Let me ask her a question. One I know you wouldn't know the answer to."

Remington's anger smoldered. She ought to just punch him in the nose. "Beth, can you hear me? Jason wants to ask you a question."

"I'm here." Beth glared at Remington.

Why was she pissed? She has no right to be pissed. "Where did you go?" Remington asked her. "Did you hear the ghosts I spoke to?"

Beth's ears turned bright red. "I didn't hear any of it. *You* forgot to invite me in. Remember, I told you I'm not allowed in a séance unless I'm invited."

Remington's mouth went dry. Her anger dissipated. "Oh. Sorry about that. Anyway, Jason has a question he wants to ask you."

"I can't answer any questions for Jason. My job was to tell his father who murdered him. Did you tell him?"

Remington tried to think. She couldn't remember. "I told Jason."

"Close enough. Now, I can't have any more communication with his dad. If I do, I'll be stuck in this veil for a very long time for breaking my contract."

Jason stood and walked to the window, pulled the quilt back and glanced out. "Ask her where I hide the passwords for all of my accounts."

"You told Beth where you hide your passwords for your accounts? Why?"

"Just ask her the question."

"You heard," she said to Beth. "Where does he hide his passwords?"

Beth looked at her, despair shining in her eyes. "I'm sorry, Remington. I can't help you."

Remington sighed. She really hated rules. "She won't tell me. It's breaking the rules if she continues to speak to you."

Jason lifted an eyebrow. "That's a bit inconvenient. For you." He dropped the blanket and walked to the side door that led to the back porch off of the bedroom and jiggled the knob. "Did you know this door isn't locked? You should keep it locked." He flipped the switch.

Who gives a fuck about the door? "I'm telling you the truth. Since you're so sure I'm a wacko, why don't you go home? Leave me alone. And leave my door alone. It's none of your fucking business which doors I leave locked or unlocked in this house."

"You're right. It isn't." He unlocked the door.

"Just go."

He rubbed a hand down his cheek. "Remington, the sex was great."

"If that's your idea of pillow talk, it's a little too late."

"It was the best I've ever had is what I'm trying to say. You're great."

"Can I move straight into your New York condo,

or do I need to get a place for a while?" There. That should show him she didn't give two cents about him or his opinion of their sex.

He took a set of keys out of his jean pockets. Pulled one off. "This is the key to my condo." He pulled a card out of his billfold and handed it to her. "This is the address and a phone number. When you get there, call… Let me know you made it safely."

He stood at the door and looked at her expectantly.

She said nothing. She couldn't.

"I will miss you." Long and Lanky turned and sauntered out of her life as casually as he had sauntered into it.

Remington sat very still until she heard the front door close. He was gone. For good this time. He wouldn't come back. They'd finished what they'd started. Now it was over.

One-by-one, tears rolled down her cheeks. She wiped at them.

Why had her best friend had to die so young?

Why hadn't her parents loved her enough to keep her?

The tears increased.

She cried for Johnny B. He would grow up thinking she hadn't loved him enough.

But she didn't cry for Jason. She wouldn't cry for him. Thank God her heart was hexed.

CHAPTER THIRTY-TWO

R EMINGTON WOKE UP STILL LYING on the floor in her séance room. She rubbed her eyes and glanced around. The room was dark, probably because the quilt still hung over the window.

How did a scaredy cat fall asleep in a ghost room? Had any watched her sleep? She shivered at the spine-chilling thought.

She stood, her legs shaky, and hurried out of the room, firmly closing the door, not wanting any goblins to follow her. She went into her bedroom. She should be happy to leave Knotty. Happy to pursue her dream designing costumes for Broadway plays.

Strange as it sounded, she wasn't. She'd grown quite fond of the town over the last several months. And Ruby Rae and Sara Ann. And of course, the guys. And she sort of liked casting spells. When they worked.

She yanked her suitcase out from under the bed. It was as battered as her. She often wondered where all it had traveled to before she'd bought it at a secondhand shop. She liked to think it had been to the moon and back.

She went to the closet, pulled sweaters off the top rack, and tossed them into the open suitcase. One got stuck. The more she pulled, the more it stretched. "Crap." She marched into the kitchen and got a chair, placed it in front of the closet and used it as a footstool.

The sleeve was latched on the knob of a tiny door. A secret door. With hinges. She grinned. She loved secret doors. There'd been a secret door in a movie she'd watched lately. What movie had that been?

She tugged on the knob, and the door opened, making a creepy, creaking noise. Like a horror movie creaking noise. Remington shivered.

Taking a deep breath, she looked inside the wall—hoping like Hades she didn't find something deader than a ghost. Something like a body part waiting to be discovered, a severed thumb, tongue, lucky rabbit's foot.

A secret drawer was built into the wall. A safe deposit box with an opened lock dangling from it. Remington reached inside and pulled out the dusty container. She held her breath and opened the treasure chest. Inside, she found a skeleton key and a picture of herself and Beth. She exhaled in relief and laughed. She had a matching one in her billfold. Nothing sinister.

Under the picture was a wad of one-hundred-dollar bills. Had Beth robbed a bank and stashed the loot here? Was that why she was stuck in the second veil? Remington set down the box and groped inside the hidden cubbyhole. Her hand came in contact with something. She pulled it out. A journal. A fat journal. She reached farther back and grasped several more journals. Not as fat as the first journal. Almost petite in comparison. She flipped the journals over, face up. The fat journal had Beth's handwriting on the front.

It said, *The first day of the rest of my life. By Beth Henderson.*

Remington smiled. "Beth, I've found your journals." She pulled them out and climbed down. She plopped two pillows against the headboard, settled in, and opened the one with the earliest date using the skeleton key in its tiny lock. "If you can hear me, come read them with me."

Max, thinking she was talking to him, climbed up the doggie stairs and burrowed under a blanket at the foot of the bed.

Remington rubbed Max with her toes. "I wasn't talking to you, but I guess—"

Beth appeared at the foot of the bed, cutting off Remington's words. She sat down on Max, causing the dog to growl and Beth to jump in fright.

Remington giggled. She didn't know ghosts could be frightened.

Beth looked under the blanket at Max. "Sorry about that." Then, she scooted to the head of the bed. "I can't believe you found them. I'd forgotten about them." Beth picked one up and ran a hand lovingly over its leather cover, *seventh grade* written on the front of the book.

There was a journal for each grade level starting in seventh. "I'm glad my sweater got snagged, or I'd never found them."

Beth rubbed both hands together like an eager addict. "I bet they'll have a clue as to what my unfinished business is." Her eyes shined with excitement. She dropped the journals onto Remington's lap and settled in against the pillows next to her.

Remington frowned. "I wish you could just go to New York with me instead of crossing over." She shifted a bit so they both had half the pillow behind their backs.

"If I don't cross over, you have to promise to come back and visit me." Today Beth wore military fatigues. On her feet were pink ballerina slippers.

"I'll do my best." Remington handed the journal, with *the first day of the rest of my life* written on it, to Beth.

Beth pushed the book away, an expression of panic on her face. "You read. I'll listen."

Remington shrugged. "Okay. Here we go.

Dear Journal:

Shit. Today I found out I have breast cancer. Stage four. It's so unfair. I eat right. I exercise. I go in for my yearly mammograms, pap smears, and dermatologist checks. WTF? Did I piss God off somewhere along the way and not know it? I feel like I need to look up toward heaven and pray, "Are you there God, it's me, Beth Henderson. WTDF? The D stands for double. "

Or did my fiancée do something that pissed Him off, and God's killing me as revenge? If I break off the engagement, will I have a miracle cure?

Obviously, miracle cure or not, I can't marry Carver. It

wouldn't be fair. He wants children and happiness. All I can give him is doctor bills and sadness. I'll have to break things off with him in a way he doesn't suspect the truth. If he knows I'm going to die from cancer, he'll insist on sticking around and watching me die. He's that nice of a guy. I can't stand the thought of that. It will be better this way. I just have to find the courage to do what has to be done.

"You were engaged?" Remington asked Beth, deciding not to tackle the whole idea of God killing her because of a he-was-mad-at-her-fiancé hang-up.

Beth laid her head on Remington's shoulder. "Yes," she said in a dreamy tone. "Maximus Carver Smith, the Third."

When Beth didn't offer any more information, Remington continued reading.

Dear Journal:

It's two in the morning, and I can't sleep. I have the perfect plan to earn Carver's hatred. I'm going to put it into action tomorrow. By this time tomorrow night, he'll despise me. I'll despise me, but I'd despise me more if I was selfish and let him go through this with me. He deserves so much better than a diseased woman. He deserves a reason to fall out of love with me so he can fall in love with someone new.

"Do you remember your plan?"

Beth shook her head. "Not at all."

"*Dear Journal:*

Carver hates me. He walked in on me with another man. I knew he was coming over. I knew it would happen, and he reacted exactly as a man in love should act. I hate myself for causing him such pain, but this way I've given him a reason to fall out of love with me, and he'll be free to fall in love with someone else. Someone with a life expectancy longer than six months."

Remington wasn't sure what to say. She wanted to say, *what the hell. You slept with another man when you were engaged.* But the poor girl was dead. It didn't seem too nice to rag on her about the decisions she'd made when she was alive.

Beth, who'd been very quiet, suddenly sat up and glanced at Remington with an expression of hurt. "You think it was the wrong thing to do."

It wasn't a question. She'd read Remington's mind. "Of course, I think it was wrong to have an affair while engaged to another man."

"No, it wasn't like that. The other man was a friend of mine studying to be an actor. I hired him to act the part. I needed Carver to stop loving me."

"Did it work? Did he stop loving you?"

Beth pulled on her ear, deep in thought. "I just remember him looking at me with a blank expression. His beautiful blue eyes naked of emotion. I don't remember him actually saying anything. He just turned and left. He didn't slam the door. Just shut it very carefully."

"Wow. I can't imagine how that must have felt to you. To love someone enough to set them free from their love of you."

"I think I cried a lot. A whole lot. I think I whispered *I love you Carver* into the universe when I died."

"Was there anyone with you when you died?"

"Jason. I was in the hospital. My parents were out of the country. I didn't tell you or them."

"We would have come. We would have held your hand. We would have been there for you. You should have let us in."

"I know. I just…for some reason, at the time, it felt like the right thing to do. I know now it wasn't. But after I hurt Carver, I just couldn't bear to see that kind of hurt on the face of anyone else I loved."

"Tell me about Carver."

"Oh, he is so sweet. Three years older than me. Charming, happy-go-lucky, handsome. Everything you could want in a husband or father for your children. His plans were to open a unique line of coffee shops called Drunken Coffee. He'd served spiked coffees after dark."

"Have you seen him since you've been dead?"

"He doesn't live in my jurisdiction."

They both sat quietly, internalizing their feelings. Finally, Remington picked up the journal and continued reading.

"Dear Diary:

I've moved back to my hometown. I thought it would make me happy, but it doesn't. It's such a sad place. No one lives here. By the way, no miracle cure. I'm still dying. It must be me God's mad at. I wonder if it's because I prayed no one would adopt Remington when we were in school."

Remington stopped reading. She didn't look at Beth. They should talk about this.

"Are you mad at me?"

"Do you think it was because of your prayers I wasn't adopted? Or do you think there was something wrong with me? Something that made me not good enough?"

"It had to be my prayers, because you were perfect. Everyone loved you. You always made the teachers laugh, and they talked about what a breath of fresh air you were."

"I think they just said those things to try and make me feel better, because I didn't have family."

"You know there might be another reason you weren't ever adopted."

"What other reason would there be?"

"Well, I don't know for sure, but the other night I was playing dress up in Sara Ann and Ruby Rae's attic, and I overheard them talking. One of them mentioned a rumor about how those who wanted to adopt you weren't allowed to."

"That's ridiculous. Who wouldn't want me to get adopted?"

"I don't know. And they didn't talk about it very long. But you never know."

"Yeah. You never know. Shall I continue with your diary?"

"Sure."

Remington picked up the diary and turned the page.

I have a neighbor who I think I will like. He's a bit horn-doggish, probably due to the hex on the town, but I bet he'll cool his jets when he discovers I'm dying. I'm thinking about calling Remington, but something tells me that would be selfish. It would be better if she just finds out after I'm dead. It won't save her the pain of my being dead, but it'll save her the pain of watching me die.

Remington reached out and laced her fingers with Beth's, surprised when they didn't slip through air. She blinked away the tears hovering on her lashes. "You should have called me."

"Maybe."

Dear Diary:

My neighbor is nice. He stayed with me the other night when I was throwing up, and we talked. I told him all about Remington.

Beth knew all of her secrets up to the point they went their separate ways for college. How many of them had she shared with Jason?

Dear Diary:

My to do before I die list: 1. Have a candlelit dinner with a dashing, debonair dastardly man. 2. Skinny dip. 3. Try to find Remington's parents—

Beth sat up straight. "Ooh, I forgot about that. I did try to find your parents."

Remington's heart flooded with hope. "Did you find them?"

Beth fell back onto the pillows. "I don't remember. Keep reading."

CHAPTER THIRTY-THREE

JASON WAS HALF-CRAZY WITH EMOTION. He didn't believe in gray. Things were black or white. Right or wrong. You either kept a promise or you didn't. You practiced honesty or you were a liar. You were sane or you were insane. You believed in ghosts, or you didn't. He didn't. Which left only one conclusion he could draw about Remington. She was crazy.

Sure, she was also sexy and fun and smart and passionate and kind. But he'd be lying to himself if he didn't add crazy. She thought she could talk to ghosts. There wasn't a gray answer. Ghosts didn't exist.

Dad wasn't stuck in some second veil dying to make amends with him, and Mom wasn't a ghost. To believe that would be to... His shoulders drooped. He couldn't even give a name to what it would be. Mom had to be alive.

Knotty obviously wasn't a healthy place for Remington. She needed to leave town and stay gone for more than just her physical safety. Beth had also believed in ghosts. But she hadn't gone around reporting conversations with them. It was best Remington left today.

He walked to his liquor cabinet and poured a shot of whiskey and downed it. In a few hours, Remington would be out of his life. This is the way it had to be.

Remington took a sip of hot tea and then continued to read Beth's diary.

Dear Diary:

Tonight, Jason and I talked for a long time. He is so anti-marriage. I guess after hearing his story, I can't say I blame him. His mom and dad's marriage was a shambles. She abandoned Jason. She told Jason she'd come back and get him someday, but she never did. Can't say I blame him for not believing in happy ever after. Just like I can't blame Remington for never feeling lovable. The two of them certainly have trust issues in common. It kills me I can't fix either of their problems. All I can do is hope someday they find true love and take a chance.

Beth made a noise of distress. "I don't remember him telling me that. I'm sure it's true or I wouldn't have written it down, but I don't remember it. Why can't I remember it?"

Remington patted her on the knee. "When you talk to the other ghosts, do they have holes in their memories?"

"I don't know. I've never asked them. It's embarrassing to admit you can't remember your own life."

"You should ask. I bet it's completely normal."

"Maybe. Keep reading."

Dear Diary,

Today, I wrote my will. I'm debating on what I should tell Remington. Or if I should tell her anything. I'm going to write her a letter and ask her to come home to Knotty. I want her to live here and grow roots. If she goes to New York, she will always be an orphan. She won't surround herself with people who love her. She'll always be running and hiding from life.

Remington elbowed Beth. "What does that mean?"

"I thought if you came here first, you'd let the town adopt you, and you'd stay with your new family and stop living the life of a cynic."

"Cynical is good when you're an orphan. It protects you. Besides, Jason's made it clear he doesn't want me to stay in Knotty. He thinks I'm bat-shit crazy."

"His wants are immaterial. Keep reading. Let's see what I found out about your parents."

Remington kept reading the journal, although her throat was crammed so full of feelings her voice had to maneuver around them before words could come out. She'd read through several entries that didn't mention her parents and then they were brought up again.

Dear Journal, I wish I hadn't hired the detective to find out more about Remington's parents. It wasn't really any of my business. It was Remington's business. I wonder if she'd want to know…

Remington turned the page, anxious to read more.

I'm not going to tell her. It wouldn't be—

There was a smudge preventing Remington

from reading the last word. How could Beth find out something about her parents and not tell her? What kind of friend did that?

"Oh God, Remington. I'm sorry. I can't believe I didn't write it down or tell you. I don't remember anything about it. I bet that's my unfinished business. If I tell you what I found out, I'll cross over. It has nothing to do with Jason's dad."

Remington tuned her out, took the journal and read the next entry.

Dear Journal, today I'm going to die. I can feel it. Right before I die, I'm going to connect myself to Carver forever by whispering to the universe I love him. That way his memory won't escape me when I'm dead. That's what my grandmother said she did right before her and grandpa died.

Dear Diary, I didn't die yesterday. Not sure why. I could have sworn it was going to happen. Jason has been with me for so long. He's tired. I can tell he's hurting. We just keep talking. I've told him all about Remington, and he's told me so much about his life. It's probably the drugs that I'm on that I think this, but I have this image of him and Remington someday getting married. I told him that, and he scoffed at me. Assured me the day he got married was the day hell would indeed freeze over.

Beth turned the page.

"That's not your handwriting," Remington said.

"I think it's Jason's. He must have written in my journal for me." Her voice cracked.

Remington took the diary and read:

Dear diary, when I woke up this morning, I could hear the death rattle in my breathing. I'm glad that it's about over. I'm ready. When I look in the mirror, I don't see me anymore. I still feel like me on the inside, but the outside is a shamble of who I used to be. Remington, if you're reading this journal, just know how much I love you, and I'm glad we were friends growing up. Remember you are worthy of love.

Remington pressed her fists to her eyes, blocking the tears she wanted to shed. Beth's last entry had been a message to her.

Beth patted her leg. "Do you think your parents died? Do you think that's what I didn't want to tell you? Maybe I saw them as ghosts while I was alive."

Remington dropped her hands and stared at Beth. Tears streamed down both their faces. The mere idea of her parents being dead felt like poison seeping into her stomach. "They're not dead."

"There's an easy way to find out. We can hold another séance. See if either of them is dead, or if someone on the other side knows about them."

Remington shook her head. There had to be a different way to find out. "You're still in contact with your grandmother. Why don't you ask her?"

"It's one of those things she wouldn't be allowed to tell me. Kind of like I wasn't able to answer any of Jason's questions."

Remington stiffened. "He thinks I'm a lunatic. Not that I blame him."

Beth wiped at the tears on her cheeks. "Do you want to hold another séance?"

Remington wished she could wave a wand and make the whole day go away. Did she want to know if her parents were dead? Did she want to lose that little bit of hope of someday finding them? Not really.

But…if one of them was dead, and they came into the séance, she'd at least have a chance to talk to them. That would be a good thing. Wouldn't it? She'd still have the hope of someday finding the other. Unless they were both dead. She released her sucked in cheeks. "Why not?"

What were the chances they were both dead?

CHAPTER THIRTY-FOUR

REMINGTON AND BETH SET UP the séance in the attic. Remington wanted to host the ghost party in the bedroom where the other had taken place, but Beth said the vibes were oddly wrong in there.

"Are you ready?" Beth asked, her tone almost otherworldly.

Am I ready to find out if the parents who left me at an orphanage are dead? Remington rubbed her hands against the goosebumps on her arms. No. She was not ready. Would never be ready. "Yes."

The damp smell of the attic reminded her of a horror-movie set, so when the doorbell rang loudly, she jumped and sneezed and practically had a heart attack. "Shi…shit," she stammered. Everyone in Knotty knocked. She hadn't even known she had a doorbell.

"Are you expecting company?" Beth asked.

"No. Should I ignore them?" Remington walked to the attic's window and glanced out. "I don't see any cars parked out front." The window gave her a clear view into Jason's kitchen. He sat with his elbows on the table, head resting in his hands. What was he thinking?

"Might as well answer the door. We can't be disturbed during the séance. Sudden noises scare spirits away."

Remington carefully back-stepped down the foldable stairs and made her way to the front door.

Ruby Rae and Sara Ann's faces were plastered to the glass screen. They took a step back when they saw Remington. She swung the door open. "Since when do you ring the doorbell?"

"We knocked, and you didn't answer," Sara Ann said.

"Didn't have any choice but ring that damn bell," Ruby Rae added.

"So formal. Hate the thing," complained Sara Ann.

Ruby Rae patted her purple hair. "Makes me feel like a church lady going around inviting people to church events."

Being new to the whole living-in-a-house thing, Remington had never had a church lady come to her house and invite her to anything. She liked the warm sound of it. "I was in the attic."

Ruby Rae's eyes lit up. "What were you doing up there?"

The sound of a door closing drew their attention next door. Jason stood on his front porch in his running gear. "Hi ladies. You're looking beautiful."

Ruby Rae, who wore a loud purple coat and matching gloves, waved. "Where are you off to?"

"I need to blow the cobwebs out of my brain. Thought I'd see if running would get the job done," Jason said. "How about you ladies? What are you up too?"

Sara Ann cleared her throat. "Remington was just about to tell us what she was doing in her attic."

Jason glanced at Remington. Was that speculation in his eyes? Did he assume she was holding another séance? Did he regret kissing her? Afraid he might now have crazy cooties? She raised a hand and gave him a stiff wave. She resisted the urge to lower all but one of her fingers.

He lifted his chin in acknowledgment. "Don't let me keep you from your gossip." He winked at them and then took off running.

"Damn, he's a cute one." Ruby Rae deeply sighed. "If I were twenty years younger, I'd teach him how much fun a cougar can be."

"Remington, what were you doing in the attic?" Sara Ann asked.

"Just looking at stuff," Remington said.

"Stuff?" Ruby Rae echoed.

Remington nodded.

"May we come in?" they both asked at the same time. They whipped off their hats and looked at her with expectant smiles.

Remington's hopes of a hit-and-run food drop-off plummeted. "Is something wrong?" She opened the screen door and forced herself to take a step back so they could enter.

"Not really. More like what's possible," Ruby Rae said.

Sara Ann took off her fashionable black coat and leather gloves and handed them to Remington as she walked in. Ruby Rae did the same with her purple accessories.

"I see. Can I get you something to drink? Some tea?" Remington placed the coats on the back of her couch, which now sat in front of her furnace, and led the ladies into the kitchen.

"We don't want to be a bother," Sara Ann said.

"Oh, you're not."

Sara Ann trailed her hand over the back of a chair. "In that case, sweet tea would be lovely." She glanced at her fingers and then pursed her lips slightly. Had she found dust?

Remington poured the tea and brought it to the kitchen table, where they sat across from one another.

"What brought you out in all this snow?" Remington took a seat at the end of the table.

"We've got some information," Ruby Rae announced.

Gossip? Remington sat back in her chair and crossed her arms. "Spill it. What do you know?"

Ruby Rae clasped her hands together and leaned in slightly, placing her elbows on the table. "Well. I went to the hairdresser this morning just like I do every other Saturday, only I went on two consecutive Saturdays, because my hair wasn't behaving in back."

"That's not true. Her hair was fine. She went so she could try to set Kevin up with that hairdresser of hers, and I told her not to bother. They won't be a good match."

Ruby Rae's eyes shot devil horns at Sara Ann. "Anyway, my hairdresser has some friends who aren't able to have children, and they checked into adoption."

Sara Ann held up a hand, palm facing Ruby Rae.

Ruby Rae sighed loudly. "Now what?"

Sara Ann glared briefly at Ruby Rae before angling her body toward Remington. "Nothing. I'll wait my turn."

Ruby Rae's lips thinned out. "Anyway, the last time I saw him I had told him to tell them about our orphanage and about Johnny B."

Sara Ann turned back around. "Yes. That's true. She did. She came home and told me the day she mentioned all of this to her hairdresser."

Remington smiled and nodded.

"Johnny B is a doll," Sara Ann said, before Ruby Rae could continue. "He reminds me of my nephew when he was that age. Now, he's grown and more adorable than any one child should be allowed."

"Yes well. That's not the point," Ruby Rae said. "The point is, they checked into adopting Johnny B, and they were told he *wasn't* up for adoption."

Sara Ann grabbed Remington's hand. "Have you ever heard of such a thing? We figured since you used to be an orphan, and all, you'd know if that was right or not."

Remington frowned. Very few of the orphans at Knotty had ever gotten adopted. The school kids had always told them it was because they were unlovable. Not unadoptable. "I have no idea why a child wouldn't be allowed to be adopted."

They nodded as if she'd given the correct answer,

and they were pleased. "Well, that's what we thought. And that's what we told them. So, they inquired further," Ruby Rae said.

"And?"

"And, they were told, for now, none of the orphans at Knotty Orphanage were up for adoption. None of them. Don't tell us that's not weird," Sara Ann said.

Remington wasn't an expert on the operation-side of an orphanage. "Maybe since the orphans are being moved to a new location, they've put all adoptions on hold. You know, to allow them time to get over the trauma of moving."

Sara Ann grabbed her other arm and nodded sagely. "I guess that's as good an explanation as we're going to get. For now."

There was a moment of silence.

A moment in which Remington witnessed a change in the two women.

They both scooted their chairs closer to Remington's. As if circling their prey.

Remington stood, knocking her chair over in her haste. She righted it and—

"Why were you in your attic?" Ruby Rae inquired, politeness oozing forth.

Remington looked from one to the other. The glow in their eyes appeared bluish. *Who knew anticipation had a color?* "Noth…nothing important."

"Sweetie, I didn't ask you if it was important," Ruby Rae said in her I-can-be-trusted-with-your-life southern voice.

Sara Ann cleared her throat. "She asked you what

you were doing." Her helpful clarification punctuated the last word as if Remington couldn't
decipher on her own which part of the question
was the most important.

Remington smiled tightly at Sara Ann and made
the mistake of looking Ruby Rae in the eyes. "If
I told you, you wouldn't believe me." The words
were out before she could pull them back in. Shit.
Shit, shit, shit. It was just like when she'd meant
to tell Johnny B no and had said yes instead. That
couldn't be a coincidence. Beth had to be jerking
her vocal strings. Or the mayhem ghosts.

She glanced around for them. Didn't see them.
But that didn't mean they weren't around.

She looked from woman to woman. Two pairs of
eyes stared at her in triumph. They reminded her
of a couple of dogs who wouldn't dream of leaving
a gossip-bone ungnawed.

"Tell us all and don't leave out a thing."

Remington wasn't sure which one spoke. Her
ears were ringing, and blackness was taking over
as a panic attack slammed her. She bent over and
grabbed her knees. Wheezed until one of them
kindly slapped her back as if she were choking.

She coughed. Now, they'd think she was crazy.
Just like Jason thought she was crazy. *Damn it.* She
stood. "I'd prefer showing you."

"Only if you feel like it," cooed Sara Ann.

"We wouldn't want to cause you stress," added
Ruby Rae.

Remington walked to the attic stairs. They were
the type you pulled down from the ceiling when

you needed them and pushed back up when you didn't. Holding the steps steady, she motioned to the ladies, "Go on."

Ruby Rae went first. When her head popped through the attic opening, she exclaimed, "What in the devil's name is all of this?"

"Keep moving up there, so I can see," Sara Ann urged.

They both scrambled through the opening with amazing agility. Remington followed.

They looked at her for an explanation.

"I'm getting ready to host a séance."

Several seconds ticked by with no words.

So much silence. Was she having another panic attack and her hearing wasn't functioning?

"Do you know how to host a séance?" Sara Ann finally asked.

Her ears worked. "I have instructions."

"Have you ever spoken to the dead?" Sara Ann asked.

Ruby Rae remained unusually quiet.

"I've spoken to Beth."

Sara Ann smiled. "I knew she was around. Didn't I tell you she was around?" she said to Ruby Rae. "I told you I heard her voice."

"You hear her?" Remington had never suspected Sara Ann of hearing the dead. Ruby Rae, yes, but not Sara Ann.

"Yes, but I've never seen her."

"Beth, are you here?" Remington called out.

Beth appeared in the attic.

"She's here. Do either of you see her?"

Ruby Rae turned in a circle, peering like an owl into the candle-lit darkness. "I don't see her, but she's standing right here." She walked to a spot and pointed.

Remington laughed. "You're right. How do you know that?"

"I can smell her perfume. The one she wore when she lived."

"Wow, that's amazing. Beth say something."

"Hi ladies, I've missed you."

Ruby Rae grinned. The corners of her lips touching her ears. "Fuck. Did you hear that?" she said to Sara Ann.

"Of course."

"I've missed you, too, little britches." Ruby Rae pulled the collar of her sweatshirt out away from her body and fanned herself.

Remington slumped down onto one of the cushions. Tears ran down her cheeks. *They hear her.* She wasn't losing her mind. Beth was here. *I'm not crazy.* "Would you guys tell Jason?" She glanced from one to the other. "Tell him you believe in ghosts, too, so he won't think I'm crazy."

Their hands covered their mouths. Shock registered on their faces. "Honey," Ruby Rae said, "we'd like to, but when those kinds of words come out of the lips of ladies our age, they think we have dementia or something and start talking about having us placed in a nursing home for our own good. No, this is something we can never share."

Beth stepped up and took Remington's hand. "They're right. People would think they were looney."

Remington nodded. "Of course. But why can they hear you and Jason can't?"

"Because they believe in ghosts. Their third eye is open to the universe."

"Oh." That didn't sound very attractive. Having a third eye.

"Shall we all take a seat?" Beth said.

They all simultaneously sat on the cushions.

"Are there any spirits you want invited in?" asked Beth.

"No, just whoever shows up will be nice," Sara Ann said.

"Do we have to invite someone?" asked Ruby Rae.

"Some spirits are shy. They won't show up unless they've been invited. They don't want to upset their ancestors."

"In that case, I invite in all of my ancestors. They are all welcome to this party," Ruby Rae said and then chuckled. "Even the criminals. And anyone dead that I once knew."

"Okay. I'm going to blow out the candles." Beth blew them out. "Now, close your eyes. Hold your palms up, and we're going to do a few alms."

Beth started the chant, and Remington joined in, followed by the ladies.

"Aaaaahhhhhmmmmmm, aaaaahhhhhhmmmmmm, aaaaahhhhhhmmmmm."

"Remington, I'm turning it over to you. Invite the spirits in?" Beth nudged her in the side.

Remington picked up her cheat sheet and

turned on the miniature flashlight. Squinting, she read, "This circle is protected by the light. By the goodness it represents. The darkness is banned from our circle. We invite in our ancestors, our acquaintances, our angels, our guardians." Not Ruby Rae's criminals. Remington didn't know who else to invite so she stopped. She turned to Beth.

Beth wasn't there. She'd disappeared. What the hell? She'd poofed into thin air. Then Remington remembered the rules. "Damn it," she muttered. "I also invite in Beth Henderson."

Beth reappeared at her side.

"Good save." She winked at Remington. "I'll take it from here."

A cold wind blew into the attic causing Remington to shiver.

"I think we have company," Beth said. "There's a Lema with us?" she continued. "Does anyone know a Lema in the spirit world?"

"Why can't I see the spirit?" Remington asked.

"Because I am acting as the medium. During a séance, only the medium can see the spirits. Does anyone have a Lema in the spirit world?"

No one said yes.

"She's showing me a school room and a rock. She's young. School age."

No one spoke.

"Ruby Rae, she's looking at you, and for some reason, I'm getting the image of a hearse."

Ruby Rae inhaled sharply. "LK," she exclaimed. "It must be her. I think her first name was Lema. She was found dead outside the school when I was in second grade. A bloody rock next to her body. We never did discover what happened. If she fell. Or if she was murdered."

"She's smiling at you. Do you feel her next to you, Ruby Rae?"

"I feel a weight on my left shoulder. Is that her?"

"She has her hand on your shoulder. She wants me to tell you to recall your visions. Does that make sense?"

"After she died, I had dreams I knew what happened. But, I don't remember the dream anymore."

"She's gone."

"Is there anyone else here?" Sara Ann asked. "Anyone for me?"

Beth squeezed Remington's hand. "I see another child. A girl. She's walking but not very well. She's probably barely one-year-old. A lady is holding her hand. Remington, do you feel them?"

Remington looked into the darkness. Wishing she could see them. "No."

"Their eyes are sad. Now, they are standing in front of you, Remington, and staring at you. Like they know you."

Remington's heart collapsed. "Who are they? Ask them who they are."

"The little girl is touching your hair."

Remington's hair lifted and fell back to her shoulder. "I feel it."

"The woman has her hands over her heart and is staring at you."

"Is she my mom?" Remington's heart pounded so loudly she could barely hear herself.

"I don't know. She's trying to speak, but for some reason, words aren't coming out. Now, she's showing me a danger sign. She's pointing at the sign and pointing at you. I think she's trying to say you are in danger."

"Why would I be in danger?" No way was Remington going to let Ruby Rae and Sara Ann in on the Linny debacle and his vague threat.

"She's shaking her head again. She's not allowed to tell us. That's why she's not speaking. Why she looks so sad. She's not allowed to talk to you. She just wanted to see you."

"Who is the child?" Remington's heart sank.

"I don't know."

A drop of sweat rolled between Remington's shoulder blades. "What does the woman look like?"

"She's tall. Long hair. Very pretty."

"Mom, is that you? Are you my mom?" Of course, it was her mom—who else could it be?

Beth sighed. "You've startled her. She disappeared."

"Get her back. That's who came into my earlier séance."

"I can't. It doesn't work that way. Let's see if any other spirits come in."

Remington wanted to run and hide. Pretend none of this had happened.

Oh God. She'd given Jason bad information. It wasn't his mom who was dead.

She had to tell him the truth. Before she left for New York.

CHAPTER THIRTY-FIVE

BY THE TIME THE LADIES left Remington's house, a fresh blanket of velvety snow covered Knotty. Like a sponge, it soaked up the late afternoon shadows. Shadows cast by things living and dead.

Remington's mood resembled something deceased. No life. No hope. No brain. She'd secretly hoped Ruby Rae and Sara Ann would march over to Jason's house and tell him they, too, had spoken to Beth's ghost.

They didn't. He wasn't there. Neither was his truck.

No doubt he was with Gnat-Brain. Why hadn't Remington quizzed him more about her?

Remington listlessly packed her car and Googled directions.

Afternoon turned into evening. Jason still didn't return. She'd leave tomorrow after she had a chance to tell him it was her mom and not his who'd made an appearance at their séance.

For dinner, Remington uncorked a bottle of red Zinfandel and fixed some popcorn.

While watching old movies, she contemplated the pros and cons of getting a boob reduction, a nose reduction, and having a gravelly voice like Audrey Hepburn.

And she cried. A lot. Mom was dead.

At midnight, a noise woke her in such a way her heart rate zoomed from resting to hard cardio in the length of time it took her to blink. She yanked the covers up over her head and listened.

Her foot touched something furry under the covers. And whatever was under there with her, it licked her ankle. She opened her mouth to scream and then realized it was just Max.

She was on the verge of shutting her mouth and swallowing the fear on her tongue, when a breath whispered down the right side of her neck. She shivered violently, and her eyelids flew open and she bit her tongue. *God, what was that?* She rubbed her ear with her shoulder to combat the creepy tickle left behind.

Under the darkness of the blanket, Max's green eyes glowed. Remington didn't see anything else with them. Did that mean there was something outside of the blanket?

Was some*thing* standing in front of the couch… looking down at her, waiting for her to make eye contact? There was only one way to find out. Counting to three, she lowered the blanket from her face…with her eyes closed.

By accident, or by help, the empty wine bottle rolled off the couch and landed with a thump. Remington yelped and her eyes flew open. Max clambered up and over Remington and shot out from under the covers with a yappy growl.

She saw nothing. The menacing spirit she'd expected to pounce, didn't. She allowed herself a shallow breath. If not a bad ghost, what was it? What had awakened her? Was someone outside trying to break into her house? A human?

She peeked over the back cushions of the couch to see out the window. "Thank god." Jason's truck was back, and a light was on in his bedroom. He was home. She collapsed against the pillowy cushions and exhaled a raspy breath.

His coming home must have woken her. Nothing sinister or dead. "Good." No time like now to tell him the truth about his mom.

He wouldn't believe her, would probably call her crazy. But it was the right thing. And it gave her the perfect excuse to leave the scariness of her place and go over to the safety of his.

She slipped on a pair of snow boots before stepping outside in her sweats and a T-shirt. Her bare arms protested against the icy wind, and the cold air made the inside of her nose hurt. Rubbing her arms and twitching her nose, she walked slowly through the snow toward his house, thinking of what words to use.

Surprise…your mom isn't dead. Good news…your mom isn't dead. That thing about your mom…my bad…she's not dead.

How would he react? Would he just laugh? Or offer to help her into a straightjacket?

As she stood in front of his door, her nerves hummed an AC/DC tune in her ears. She could do this. She could—

Her goosebumps told her to hurry the hell up with the pep talk and get her ass inside to the warmth of a fireplace.

Listening to her bitchy goosebumps, she grabbed the doorknob and twisted while raising her other hand to knock. But before she could actually knock, the wind caught the unlocked door out of her grasp, and it hit the wall in a full-on slam.

Her heart jumped out of her body and ran back toward her house like a dog with its tail between its legs.

Scotch growled.

"It's just me," she called out to Jason.

"I'm in the bedroom," Jason replied.

Scotch lumbered over and licked her leg. Stayed long enough to get his ears scratched before plopping down on an oversized cushion located by the fireplace and eyeballing Remington.

Using the moonlight as a guide, Remington padded into Jason's room.

He sat on his bed, wearing a pair of plaid pajama bottoms, a book propped open by his side.

Long and Lanky's nickname could be Sizzled Sexiness. Remington giggled. She slapped a palm over her mouth. She must still be under the influence of the bottle of wine she'd consumed. Even so—no need to give him more reason to think of her as wackier than a demented fruitcake.

He fluffed the two pillows next to him. "I saw you through my bedroom window. I thought you were leaving today." He sounded like he had a frog in his throat.

"I was going to but something came up, and we need to talk." She tried to remember which turn of phrase about his mom not being dead had sounded the best in her head. But her brain had fuzz balls. Damn it. This was important. She didn't want to get it wrong.

If he'd just put on a shirt and dry his hair, she could think better.

He pulled back the covers and patted the spot beside him. "Okay, but it's cold. Get in."

She took a step back. That was not going to happen. She would speak her piece and march home with her head held high. She would leave for New York in the morning with a tad bit of dignity intact.

He patted the spot again. "I don't bite."

Staying intact wasn't her strength. And her house felt scary. And the bed looked warm. And she was cold. And it was her last night in Knotty.

And who says no to sizzling sexiness?

She tugged off her boots, crawled into his bed, and pushed her cold feet against his strong calves. His body jerked, and he hissed, but he didn't protest.

He opened his arm and said, "I was an ass today."

She curled into him, laying her cheek on his chest, inhaling the scent of soap and beer.

She wrapped her arm around his middle and snuggled firmly against him. "You were." She listened to the steady rhythm of his heart. And hiccupped.

His lips brushed the top of her head.

"I held another séance."

Silence, followed by more silence, and then, "I thought you might have."

She resisted an urge to sneak a peek at his face. She didn't really want to know what he was thinking. "Ruby Rae and Sara Ann were there." She hiccupped again.

He laughed softly, causing his chest to move and her lips to accidentally brush his skin. They both jumped.

"Did they see ghosts?" he asked in a crooked-grin tone.

She swallowed. If she told him they did, he'd be more likely to believe her. "They weren't there to see ghosts." She couldn't tell their secret. There were codes among gossips. She hiccupped.

"Did you?" He sounded like he had to make himself ask.

She wrinkled her nose. "Maybe if one would show up now and scare me, I'd get rid of the hiccups."

He didn't say anything, but she could sense his confusion. She dug her hole deeper and explained. "Ghosts only show themselves to the host of a séance. Beth hosted our séance. She saw a few and described them to the girls and me."

"Who showed up?"

Remington plucked at the blanket. "My mom." The two words left a dull ache in her stomach. She'd grown up being nobody's child. But even so, she'd still dreamed of Mom finding her. Of Mom taking her out to lunch and shopping. Never of Mom finding her in a séance. She was truly alone in the world. Truly nobody's child.

Jason pulled her closer to him. "Now, you think your mom is dead as well as mine?"

She leaned her head away from his chest and surreptitiously wiped away the tears on her cheeks before he felt them on his skin. "I don't think yours is dead anymore. The woman I thought was your mom was mine. I fucked up. I'm sorry."

He shifted, and she found herself on her back, looking up into his dark eyes. "You didn't fuck up."

"I didn't?"

He kissed her lips. "I never believed you."

She touched her lips. "You just think I'm a liar."

"I don't think you're a liar." A pulse ticked under his right eye. "I think something is going on with you and it makes you think you can talk to ghosts."

Remington flinched and rolled to face away from him. *Yep, crazier than a demented fruit cake.* "What do I have to do to make you believe me?"

He spooned against her, wrapping an arm around her middle, pulling her tightly against him. "Give me proof."

He might as well have said, *give me a million dollars.* "I don't have proof."

A movement at the window caught her eyes. She looked out and saw Beth frantically waving her arms.

"We need to talk!" Beth shouted.

Remington glanced over her shoulder at Jason to see if he'd heard Beth.

He rolled onto his back, pajamas tented. He looked like the Greek God of Pajama wearers.

"Did I cause that?" She pointed, then hiccupped.

"Remington Smith, look at me," shouted Beth.

Remington dragged her gaze back to the window. *Not now.*

Beth's hair stood out straight. "It's urgent."

Urgent. Remington stilled. Beth's normally white complexion looked a little green. Was Beth about to cross over? *Oh God. Not yet.* Remington wasn't ready to lose her best friend.

She scrambled out from under the covers, threw her legs over the side of the bed, and stood. She glanced back at Jason. At his pajama bottoms. "Sorry. That was rude of me to ask. Please don't answer. I don't want to know."

Jason gave her a look of what-the-hell.

Remington hiccupped. "Sorry to give you an erection and run, but I'm just going to go back to my own bed. Thanks for listening." She pulled on her boots as she talked. "By the way, don't worry, I'm for sure leaving in the morning for New York." She walked to his bedroom door. Turned. "Sorry. I just...need to go."

"Don't go." The sensual darkness of his tone caused her to gulp.

"Don't go to New York, or don't go home?"

"Move your ass," shouted Beth.

Remington looked at Jason. "Never mind. I have to go. I'll just see myself out. Thanks for the hug." She slipped out of his bedroom and headed toward the front door. If Jason didn't think her crazy before, he would now.

"Remington?"

She stopped. Her hand on the front door. "Good-bye, Jason."

Not turning to face him, she left and hurried to her house. Jason was just a man. Beth, on the other hand, was her best friend. She couldn't let her crossover without saying goodbye.

Beth waited for her in her living room.

"Is everything okay? What's wrong?" Remington asked.

"I'm scared." Beth wore blue jeans and a Kansas City Chiefs sweatshirt.

"Why are you afraid?" Was she afraid of crossing over?

Beth wrung her hands together like a worried mother. "There's an evil cloud over Knotty tonight."

Remington glanced out the window. The noise that had awakened her earlier came to mind. Was there something out there, hiding in the snow, behind the undressed trees? Waiting to strike? "What do you mean?" She walked into her living room and told her imagination to behave.

"I don't know. I can't explain it. Just lock your doors and be aware of strange noises."

Shit. The strange noise she'd heard earlier had been a strange noise. "Okay." She should have stayed in bed with Jason where she'd felt safer. *Damn it.* She sat.

Beth did the same. "In fact, I shouldn't have bothered you. It's just so peculiar. I feel all tingly inside like something major is going down."

Remington pulled her knees up to her chin.

Her friend was genuinely freaked. This wasn't just a drama queen being dramatic. "Are you sure it's evil? Maybe this is how you're supposed to feel before crossing over?"

Beth shook her head. "It's not that. I don't think so, anyway. I think I'll go explore. Why don't you go back over to Jason's? You might be safer there."

Remington threw a pillow at Beth and it went right through her. "Your timing sucks. Now he for sure thinks I'm beyond weird."

"Sorry. I just had to see you. Sleep with your gun tonight?"

The hairs on the back of Remington's neck rose, Beth's fear tangible. "Okay."

"Good." Beth exhaled hard. "And, there's one more thing." A smile tugged her lips upward.

"What?"

"Jason's erection...wow!"

CHAPTER THIRTY-SIX

THIRTY MINUTES AFTER REMINGTON LEFT his bed, Jason received a call to come to the orphanage because of a murder. He drove to the orphanage with dread in his stomach, fear in his throat, and Remington on his brain.

Agent Meek met him at the door. The guy's hair stuck out in a haphazard pattern and his clothes looked like they'd been stomped on by a pregnant elephant. "What can you tell me about this man?" Meek shoved a picture at Jason.

Jason glanced at it and blanched. "That's my neighbor's ex-boyfriend. Linny something. Why?"

Meek motioned for Jason to follow and led him to an empty room. "He broke in tonight. Tried to kill Sue."

"Tried?"

Meek chuckled. "Sue pulled a gun on him, surprising him. Shot him in the balls."

Jason winced. "Christ." A sheet-draped body had been carried out of the orphanage as he parked. "Did he bleed to death?" The thought of getting shot in the balls made him nauseous.

"He bled plenty, but not to death. Lucky for him, her shot went astray."

An eerie silence engulfed the room as both men fell quiet. An odor of dust and the whisper of broken hearts permeated. Jason waved a hand toward the door. "Then who went out on the stretcher?"

"Oh, that was Linny."

"I'm not following?"

"We want anyone who might be watching from the outside to think he's dead. That the gunshot was fatal. That's why we called you and said there'd been a murder."

Jason pinched the bridge of his nose. "Still not following."

Agent Meek widened his stance. "The scum's offered to turn over federal evidence in return for witness protection. It's easier to keep them safe in the protection program if the people after them think they're dead."

"Where's Sue?"

"We took her statement and then an officer took her to stay with her sister."

Jason walked to the window and looked out. An abandoned playground stared frostily back at him. "I take it he wasn't just after money or something he can pawn for cash?" Jason leaned a hip against the wall. He wished like hell he had Remington's phone number. He wanted to check on her.

"He wanted information on the orphans."

"Why would he want information on the orphans in the middle of the night?" Jason pulled out his phone. Punched in Kevin's number. He would have her number.

"Who are you calling?" Meek asked, taking the

phone out of Jason's hand and ending the call.

"An employee," Jason snapped, taking the phone back. "I want him to check on my neighbor."

"The fewer people who know about this, the better." Meek rubbed his chin.

Jason kept the phone out. "I won't tell him anything, just ask him to check on her."

Meek shook his head. "You could be placing her in danger if you draw attention to her."

Jason shoved his phone in his coat pocket. "Could we speed up to the part where you say something that makes sense?"

"Linny wants to talk with you."

"What the fuck for? Last time I saw him, I threatened to kick his ass."

Meek's phone rang. "We'll talk about it at headquarters. That's where they are taking him after they go by the morgue and pretend to drop his body off."

"I can't just not check on Remington."

"If you care about her, you'll do as I say. If someone's watching him, they'll know Linny tipped us off if they see you go to her house. Which could place her in more danger."

Jason ignored the speed limit driving the twenty miles to the police station where the FBI had set up makeshift headquarters. When he marched inside the stark building, Agent Meek stepped out of a room and motioned for him.

The room Jason entered was a basic interrogation room. A large two-way mirror took up one wall. The other walls were bare. In the middle of the room stood a table and two chairs. Jason took a seat on one side, Meek on the other.

"I'll be on the other side of the glass and will hear everything. Are you ready?"

"Before I agree to speak with him, I want to know about the orphanage." There had to be more going on than he'd been told.

"The orphanage is a safe house for children of individuals in the witness protection plan," Meek said.

Jason's mouth went dry. "Their parents are in hiding?"

"Exactly."

"Are you talking about all the orphans? Or just part of them?" As the reality of the situation hit him, his stomach threatened to empty itself.

The orphanage wasn't just owned by a former FBI agent.

Children had been placed there for protection.

"Half of them," Meek answered.

"And that's why none of them could be adopted?" Jason said, more to himself as he tried to make sense of what he was learning.

"None of the hidden children were ever open for adoption. The risk of danger to their new parents was too high should the adopted identity of their child be discovered."

Jason pounded his fist on the table and stood. "Jesus, is Remington one of them?" He paced the length of the room. "Are her parents in protective custody?"

Meek rubbed the middle of his forehead. "She's

one of them. Her mother and little sister died from a hit and run shortly after her family was placed in protective custody. That's when Remington was brought to the orphanage. She had been in the car but didn't die. We made it look like she had."

Jason turned away. Faced the two-way mirror. "She said that she went home on a trial basis twice."

"A necessary arrangement to make sure the outside world believed the orphanage was legitimate. Those who took them home worked for the agency." Meek's tone said he supported the cruel practice.

Jason picked up a chair and threw it across the room. "Do you know how messed up those orphans are as a result of never getting adopted? Of trial runs?"

Meek opened a pack of gum, offering Jason a stick. He declined. "The alternative would be to leave them with their parents, who are constantly in fear of being discovered." He unwrapped his gum and tossed the wrapper in the trashcan.

"Is her dad still alive?" He replayed his conversation with Remington...the séance... his dad's declaration of having set something in motion... Was this... No, he didn't believe in ghosts.

"I'm not allowed to say."

No wonder the orphans thought they were unlovable. It didn't matter how good they were, they weren't going to be adopted. "Tell me about the leak."

"Your father is behind the leak. He's been on our radar for a long time because of some of his business acquaintances."

Jason grabbed the table for balance. She'd been right. His father was behind this. How had she known that? "How?" Could she really talk to ghosts?

"Once he discovered your plans to rebuild Knotty, not come to work for him, he hired a man to scour Knotty and find a reason for TTI to remove their financial backing of your plan for the town. He uncovered Knotty's secret."

Jason exhaled heavily. "How in the hell did he do that?"

"We don't know. There are only a few who know of its existence."

Jason pounded a fist on the table. "Did you ask him?"

"We brought him in for questioning. He told us that a list of the names of the hidden orphans landed in his hands by accident. He offered the list in exchange for our shutting down your plans and not pressing any charges against him. We agreed."

Jason pinched the bridge of his nose. "And he got the list from someone inside the agency?"

"He said he did. But he had the heart attack before we could get full disclosure from him."

"So, trying to force me into the family fold was the final undoing of the old man." Jason blocked the emotions brewing inside of him. "Did Linny work for my dad? Is that why he wants to cut a deal?"

"We don't know. You're going to find out for us."

Sourness rose up in Jason's throat. The asshole

had probably been using Remington the whole time. "Get him in here. I'll pulverize the bastard until he tells us whatever we need to know."

Meek stood and left the room.

Within minutes, the door opened again, and Remington's ex-boyfriend shuffled in, shackles on his feet and hands. Jason didn't say anything.

Linny sat, wincing as he did. "I couldn't care less what you think of me."

Jason cracked his knuckles, leaned in close. "I think you're slime of the underworld. If I ever see you in a dark alley, I'm going to rid the world of a rat by skinning it." His words were barely a whisper. For Linny's ears only.

Linny grunted. A harsh sound that didn't match his outside look. "I'd be careful threatening someone from the criminal society. Rats breed rats."

Jason leaned back. "Did you work for my father?"

"He paid me well to sleep with Remington. Did you know I was her first?"

Jason jumped across the table, grabbed him by the collar, and yanked him up, the pounding in his ears shouting at him to kill Linny.

Linny sneered. "Careful, or I won't tell you anything else."

Jason released his collar and shoved him back. "Start talking."

"Daddy dearest wanted me to kill her," Linny said. "I would think you could show me a little gratitude that your girlfriend is still alive."

Jason stilled his expression. He'd always known Dad was dangerous, but to actually hear he'd hired a man to kill a woman torched what little respect Jason had ever had for him. "I don't have a girl-friend."

Linny kicked the leg of the table. "Don't fucking fuck with me. I saw how you looked at Remington when she was doing the walk of shame between your houses."

Jason flat-lined his emotions. "If you were hired to murder her, why isn't she dead? Do you suck at your job?"

Linny's eyes narrowed. "Ask that question of the men at the bottom of Table Rock Lake whom I've made brief acquaintances with… Not that I killed them."

"Why didn't you kill her?"

Linny grinned, showing a gold incisor. "I was supposed to get information out of Remington first. By the time I realized she didn't have any information about her dad's new whereabouts, I'd gotten attached to her myself. I couldn't bring myself to kill the mouthy thing. Tell me, has she ever shown you the picture of her fake family?"

Jason vaguely recalled seeing a picture of a family somewhere in Remington's house. He hadn't taken the time to glance at it carefully. "She's an orphan. I don't know anything about a fake family."

"Well, as an adult, she doesn't want people to know she's an orphan. So, she has a family picture in her living room and a story that goes with it. It's really quite touching. She's an excellent liar."

Did she want to shed the orphan tag so bad that she'd made up a family once she'd left Knotty?

"What kind of information about her dad were you looking for?"

"Your dad was told they were the children of parents who were in protective custody. But he didn't have proof. When he discovered Remington talked about having parents, he thought she knew who hers were. He wanted their whereabouts so he could prove what he knew, and then he wanted her dead. Hired me to kill her. He wanted the news to leak out that your town wasn't a safe place to live."

"Who else did he tell all of this to?"

"Once I have a written statement giving me immunity and contractual guarantees, I'll be placed in protective services, I'll be happy to fill you in on the rest."

Jason glanced at the mirror. His town wasn't safe for Remington. He had to get her out. Cut all ties with her. There was no telling who Dad had already sold the information to. "Why did you break into the orphanage tonight? My dad's dead. You weren't working for him."

"That's a good question. One I'm not answering. Yet."

Jason stood and shoved the table into Linny, causing his chair to fall backward.

The door opened.

"Is that what you needed?" he said to Meek.

Meek came in. Clapped him on the back. "It's a start."

Jason strolled out of the room. It was time to check on Remington. He didn't trust Linny. He could be lying. He could have killed Remington

before he'd gone to the orphanage. He tried calling her. No answer.

CHAPTER THIRTY-SEVEN

REMINGTON WOKE TO A CREAKING noise. She tried to think, but her brain floundered for more sleep, and her eyes begged to remain closed. Had she forgotten to lock the front door? Nah. She'd locked it.

Beth had spooked the hell out of her with her talk about the air being filled with evil.

In fact, not only had Remington locked the freaking door, she'd stuck a knife between the door and the frame for good measure. And then what?

Then she'd conked-out listening to Frank Sinatra's Greatest Hits.

Remington reached to remove her ear buds and found they weren't there. They must have fallen out. Maybe the music had awakened her. She turned the music off and listened.

A soft clicking noise.

She frowned. It was coming from the spare bedroom. The noise grew volume. *Scrape. Thump. Clunk.*

Damn it. She'd never locked the spare bedroom's side door. Remington yanked the covers over her head. Heart-in-your-throat, panic-in-your-belly fear shook her body like a gigantic earthquake. She had an uninvited guest.

"Beth? Can you hear me?"

No response.

Oh God, I'm going to die.

She gulped a hefty breath, leaned over the side of the mattress and grabbed Hank under the bed. She checked to make sure he had bullets and then slid into the crevice between the bed and the wall—ready to shoot. If death had found her, she was going with her eyes open and her gun firing.

No cry-baby death.

Whoever had broken into her house wasn't even trying to be quiet. Did he think just because this was Knotty that the residents were dense? That they didn't know when they were being broken into? That they didn't sleep with guns?

Her bedroom doorknob twisted and so did her insides. Someone was truly in her house in the middle of the night without an invitation. *Damn it. Damn it. Damn it.*

Her heart slammed her chest, and she pointed the gun at the door, nearly dropping it when the mayhem ghosts materialized.

"This is bad. Really bad," the fat one said to the skinny one.

Before Remington could question them, a large shadow emerged from the other side of the door. Like a thwarted shrew, she screamed and pulled the trigger.

"What the fuck. Fuck."

The voice had a ring of familiarity. Not enough to keep her from shooting again. Pieces of the ceiling exploded.

The mayhem ghosts were on the ceiling, laughing their asses off. Clasping their sides as if gas pains consumed them.

"Son of a bitch. Remington, stop shooting that damn gun."

Remington gasped. "Oh God." Jason. She'd shot at him...and...he was him. Not a burglar. *Him*. Her heart somersaulted all the way down to her curled toes, and she jumped up.

"Put that gun down," Jason bellowed. He flipped on the light. A crimson stain spread through his fingers where he clutched his arm.

"Shit." Remington scrambled across the bed. "I hit you." She grabbed Jason by his good arm and pulled him toward the bathroom. "I'm sorry. So, so, so sorry. I can't bel—"

"It's just a scratch." For someone who'd just been shot, he sounded oddly happy.

Remington grabbed the gauze out of the medicine cabinet, removed his hand from the wound and looked. Soothing relief, distorted with hard-rock-pounding adrenaline, poured through her. She bent over, grabbed her knees, and concentrated on her breathing. "Why in the hell are you acting such a baby about a barely-there nick?"

He grunted. "Why in the hell did you shoot me?"

She glanced up. "Because you were breaking into my house. Why in the hell were you doing that?"

He tucked a curl behind her ear. "I came to check on you."

She straightened up and pushed his hand away.

"Check on me? In the middle of the night?"

He let loose a long breath. "I remembered your unlocked door and thought I'd checked to see if you got it locked."

The answer smelled of thick malarkey. "I'm fine." They were living in Knotty. Not East St. Louis.

He smiled, and his eyes twinkled. "Yes, you are." He yanked her into his arms, knocking the breath out of her, and wrapped her in a bear hug. "God, I'm glad you're okay."

"Are you drunk?" She pulled back and sniffed for alcohol. None. Just manly soap.

"With joy." He took her hand and tugged.

She dug her heels. "What aren't you telling me?"

He kept tugging until they were back in the bed-room. He sat on the edge of her bed and glanced at the ceiling. "I heard a crashing noise."

"You did?" She tapped her barefoot on the floor.

"I thought perhaps your roof had caved in from the weight of the snow. I had visions of you pan-cake flat. I came running like a Prince Charming." His eyes met hers on the last word.

"What you're saying is—I shot Prince Charm-ing?"

He nodded. "Yes."

"He's lying," the skinny mayhem ghost said.

Remington ignored the ghost and concentrated on Jason. "Want to stay until the sun comes up?" The question was out before she could analyze its origin.

"I thought you'd never ask." He took his jeans off, left his boxers on, and climbed under the skewed covers.

"That makes two of us." She climbed in on the side closest to the wall.

Without saying anything else, he pulled her into his arms and held her tightly against him, his heart thumping beneath her cheek. He whispered something. Something she couldn't hear.

She closed her eyes, and an ache settled inside of her, close to her heart. But not her heart. Her curse still held.

Jason stroked his hands down her back until his fingers rested on her bottom.

She shivered.

He shifted on the bed, rolling her onto her back.

She blinked up at him. The last twenty-four hours had had more twists and turns than a manic-drawn roller coaster. Was she about to experience the ride's final heart-pounding plunge?

He angled down, brushing his lips against hers, a mere whisper of contact.

She'd only ever been on one roller coaster. But she vividly remembered how much fun the final hill had been. She'd be dumb to jump off this ride before its big plummet.

Jason took her lips again. An unhurried kiss. Exploratory. Insanely sexy.

She closed her eyes. Tonight, what little remained, she'd use all of her feminine wiles to become a roller coaster ride he couldn't easily forget.

He sucked her bottom lip between his teeth, stroking the flesh with his tongue until she arched against him. Longing building like a summer thunderstorm.

Bittersweet sex between a woman and a man both under the weight of knowing this would be their last ride.

His lips skimmed down her cheek. She moaned, placed her palms on his head and shifted until her lips were at his ear.

She silently mouthed, "I want to love you."

Jason spooned with Remington and watched the sun rise while she slept. The softness of her body and her sweet scent overwhelmed him with new desires and impossible dreams.

They'd made love until the early hours of the morning. For a few brief hours, she'd been his everything. And he'd been her one-night-stand man.

The thought of her leaving Knotty caused his head to ache. But she had to go—today. But before she left, he wanted to tell her about her parents, and about why she was never adopted. Only he couldn't. He'd been sworn to secrecy.

He'd been thinking the last hour about what it would be like to spend the rest of his life with her. Fantastic. But he'd come to one conclusion. She deserved better than what he had to offer. He didn't even have a family to share with her, and someone who had grown up an orphan deserved to marry into an enormous dynasty type of family.

"You need a husband with more relatives than the sky has stars. One with grandmas on the ready to spoil all of your future babies," he whispered into her hair. "And aunts and uncles. And cousins."

She stirred.

He rubbed her hip with the pad of this thumb, right beneath the lace edge of her panties. Red string bikini panties. When had she put those back on? God, she was passionate.

He kissed her naked shoulder.

She moved her hips and rolled onto her back. "Good morning," she said in a sleepy tone, not opening her eyes.

"One of the best in my lifetime."

"Was last night a dream?"

"I certainly hope not."

"Me too." She opened her eyes and a shadow filled the room. "But today *is* the day I'm being evicted from Knotty…isn't it?"

He blinked. Girded his loins. "Yes."

She shifted and straddled him. A marvelous move on her part. No man worth his salt could look at that body and remain focused on the better good.

"I do believe we should have one last goodbye romp. Don't you?" She pushed her panties aside with one hand and guided him to her with the other.

He swallowed a groan. This wasn't a move on her part to change his mind. She was as unpredictable as the stock market.

She sank down just enough for his cock to penetrate her. Barely. Causing his thoughts to scatter. This moment was all he could focus on.

She closed her eyes, her breaths coming fast, and

leaned down and kissed his lips. The caress started gently but quickly morphed into needy. Jason's hands came up and grasped her hips. Ready to take over.

She rose up. "Not yet."

His fingers ached to touch her. "You're killing me, Smith."

She smiled like a fallen angel—all siren and sexual contemplation. "I'm working on my Tantric seduction moves. By the time I'm finished with you, you're going to be begging me to love you."

Begging me to love you. The words scraped his conscious.

He grabbed her and rolled them over, balancing himself above her, ignoring the tightness in his chest. "Sorry babe, right now, I need to be the one in power." He grabbed a condom off the nightstand, slid it on, and positioned himself between her legs. "Open your eyes. I want to see them."

She did, and he slid inside her.

She gasped and wrapped her legs around him, squeezing.

Together, they found a rhythm that shattered the earth.

Later, they laid sprawled out and spent. Neither of them ever saying the L-word.

"I should get up and get a move on. New York isn't going to come to me."

"That's probably for the best."

"Or I could stay." She stared at him with what she probably thought was nonchalance. It wasn't. It was a look of a woman begging to be wanted.

He searched for the right words to kill her affection for him.

Remington waited for Jason's reaction. In a perfect world, he would tell her he thought her idea of staying in Knotty was fabulous.

"Darling, that's not going to work." Jason frowned. "Bernadette and I are engaged."

Her body turned clammy and her vision blurred. "Still?" Wasn't that where he'd gone yesterday? To break things off with Gnat-Brain? If not, why had he let Remington crawl in bed with him last night? Was he that kind of guy?

He nodded, not looking her in the eyes.

Her bottom lip trembled. "Oh." Fuck.

He raised his head and their eyes met. "Did you think I picked you over her?" The words were spoken in a hard-icy tone.

She blinked hard. "Of course not. I just thought… It was a stupid idea."

He gave her a fractured smile. "It wasn't a stupid idea, but not one of your best ones, either."

Damn it. Damn it. Damn it. "Don't worry… I get it. I was your itch. Your scratching post. You were my one-night stand."

"Exactly." Jason grabbed her shoulders and pulled her against his chest. His mouth came down on hers in a kiss that severed ties.

When he pulled back, he dropped a soft kiss on her forehead, dressed, and then turned and left the room.

Remington touched her lips. "And that's how a pro ends a one-night stand," she said to Max, who looked at her crossly from across the room. "Him. Not me. I'm a fool."

"Boy, you've got that right," said the skinny mayhem ghost, drawing Remington's attention to him and his buddy, who were standing on their heads in the middle of her bedroom.

The fat one elbowed him, knocking him over. "Not now. Can't you see her heart's trying to break free of her hex?"

CHAPTER THIRTY-EIGHT

REMINGTON PULLED ONTO THE SIDE of the road. She turned in her seat and smiled through teary eyes at Beth who sat beside her in the passenger seat. "This is it. Fifty miles from Knotty. Your getting off spot."

Her best friend had appeared in her bedroom after Remington's shower. A shower to scrub off the ugly feels of what had happened between her and Jason.

Beth placed her hands on Remington's cheeks, turning her face, and staring intently at her. "I'm not sure you should be driving by yourself. You look awful." She let go of Remington's cheeks and sat back. Today Beth wore a hideous Christmas sweater that had garland for a neckline, and bells on her boobs.

Remington burst into tears. "I don't know why I'm crying. I'm under a spell not to love anyone."

Beth handed her a tissue. "Oh honey, your spell doesn't work outside of Knotty unless you added that to your intention when you cast it."

"I didn't," Remington cried. "I don't even want to go…but, I have tooooooo."

"You don't have to," Beth said. "You can stay."

Remington hiccupped and shook her head. "I don't want to stay if he doesn't want me to stay. And he doesn't. He chose Gnat-Brain. Only a loser would choose to stay and watch."

Beth patted her arm awkwardly. "Look at it this way. New York has always been your dream. Your first dream is about to come true."

Max crawled out from behind Remington's back and to the backseat.

Remington wiped her eyes. "You're right. And it's a fine dream. I mean, it's not family. And it's not playing cards on Sunday afternoons with crotchety old ladies and sexy men who think of me as their kid sister. And it's not talking to you whenever you pop in. And it's not matching wits with mayhem ghosts. But it's a fine dream."

"That's the spirit." Beth gave her an over-bright smile. "How about a joke?" She pulled out her joke box from a beach bag. "What does a ghost say when their best friend is leaving them?"

Remington blew her nose noisily. "I don't know… What?"

"Ghoul-bye." Beth waggled her eyebrows at Remington.

"Ghoul-bye to you." Remington gave her a trembling smile. "I'll miss you."

"And you're one-hundred percent sure this is what you want to do?"

"Even if I go back, and the spell takes away my heartache, it won't take away the memories. I'd be miserable watching him married to that woman." Remington's strength had been all used up. "It would be a constant reminder she has something to offer him I don't. He told me that…to my face… did I mention that?" She just wanted to crawl into bed and sleep forever. "I'm really looking forward to New York."

"Oh, Remington…" Beth's breath caused the car windows to frost over. "I should have never told you about the curse, or given you the spell book, or left you my house. I should have sent you straight to New York with my blessings and my insurance money. You'd be happy right now. Living your dream."

Remington shook her head, her hair whiplashing around her face. "If you hadn't brought me back to Knotty, we'd never had the chance to be together again." She smiled—a genuine smile. "Having time with you is worth all the tears."

Beth hugged her. "Don't forget. You promised to come back in May to run the Unorphanage Marathon."

The ladies had decided they were going to run the marathon even if there wasn't going to be an orphanage sponsoring the run. "I won't forget." Remington grabbed a tissue and blew her nose. "Even though I may die from the effort."

"If you die, we'll just be ghost buds together."

Remington lifted an eyebrow in acknowledgment.

"You knock them dead on Broadway with your designs. Pull out your T-shirt designs if you fail at the Broadway stuff."

"Don't you dare cross over before I come back."

Beth sat back in her seat. "I've decided to stop looking for what my unfinished business is until after I see you again."

"Promise?"

Beth nodded and smiled big, warming up the car a little. "There's no way I can cross over until I know you're happy."

"I thought for sure you would have crossed over yesterday after helping me discover about Mom's death."

"I know. Right? For the dead of me, I can't figure out what my unfinished business is. Which is fine. It just means more time here on earth."

Remington leaned in and gaze intently into Beth's eyes. "I love you."

Beth started fading in and out. "I think we might be a little past the fifty-mile mark. I'm being pulled back toward Knotty. I have to leave."

"Okay." Remington didn't want Beth to worry about her. "I'm sorry I've been such a cry baby today. But I'm good now. New York is going to be fun."

Beth floated out of the car and then stuck her head through the driver-side window. "Be careful. I have this feeling that something still isn't right with your aura."

Remington didn't know a lot about auras, but she was pretty sure what was wrong with hers. "It's called sadness." Mom was dead.

Beth stared. No smile, eyes narrowed, head tilted, mouth twisted. "Maybe."

Remington placed her hand on Beth's forehead

to push her out of the car. Of course, it went right through and landed on the door's window. "Get out of here, I'm fine."

Beth smirked. "I know what you need. You need another joke." She pulled out a card. "What do you call a cat that has seen a ghost?"

Remington started her car. "I don't know... what?"

"A scaredy cat."

Remington smiled. A tiny lifting of her lips. "Ha. That's pretty good."

Beth blew her a kiss. "Ta ta for now."

Remington's smile evaporated. It was just her and Max against the world once again.

Beth reappeared, startling her. "I almost forgot! Here." She plopped a big beach bag on the seat between them.

Who carries a beach bag while wearing a Christmas sweater?

"It's a Christmas present," Beth said.

A lump of nostalgia formed in Remington's throat. She bit her upper lip and looked away until the tears wanting to fall dried up. Then she gazed at Beth. "Thanks. I'll have to owe you one."

Beth waved a hand in the air. "Nonsense."

"Bye," Remington said.

"Smile if you love me," Beth responded, and then poofed away feet-first.

Remington caught her breath. Beth had used her signature exit line. Beth really was Beth. Not an imposter.

Remington stopped in Branson for gas and a

fresh box of tissues. At the gas pump, a car pulled in behind hers, and she glanced at the driver, hopeful it would be Jason chasing after her.

A heavy-set man got out of the car. He glanced at her and smiled. "Hello."

"Hi." She swiped her gas card and started the gas and reminded herself it wasn't wise to talk to strangers.

The man pointed to her suitcase in the backseat. "Are you traveling for Christmas?"

Christmas. She'd never gotten the tree up. Another year without a tree. The realization threatened to set off a fresh set of tears. She bit down on her tongue to keep that from happening.

She and Max should be in New York by Christmas. In a condo. All alone. Would the furniture smell like Jason? "I'm headed to New York. Moving there." She'd have to remember to pick up something for herself as a treat for Christmas morning. Maybe some wine. A doggie bone for Max.

The man smiled broadly, showing a gold tooth. "What a coincidence. That's where I'm headed. I have family there. Making my annual trek. Maybe we'll see each other on the road."

"Maybe. Merry Christmas."

"You too," he said.

Remington finished up and went inside the store to buy a cup of coffee and tissues for the road. Christmas was about family. Until the last several months, she'd never had family. Should she at least try living in Knotty, alongside the happy couple, before giving it all up? Or try New York before giving it all up?

When she came out, the man had finished gassing up as well and was on his cell. He waved at Remington. Remington waved back as she pulled into traffic.

A mile down the road, the mayhem ghost appeared in her passenger seat. "What's up, doll face?" the skinny one said.

"You guys are not coming to New York with me," she said. "Go back to Knotty."

"You didn't hear this from either of us but going to New York is the wrong thing to do," the fat one said. "Turn around. Go back and fight for what you want."

"I have no idea what you're yapping about."

For the next ten minutes, they proceeded to tell her a fanciful tale.

CHAPTER THIRTY-NINE

THE SLAM OF A CAR door caught Jason's attention. He walked to his window and glanced out. What he saw caused his heart to raise a hand for a high-five and his brain to scowl.

Remington. Standing at her car. Sparks shooting from her hair.

He opened his door and stepped out on his porch.

Remington's glare dared him to say the first word.

He obliged. "What are you doing here?"

The sudden pain in her expression tore at his gut. He wanted to pull her into his arms, hug her tightly, absorb all of her hurt. But he couldn't.

"Knotty's my home, too. If it's not big enough for the both of us, you can leave," she said.

"Don't—" Exploding sparks caused his words to falter.

As if unaware of what her hair was doing, or simply not caring, she marched to his sidewalk. Leaned in. "Don't what?"

"Don't stay." He resisted an urge to call the fire department. "I can't give you want you want."

Another explosion. "Can't give or won't give."

He exhaled hard through his nose. "Does it matter?" Where in the hell was all the static electricity coming from?

She smoothed her hair with her hands and the sparks fizzled. "As it turns out, there's nothing I want you to give me. I'm here for me. So, you don't have to worry about the crazy orphan who talks to ghosts trying to win your heart. Or the witch who cast spells on your town telling others she wants you. Go ahead and marry Gnat-Brain. We'll coexist."

He stuffed his hands in his pockets. "For what's it worth, I'm beginning to believe you can talk to ghosts." For the first time in his life, he allowed the color gray into his world.

"Really?" It was a smart-ass really, not a sincere really.

Something had to account for the way her hair did its thing. And what she knew about his father. Hell, she told Jason during the séance that his dad tried to sabotage his Knotty project. "I'm willing to believe it's possible."

She tilted her head. "And the fact I can cast spells? Are you willing to believe that's possible as well?"

He could hear her shallow breathing, smell her perfume, see the tiny pulse beating in her tense jaw. And if ghosts exist, who was he to say witches couldn't? "That one's going to take a while."

She opened her mouth. Shut it. Opened it again. And then gave him a rueful look. "Fair enough."

Remembering to be an asshole, he said, "Why

did you come back?" She still couldn't stay.

"You didn't really think you could dictate to me where I'd live, did you?"

He shoved his hands back in his pockets. Ordered himself to do whatever it took to keep her safe. "If you came back because you're under some delusion I love you, you're wrong."

"Don't be so full of yourself. I'm my own person. I come and go as I please. And I please to live in Knotty. Where I own a house and have friends. And the roads are only two-lanes."

"I want you to go to New York."

"And I wanted you to fall for me but that didn't happen, did it?"

"Only because falling…loving…you is complicated."

"Oh, trust me…I know that. My parents found it complicated to love me as well. Just like you, they found it easier to ship me off. Out of sight—out of mind. Yes, Jason Hart, I know that loving me is complicated." She turned toward her house.

"Remington—"

She jerked back around. "What?

He grabbed her fisted hand. Kissed her knuckles. "Do you think this is easy for me?"

She ripped her hand out of his grasp. "Absolutely."

"You're wrong. There's nothing easy about letting you go. It's the hardest thing I've ever done."

"Then you've had a shit-easy life," she said. "Because you left me without so much as a stammer in your steps."

"How do you define love?"

"Someone who will fight to keep me in their life." Her words were barely a whisper. "Someone who loves me so much they fight to keep me next to them…not send me away. Not give me excuses as to why I'm better off away from them."

Her words gathered force and rushed him like debris from an opened floodgate.

She continued. "I want someone who loves me not *just enough*. I want someone who loves me so-freaking-much-enough they are willing to face all the challenges that come with staying beside me. Not marry someone else."

He could hear her labored breaths. Knew she wasn't done.

"I want someone who knows I'm better off somewhere else, but who loves me too much to do the right thing. Who loves me too much to let me leave."

"Remington, I can't give you details, but it's not safe in Knotty for you. That's why I don't want you to live here."

She laughed. A sinister sound. "I know that. I talked to the mayhem ghosts. They told me there are bad guys who want me dead."

"Mayhem ghosts?"

She shook her head. "It's a long story. But if those bad people want me dead, they're going to find me no matter where I am. Hell, I think I met one of them at the gas station."

He frowned. "But it would be harder for them to find you if you weren't here." Then again, if she was here, she'd have ghosts protecting her. That's something she wouldn't have in New York. Hell. Was forcing her out of Knotty a mistake?

She stilled. "Do you know who they are and why they're after me?"

"I do. But if I tell you, I lose everything in Knotty. Can you just trust me when I say they're bad?"

She nodded. "If you won't fight my staying."

He didn't reply.

She gave an exasperated sigh. "Jason, don't you wish your mother loved you too much to leave you behind? Don't you wish she'd had the courage to take you with her or stay there with you?"

Her words reverberated through him like a rumble of thunder. She'd just given him a definition of love he'd never considered. Why should he? It was a typical, female, romantic definition. An impossible definition. An impractical definition. "I can't love you like that."

"To hear you say it, you can't love me at all," she yelled.

"Damn it, Remington Smith. I do love you. There, I said it. Are you happy? I've loved you ever since Beth told me about her very best friend in the world." His voice was loud. "But some loves aren't meant to be. I have to send you away."

"Aren't you listening to me? It doesn't matter that you don't love me enough. You don't have the fucking option to send me away."

"You're asking the impossible." His breaths were

as ragged as hers.

She sighed. Closed her eyes. "Of course, I am. I've dreamt of the impossible my entire life."

He grabbed her by the shoulders. "Then stop choosing impossible dreams. Be realistic. Go to New York. The bad guys won't know where to look for you in New York."

"Not going to happen."

He let go of her shoulders. "We have a verbal contract. You no longer own a house in Knotty."

She shook her head stubbornly. "I haven't signed over my house to you. I can live in it and you can't do a damn thing about it."

"Why are you being so obstinate?"

"Because the only family I have lives in Knotty and I'm not leaving them."

"They're not your real family."

"Ruby Rae and Sara Ann are my chosen family. And the guys. And Beth."

A look of panic filled his eyes. "What can I do to change your mind?"

"You can't."

"You're hell-bent on behaving like an irresponsible, frustrating child?"

Her hands fisted. The guy was infuriating. "I'm hell-bent on living my life under my terms. If that makes me childish, so be it."

"How about Bernadette? Remember, I'm going to marry her."

Remington gasped. Was he fucking... "You're going to marry Gnat-Brain? After just telling me you love me? What kind of guy—"

"Of course, I'm not marrying her," he said on an exhaled breath. "I was never going to marry her. She blackmailed me. I just want you to be safe."

The mayhem ghosts had actually told her the truth. "You allowed a gnat-brain to blackmail you?"

Jason chuckled. "Gnat-Brain suits her. I only allowed the blackmail for your safety. It's you I love."

Remington's knees wobbled. "You don't get to just go from I'm marrying a gnat-brain to *it's you I love.*"

"But it's true."

"Will you feel the same when I tell you I'm going to help Beth solve mysteries from the second-veil?" She needed to fly all of her freak flags. See which one sent him running.

He blinked. "I still feel the same."

"You should know my heart is hexed. I'm currently incapable of loving you back." On the word *incapable*, her heart mule-kicked her chest as if ready to throw-down over its confinement. She grimaced. Who knew a heart could kick like that.

His expression, on the other hand, showed no signs of worry and a whole lot of cocky. "You should know…I'm struggling with the whole hexing thing."

"Struggling?"

"I'll give you ghosts. You're going to have to give me more time to wrap my brain around the idea of hexes."

"Does that mean there's a chance you might come to the conclusion I'm capable of hexing?"

This took the cock out of his cocky and his face paled. "It's an explanation for so much of what has happened in Knotty, but I'm not willing to commit to it yet as the legit explanation."

She grabbed his shoulders, stood on tiptoes, and gazed into his eyes. "Cross-your-heart-risk-being-double-hexed promise you'll try to believe me?"

He wrapped his hand around the back of her head and tugged her closer. "I cross my heart, risk being double hexed, promise I'll try to believe you're a witch."

"Shall we seal the promise with a kiss?"

He groaned, and their lips united and fireworks lit up the sky. Fireworks that would have the whole town in a dither.

When they drew apart, he said, "If you're hell-bent on staying, I have a few requests."

Fair enough. "I'm listening." She took a step back.

"Would you help me choose which businesses I allow to open in Knotty? I have a sky-high stack of applications to narrow down to twenty."

"Can one of them be mine?"

He nodded. Didn't even ask what kind of business she wanted to open. For all he knew it could be a séance practice. Which wasn't a bad idea.

"And I want you to take shooting lessons," he continued.

She twisted her lips. "I beg your pardon?" Just because they'd had that small mishap didn't mean she couldn't shoot.

His jaw tightened. "That's a nonnegotiable

request."

She rolled her eyes. "For the sake of our friendship, I guess a few classes won't hurt." He was damn lucky her aim had been off.

"And a self-defense class." If anything, his jaw got tighter. "Just in case your ghost friends aren't really capable of protecting you here in Knotty."

"Not a bad idea." Even though the mayhem ghosts had agreed to keep an eye out for possible trouble coming to town—in return for her allowing them to live in her attic—it wouldn't hurt to know how to kick ass. "Can I invite Sara Ann and Ruby Rae to join me?"

Jason chuckled. "God help Knotty if you do. Oh...and there's one more thing."

"You're pressing your luck, Mister. What?"

A smile lit up his face, turning Mr. Long and Lanky into Mr. Smooth and All Hers. "You can never stop giving me a chance to win your love."

Happy slid from the tip of her head to the tips of her toes, taking its time like a lazy setting sun in the summer, leaving contentment and warmth in its path. Someone, not just someone but Jason, wanted a chance to win her love.

For the first time in her life, Remington Smith belonged.

Spells I've done now be undone.

Except on me, let that one be.

For now, she'd keep her heart until Jason proved worthy of her setting it free. She tossed her spell into the air and sparks lit up the air it traveled through.

"Was that a yes?"

"It was a let's take this slow and see how things go," she said. "I don't want our relationship to be nothing more than an after-spell hangover."

Jason held out his arms. "Are you playing hard to get?"

"No playing... I am hard to get." She walked into his arms, ready to move their reunion inside where it was warmer.

Right as she did, the snow on the roof skidded off and onto their unsuspecting heads, tumbling them to the ground in an unceremonious heap. Their surprised laughter faltered when not one, not two, but three additional rounds of snow encased them in a cold blanket.

Like newborn giraffes on trampolines, they struggled to stand. Muffled snorts wound themselves around Remington and Jason's grunts.

Remington recognized the sound of at least one of the snorts. As soon as she could stand, her gaze cut straight to the roof to verify what she suspected. Yep. Beth and the mayhem ghosts floated slightly above the roof, with drinks in their hands and snow on the toes of their assorted boots. Not even trying to look innocent.

Remington resisted an urge to hex and, instead, discretely flipped them the bird. Their snorts became all-out gales of laughter.

"Know what I'm hungry for?" Jason brushed the snow off her head and shoulders. The dude was utterly oblivious to the ghosts.

Remington gave him her full attention. "Pizza?"

"Ghosted Flakes." A snowball hit him in the face.

"I'll give you Ghosted Flakes," the fat mayhem ghost said.

Jason's gaze jerked to the roof.

Remington held her breath. Would he see?

"I'll get up there and knock the snow off the roof later."

She smiled. His third eye wasn't quite open yet. "You do that." She slipped her palm into his.

Later, she'd cast a truth spell on him. Discover the facts he didn't want her to know. No sense in being a witch and not making the most of her power. Did Jason's secrets concern her parents? Johnny B?

Beth flew down from the roof and slid between Remington and Jason. "Took you long enough to get back."

"*You knew I was coming back?*"

"Of course. We're a team. Now that you are, we need to talk."

The mayhem ghosts crowded around Beth.

"It's getting colder out here. Let's get inside," Jason said.

"*Talk about what?*"

"We've got our first murder case to solve."

Remington tugged her hand out of Jason's. "I've got a few things I need to take care of. You go on inside and I'll be there shortly."

He studied her. "Is there a ghost standing between us?"

"Three of them."

"Life in Knotty is never going to be the same... is it?" Jason said over his shoulder as he walked toward his house.

DEAR READER:

Without you, writing wouldn't be nearly so much fun. When you click buy, anticipation for the journey you are about to embark upon zaps me with excitement. My hopes and dreams are that you fall in love with the worlds I create. Worlds meant to enchant and intrigue you enough you forget about doing the dishes, or cooking dinner, or wearing pants to work. And when you take the time to leave a review, I wish for the superpower to reach through the computer and wrap you up in a big hug of gushy happiness.

So, from the bottom of my heart, thank you for being one of my readers.

If you haven't already, please sign up for my newsletter. And please, please, please leave me a review. And, if it's not too much trouble, share on social media your enjoyment of my book.

Your author friend,

Lisa Wells

About the Author

Lisa Wells write romantic comedy with enough steam to fog your eyeglasses, your brain, and sometimes your Kindle screen. On the other hand, her eighty-year-old mother-in-law has read Lisa's steamiest book and lived to offer her commentary. Which went something like this: *You used words I've never even heard of...*

She lives in Missouri with her husband and slightly chunky rescue dog. Lisa loves dark chocolate, red wine, and those rare mornings when her skinny jeans fit. Which isn't often, considering the first two entries on her love-it list.

To learn more about Lisa Wells, follow her on social media, and sign up for her newsletter.

WEBSITE
www.lisawellsauthor.com

NEWSLETTER
www.lisawellsauthor.com/contact.html

TWITTER
www.twitter.com/lisawellsauthor

FACEBOOK
www.facebook.com/lisa.wells.737

INSTAGRAM
www.instagram.com/lisawellsauthor

BOOKBUB
www.bookbub.com/authors/lisa-wells

Made in the USA
Coppell, TX
18 February 2020